The Horro

Includes brand new stories from:
Bentley Little
Joe R. Lansdale
Elizabeth Massie
&
Graham Masterton and
Dawn G. Harris

**Edited by Jeani Rector**
**and**
**Dean H. Wild**

**A HellBound Books Publishing LLC Book**
**Austin TX**

**A HellBound Books LLC/Horror Zine Publication**



Cover and art design by
Kevin Enhart for
HellBound Books Publishing LLC



**www.hellboundbookspublishing.com**

The Horror Zine's mission is to provide a venue in which writers, poets, and artists can exhibit their work. The Horror Zine spotlights the works of talented people, and displays their deliciously dark delights for the world to enjoy.

The Horror Zine accepts submissions of fiction, poetry and art from morbidly creative people.

Visit The Horror Zine at www.thehorrorzine.com



Bat art logo created by Riaan Marais

**Printed in the United States of America**

# Praise for
# THE HORROR ZINE'S
# BOOK OF GHOST STORIES

"This collection of ghost stories is fresh, varied, and entertaining. Perfect company for long a winter's night." – Owen King, co-author of *Sleeping Beauties*

"An incredibly creepy collection of stories of the recently and not so recently dead, written by some of the finest writers in horror. I suggest that when reading, do so in the daylight, because reading these at night will only make you more aware of your own, unempty house." – Susie Moloney, author of *The Dwelling* and *The Thirteen*

"Gruesome, eerie, horrific, sometimes uplifting; this is a terrific selection of ghost stories that satisfy the soul—they chill the blood, too." – Simon Clark, author of *Whitby Vampyrrhic*

"Looking for a perfect evening? Spend the night hunkered down in your favorite chair with only a reading light on, and dive into *The Horror Zine's Book of Ghost Stories*. Forget sleep, these tales will keep you enthralled till daybreak." – Tony Tremblay, author of *The Moore House*

"Nobody keeps the supernatural alive like The Horror Zine." – Scott Nicholson, author of *The Red Church*

## HAUNTED HOUSE

D.J. Tyrer

Left empty
An empty shell
It exudes either sadness
Or terror
Depending upon your romantic outlook
Cobwebs drape it
Bats hang from rafters
Footsteps echo through it
Even when no-one walks its halls
Floorboards creak underfoot
Shriek as if in pain
Sometimes the house shrieks
For no reason at all
Shadows shift
Shapes at grimy windows
Flapping drapes
Caught in a breeze
Or unhappy souls
Looking at a world that passed them by

# TABLE OF CONTENTS

# FOREWORD

Lisa Morton

"If I tell you the order of the nether world, sit down and weep!"

From *Gilgamesh, Enkidu and the Nether World* (around 1000 B.C.)

Right from the beginning of fiction—a beginning that usually consisted of epics featuring mighty warriors battling gods and monsters—ghosts have played a prominent part. Gilgamesh encounters his friend Enkidu returning from the subterranean land of the dead; the ghost of Patroclus appears to Achilles (in *The Iliad*) and begs him to complete funerary rites so the unhappy shade can move on; and the world of Beowulf is stalked by "fatherless creatures" whose "whole ancestry is hidden in a past of demons and ghosts."

Now, here we are all these centuries later still telling each other ghost stories.

What is it about the ghost story that we find so appealing? How is it these insubstantial shades have held such power over our collective imagination ever since we sat around a fire at night, dressed in the skins of the animals we'd killed and peering fearfully into the night, wondering what lurked just beyond the flames' glow? We'd have little in common with an ancestor from 10,000 years ago, except perhaps that both of us would thrill at a good ghost story.

Maybe the question we really need to ask is: why is the mere thought of encountering a ghost so terrifying? Shouldn't encountering the spirit of someone who has passed be a reason for extraordinary joy? Shouldn't you experience overwhelming happiness at being given proof that we survive after death?

There are a few bits scattered here and there throughout history in which visits from ghosts are good events. Early Christian scholars, for example, believed that the ghosts of saints might visit the dying to offer comfort. Festivals like the Mexican *Dia de los Muertos* or the Chinese *Yue Laan* welcome the spirits of deceased loved ones into the home, where they are honored with favorite foods and drink. Ghosts may even be played for laughs, whether in the Roman play *Mostellaria* from the second century B.C. or 1988's *Beetlejuice*.

But even those comedies have a dark side: in *Mostellaria*, a ghost (who is actually a deceitful human—shades of *Scooby Doo*!) tells the audience, "My host slaughtered me, and buried me in secret." And dire consequences await those who fail to pay proper homage to their ancestors during *Dia de los Muertos* or All Souls' Day. The great Roman historian and poet Ovid tells of a time when the Romans were so preoccupied with war that they neglected to pay the proper respects to their dead kin, and consequently "the ancestral souls did issue from their tombs and make their moan in the hours of stilly night, and hideous ghosts, a shadowy throng, they say, did howl about the city streets and the wide fields."

In other words, despite the occasional respect for ghosts, they are universally feared. Their appearance brings no relief or joy to those who are unfortunate enough to stumble upon them.

It's easy to simply suggest that the fear of ghosts derives from the way they defy nature—that things don't naturally reappear after death—and while there's certainly some truth to that, it's still not an adequate explanation.

Look again at all the great ghost stories throughout history, and you'll find one thread that ties them all together: failure. In the Gilgamesh story, Enkidu has gotten trapped in the nether world because he's ventured there on behalf of his friend, but has failed to heed Gilgamesh's warnings about traveling through that gloomy realm. In perhaps the greatest ghost story ever written, Charles Dickens' "A Christmas Carol," Scrooge is visited by ghosts because he's allowed greed and cynicism to replace his younger kindness. In Stephen King's modern classic *The Shining*, Jack Torrance is haunted by his alcoholism and his failed writing career.

Perhaps, then, what we really fear about ghosts is less their unnatural state than the very naturalness of the tragic failures they represent. Is there one ghost in all of fiction (or legend) that led a happy, or even just a normal life? Can you think of one who died in their bed of old age, or who had a massive coronary at 93 and dropped dead instantly?

No, because ghosts represent our deep-seated fear that in the afterlife, we suffer by reliving our own personal failings over and over. What if there's no paradise awaiting us, or even a non-existence free from pain, but instead we find ourselves stuck in some kind of dreadful loop, forced to act out the worst moments from our life, replaying them throughout all of eternity? When we encounter a ghost, we encounter the part of the once-living human being that was about rage, or sadness, or neurotic fixation, or psychosis. We encounter not the day they were united in wedded bliss, or their greatest business success, but the night they were murdered, or when the bad deal caused them to take their own life. We encounter hatred or fury so great it survived even death.

The setting is equally important in the ghost story. Rarely do we read a work of uncanny fiction set in a modern suburban home, or a working office (and when we do, the story will likely present an unnerving visitor who upsets the order of those places, planting the seeds of ruination). If we look at the time when the modern ghost story was born—the eighteenth century—we should note that it coincides with the Enlightenment, when much of Europe was looking beyond monarchy and the Church for new ways of governing and belief. Superstition was cast aside in favor of reason, and supernatural entities were plucked from myth and thrown into fiction. And where were the new ghost stories set? In the ruins of the Dark Ages: crumbling abbeys and castles. Just look at the title of the 1764 book that gave birth to the Gothic novel and is considered to be one of the first great ghost stories in the western tradition: *The Castle of Otranto.* That setting from the Middle Ages is right there in the title.

Now, 250 years later, we're still telling ghost stories set in locations that are ruined or neglected, but we've come a long way from castles and cathedrals.

*The Horror Zine's Book of Ghost Stories* is an excellent example of a modern ghost anthology. The stories within still reflect characters and places that have failed, but these are people and locations that twenty-first-century readers will instantly recognize. There are abused women here, on the run from husbands as they strive to protect their children; there are college students who've had too much to drink, too-curious paranormal investigators, adults struggling with memories of their childhood, and middle-aged men full of regret. There are haunted houses, of course, but there are also subways, basements, hotels, and even a terrible restroom at one of those no-one-stops-there-anymore filling stations we've all driven past (and wondered about) at some time. And there are glimpses of an afterlife that offers little comfort.

Millennia ago, the unknown author(s) of Gilgamesh's adventures told us the afterlife would make us weep. While they wouldn't recognize a car or a train or a cell phone, they'd undoubtedly consume many of the entries in *The Horror Zine's Book of Ghost Stories* and shiver in recognition…just as I suspect you will, too.

# The Horror Zine's

## THE VACUUM

M. N. Nichols

We'd been in the house for a while. About a year, I think. Mom and Dad weren't here with us. They were outside during the storm when the tornado came down. Parker, the dog, ran out through the front door, so he was gone, too.

It was my fault about Parker. I didn't lock the door like I should have when I came inside, and when Parker hit it, it came right open and let him out into the front yard. He started barking and howling at the storm, and Mom told me to watch out for Seeley and Savannah before racing out to bring Parker in.

Dad was already outside, trying to lock down the things in the yard that he didn't want blown away.

And that was that.

I remember seeing the tornado when it came down. It birthed itself from the swirling mass of clouds in the sky and spun down to the earth—long and skinny—like the gnarled finger of a crone scraping up the earth. At least, at first. Then it started getting wider, and the sheer spectacle of it kept me rooted in place until Mom grabbed my arm and pulled me back towards the house right before she went outside herself.

*****

I bring my little brother Seeley a bowl of soup because he is sick.

My younger sister Savannah is down for a nap in her room. As always, wind rattles the windows and the whole frame of the house groans threateningly. It never abates. It will someday, though. I have faith that it will, as long as I stay the course.

I rap once on the door, then peek inside. Seeley lies on the bed, eyes closed, chest rising and falling underneath the covers. I've never liked the raspy wetness suffusing every breath he takes. It reminds me too much of my father's phlegm-soaked coughs from all the years he spent smoking, and Seeley was far too young for his lungs to sound like that.

I gently nudge the door open with my shoulder and walk across the space between it and Seeley's nightstand. A heavier gust of wind buffets the house and I stop, hoping it would wake him up. I breathe a soft sigh of disappointment when it didn't. I move Seeley's lamp off to one side so I can set his soup down on the nightstand with a plastic covering on top of it to keep it warm.

"Mia."

I recoil a little in surprise. Seeley looks up at me, his eyes unblinking. His stare is unnerving. Then his eyes dart around the room, his expression growing more and more concerned with every eye movement. It's like he recognized his room, but didn't, and though I hoped and prayed he wouldn't say what I know he is going to say, he did anyway.

"Something's wrong here in this house."

My heart sinks, as it has sank so many times, weighed by sorrow. I act like nothing was wrong as I set his water next to the soup.

"What do you mean?" I ask him, trying to come off all innocent and unknowing, but Seeley isn't stupid. He's never been stupid.

"We shouldn't still be inside the tornado," he says. He sits up and looks at me. "How can the tornado never end? It doesn't make sense."

I figure that he must've looked outside, and now it's all coming back to him one realization at a time.

"But we're *not* inside the tornado, goober," I say.

He abruptly turns and pulls open one of the curtains, then faces me again.

"Look at that!" he says, pointing at the churning wall of blackness just beyond our yard.

He turns back to the window, and I decide not to wait until he turns back around. I grab his shoulders and throw him down on the bed so he is lying supine. I leap on top of him so he can't move. He starts to yell, but by then the pillow in my hand is over his face. I press down as hard as I can to make the task of smothering my younger brother go more quickly.

"I'm sorry," I apologize through my tears. "God, I'm so *sorry*."

It never takes long for his struggles to grow weaker, then weaker still before ceasing entirely. I lift the pillow from his face. His eyes are open this time. I close them with a sweep of my palm, then I go over to the rocking chair and pull it out from the corner. I sit down and wait. While I wait, I take the Bible resting inside Seeley's nightstand and open it to Galatians. The same spot every time. I make a show of leafing through the pages in case Savannah makes her way up here.

*Savannah. Shit.*

My heart in my throat, I set the Bible next to the soup, then stand up and check the hallway. She isn't out there. I pad down the hall and peek into her room, then sigh in relief. She is still asleep in her bed, hugging her teddy bear to her chest, her thumb in her mouth.

*Should've checked before you did it,* I admonish myself. I hope there wouldn't be a next time even as I *know* there will be a next time, and I know I'm going to have to be more careful. She'll never grow older, but she doesn't have to know that. Neither she nor Seeley have to know that. Not yet.

I head back to Seeley's room. I sit back down in the chair and pick up the Bible. I've only been pretending to read it when I hear Seeley stirring. I look up in time to see him open his eyes and look over at me.

"Mia?" he says.

I close the Bible and put it back in his nightstand drawer.

"Hey, goober," I say, smiling as I stand up and sit next to him on the bed.

"What happened?" he asks, rubbing at his eyes.

"It's over," I lie. "The tornado didn't do any damage."

"Where's Mom and Dad?"

"Getting emergency supplies and helping some of our neighbors." God, the lies come so easily now.

Seeley accepts this and lays back. He looks at the bowl on the nightstand.

"Soup?" he asked.

I nod. "You're still sick. We've got to get you better, right?"

Seeley nods. "Do you have the tray?"

"Of course I do," I say, then stand up to go get it.

*****

I figured it out a while ago. The solution came to me because, really, it was the only thing that made sense.

I woke up on the floor of the basement. Mom and Dad weren't there. Neither was Parker, our dog. I remember struggling my way up out of the basement and into the living room, where Savannah was playing with her toys on the living room floor. Everything was spread out all over the place. No Mom or Dad to enforce the rule of one set of toys at a time.

Savannah smiled when she saw me, then went back to playing with her toys. The lamps throughout the house were all turned on, and the curtains were drawn. I remember thinking how weird that was, because right before the storm, the curtains were all open, and the lights had been flickering madly. Now the lights were steady, and the curtains were all closed. I also got this sense that it was night outside, and not night in the traditional sense. A *deeper* night, like the whole house rested at the bottom of a well.

I figured it wouldn't be a good idea to open the curtains with Savannah in the room. Seeley, either. So I went back upstairs, listening for my younger brother. I didn't hear anything. I checked in his room, and he was still in bed, in his pajamas, coughing with an open package of saltines and a can of ginger ale on his nightstand.

I went into my room and closed the door. I should've locked it, but I didn't, and I'm still paying for it now. I went over to the window next to my bed. Through the crack in the curtains, I could see flashes of light, but heard no accompanying thunder. Tentatively, I reached forward, biting my lower lip, and my stomach clenched in anticipation in the moments before I pulled the curtains open.

I almost screamed.

The impression I'd gotten downstairs had been partly right. We *were* in a deep well of blackness after all, but every now and then it was lit up by a latticework of lightning that connected, synapsed, then moved along. What they illuminated was a shifting, boiling mass of what looked like wind…yet wasn't. I don't know how else to describe it. It looked like what you'd expect to see in the wall of a tornado, except it was like I was looking at the tornado through water.

I looked down at the lawn. There, lying on the lawn next to the road, were my parents. Their bodies were broken and mangled, bleeding from a thousand lacerations. Parker lay across both of them, protecting them in his final hour, his body equally shattered. I was balling up the curtains in both of my fists, eyes bulging, mouth agape.

I started screaming for real then. The horror of what had happened to us drove me to my knees. I was still gripping the curtains and I ended up ripping them down as I collapsed to the floor, crying.

"Mia?"

My head snapped towards the door. Seeley stood there on the threshold. He was looking between me and the window, eyes wide. He'd already been pale due to his sickness, and I hadn't thought it'd be possible for him to lose any more of his color. I was wrong.

"Mia?" he said again, walking forward like his legs had a mind of their own. His eyes were about as big as mine, I imagine. I went to him and wrapped him up in a hug.

"Don't look outside," I told him, turning so he wouldn't be able to look out the window. I picked him up and started to carry him out of the room.

That's when the house came apart.

I turned and looked back out the window right as it happened. The watery tornado wall rushed around the house in an instant, coming right up flush with it, and then the force of the house lifting off pushed me and Seeley to the floor. It was like we were in a hose attached to a vacuum cleaner, house and all getting sucked up.

It's why I call it the Vacuum.

I didn't intend to smother Seeley. I was holding him close, yelling into his ear to just hang on, that everything was going to be okay. I had my hand cupped around the back of his head, pressing it into my shoulder, and I guess that's what did it. His body went limp, and then suddenly we were falling. I hate that feeling of falling. It's why you'd never catch me on a roller coaster.

I screamed again as the house landed, and then suddenly everything was like it had been before the house lifted off. I relaxed my hold on Seeley so I could get a look at him. His eyes were closed, and he wasn't breathing.

*Oh, Christ, he's dead all over again and I made him that way,* I thought. I started shaking him, screaming in his face, then slapping it lightly once or twice until his eyes fluttered open. I can't describe the relief that flowed through me in that moment.

"Mia?" he said softly. "Is the storm over? Where's Mom and Dad?"

*They're gone*, I almost said, but I bit off the words. They *were* gone, which meant I was the grown-up now. I'd been the grown-up before when Mom and Dad had to stay late for work, but this was different. This was much, *much* more than fixing Seeley and Savannah dinner and making sure they brushed their teeth and had all their shit put away before they went to bed. I didn't know what else to do.

So I lied.

"They're out helping the neighbors," I told him. "Then they've got to go and get some emergency supplies for us. They'll be back in a few hours."

Seeley accepted this with a nod, then let his head fall onto my shoulder.

"Can I get some soup, Mia?" he asked. "Please?"

I wiped my tears away and set my jaw.

"Of course," I said.

*****

I've lost count of the number of times I've had to smother Seeley. I've never had to do it to Savannah, thank God. She's only three. She doesn't seem to remember the outside, and isn't all that curious about why all the curtains in the house are drawn. She was never a big fan of the outdoors to begin with. Whenever Mom or Dad took her outside, she'd just plop down in the backyard and just sort of stare around, never doing much anything until they took her back inside.

The Vacuum tries to suck us up, but I won't let it. I don't know where Mom, Dad, and Parker have gone. For all I know, it could be Heaven. For all I know, it could be someplace else, someplace worse. I am a big reader, and am often enthralled by stories of alternate dimensions, hell-dimensions, specifically. What if the tornado wasn't just an ordinary tornado? What if it was some kind of gateway to some other, horrible place?

It doesn't seem to try anything unless Seeley starts to realize something's off. Smothering him *resets* him somehow. I don't understand how it works, but what I know is that it *does* work, and I fully intend to keep us here until I figure this out. Until I can determine whether or not it's safe for me to let go, let the house come apart, and let the Vacuum take us.

*****

It's a couple of days after smothering Seeley yet again. I'm coming back down the stairs and happen to look towards the front door. It's hanging open. Feeling panic, I jump the last three steps on the stairs and bolt for the door. I plunge onto the front porch and skid to a halt just shy of the steps leading down to our front walk, looking around wildly.

Savannah is sitting in Mom's old rocking chair, staring out across the yard at the windy, watery expanse churning in the dark beyond, illuminated by silent lightning. I close the door and go to her.

"Savannah? Baby?" I say, forcing sweetness into my tone. "What are you doing out here all by yourself?"

"Wanted to see the storm," Savannah says, looking up at me. "Mia?"

"Yes?"

"Why's the storm still here?" she asks.

*Goddamnit. She knows something is wrong.*

"Well, I don't know, baby," I lie, looking over at it. "I guess it's here to stay for a while."

Savannah's brow knits together. I can see the little gears turning in her head, and it fills me with a sense of deep, cold dread.

"But storms move," Savannah says. "They don't stay."

"Not usually, no," I say, and that dread turns into a sense of numb horror as I realize I'm falling into the same routine I do with Seeley. Has it really become this commonplace? This easy?

"Are Mommy and Daddy coming back?" Savannah asks.

"Soon, baby," I tell her. "Very soon."

"You say that a lot," she observes. I have to choke back a sob.

The porch slats under my feet vibrated a little. The house quaked, but it was so miniscule that someone who didn't know to look for it wouldn't have noticed. But I do. I've felt it so many times, and I know exactly what it means. I look across the yard and road, and sure enough, the wall of the Vacuum has gotten a little closer to the house.

"Savannah," I say. "Come on inside with me. It's time for your nap."

"But I'm not sleepy," Savannah protests weakly. I take her tiny hand in mine and lead her back inside the house. I pick her up and hold her close, carrying her up the stairs. I gently rub her back in circular motions, trying to ease her to sleep.

When we get to her room, I lay her down on her bed. I don't want to do this. *God,* I don't want to. But I have to. I have to keep us safe. I pick up one of her pillows as she turns onto her side, her eyes closing. I look up at the ceiling as I lower the pillow towards her face.

"Stop."

I jump and turn, dropping the pillow. Seeley stands in the open doorway. He doesn't look sick anymore. He isn't using the door jamb to prop himself up. He doesn't look angry. Just sad.

"Seeley," I say breathlessly. "What're you doing out of bed? You need your rest if you want to get better."

Seeley slowly shakes his head, those sad, sad eyes of his cutting through the deception I am trying to maintain.

"I think we both know I'm not sick," Seeley says, stepping further into the room. "At least, not since the storm hit. I was sick before the storm, but not after."

I feel confused. It had worked every other time. Why not *this* time? What had been different?

The house shakes again. There is more force behind it this time.

"Seeley," I say, "I don't know what you think is happening here, but—"

"Just *stop*, Mia," Seeley says, putting some more oomph behind his words. "Just stop, and accept the truth. The storm killed us all, and we need to move on. That's where Mom and Dad and Parker went. I saw it, Mia. They went up into the sky."

"You don't know what you're—"

"I *do* know, Mia. I *do.* And I get it. You're scared. You don't know what else to do. You're trying to protect us. You were always a good big sister, you really were. But you need to let us go. For all of us. Please."

Seeley is crying now. I'm crying, too. I had plans. So many of them, so many things I wanted to do with my life. In the blink of an eye, it's over. An unlucky twist of fate that put us in the path of that tornado.

"I'm sorry, Seeley," I say, falling to my knees. He comes to me and hugs me, and I hug him back. Savannah comes down from the chair and joins us and she is crying as well, mostly because *we* are crying and she doesn't know what's going on. She's scared. I hug them both close.

This time, when the Vacuum rushes around us and lifts up the house, it is gentle and smooth, not rough like it is trying to uproot a plant. I don't hear the sounds of tearing foundations or splintering wood like I heard every other time. All I hear this time is a breeze sighing around the house; and through the curtains, light like a sunrise slowly begins to spill through.

"Where're we going, Mia?" Savannah asks. I wipe her tears away.

"I don't know, baby," I tell her as the light grows in intensity. "Hopefully somewhere good."

## WARM

Nicholas Pascall

The starless void of the world would make me ill, if that were somehow possible for me anymore. In any direction I decide to look, I find only windows peering into my darkened world; and my mirror is equally dim in nature. It's been years since someone has made light for me. How I miss light…the warmth, the brightness that causes you to see spots, and the way it chases away the shadows.

As I drift through the void, my whispery edges are fluttering about like a tattered cape on the chilled wind. I know I'm losing the battle with time. Every day I become less and less, and the void grows more and more.

My form becomes more vapor, more shadows…it's almost to the point where I can't see my legs anymore, just a simple tattered cloak that was once my burial shroud and my upper body. The glass panes, stark and twisted into absurd, jaunty shapes mock me, teasing me with the hope that someone will come by and actually shine some light into my world.

But I fear that will never happen now.

I fill my days searching for warmth; sending feelers in different directions. I don't know how long it's been this way because time is becoming meaningless. Sometimes I think I can hear people; living beings who I know must exist outside the borders of my world, but I am never able to cross those borders.

And just like that, a beam of piercing white spears through the bleak Gahanna of the world, draining the inky murk from the surroundings. Suddenly I am given an invitation to cross to the other side and it is compelling.

A voice.

"...over here, come here," a voice is whispered, the barest breath above my ear. I jerk, twisting in the void to see where the voice is coming from. One of the panels glimmers for a moment, the light dancing across it. I glide to the mirror, hovering in front of it, peering through to see who requests my presence.

All this time and no one knew I was here. Now I have a chance.

It's the room with the long couch and two high-backed chairs. The beam of light is shining from within the glass, most likely from the fire in the fireplace. Five figures are in the room, and all are sitting in a circle. One of them, a young dark-haired woman dressed in a sleeveless tunic that is shorter than I would have ever imagined, has her hands on the planchette of a Ouija board.

Warmth.

"This is the room where it happened," the thin man with a hand rolled cigarette says, his eyes narrowed as he looks around the room.

"At least, per your cousin," teases the dark-haired beauty, her glimmering eyes drawing my attention at once.

"This is the room where they say the murder happened. You should be able to contact the spirit, Jessica, if you really are psychic."

"I am!" Jessica, the dark-haired woman, assures him.

*Contact the spirit? I haven't been contacted before, ever...but I am eager to respond.*

I swirl around in a haze of excitement at the very thought of being pulled from this endless void into the world of the living once more. *No more darkness, only sunrises.*

Three of the five are women. They sit on the floor around the spirit board. The two men are not participating in the séance. The larger man is sitting on the couch, drinking from one of the metal cans, while Marty is sitting on the arm of the high-backed chair, smoking his cigarette.

"My name is Jessica and I am speaking out to the spirits within this house," the woman says aloud, holding her fingers ever so lightly over the planchette. The other women also place their fingers on the planchette as they sit in a triangle around the board. "If there's anyone there, give me a sign."

I feel the pull of ancient magics: the glass parting in the middle like a seam, a blast of warmth pouring into the void to tug at me. I follow the tug and pour myself into the room, where I'm assaulted with light so bright that I'm almost blinded. The first thing I notice are the colors, which are so incredibly vivid that they seem to pulsate. I can smell the smoke from the fire, the scent of cheap alcohol and the pungent smell of whatever it is that Marty is smoking…I almost feel like I'm alive!

I need for them to make a mistake, to break the circle before they say goodbye…or even better, to forget to say goodbye at all. If they make a mistake, I can be free. I hope they believe that this is simply a game with no consequences.

"We implore you, spirit of the house, if you are here among us, give us a sign!" Jessica calls out again.

*All right, a sign…*I extend out with my senses to the roaring fire in the fireplace, pushing the ever-chill of death into it, causing it to suddenly go dim, casting deep shadows across the room. All five of the group gasp, Marty coughing as he chokes on a lungful of smoke.

"Did you do that, spirit?" Jessica asks.

I extend a tendril of my fluttering cloth, setting it atop the planchette, and slowly push it along the smooth surface to the word "Yes" on the board. All three women are silent, looking at each other as it slides smoothly. The larger man, drinking his cheap alcohol, shakes his head. Marty just stares at the movement with bleary eyes.

"Oh my god, did either one of you do that? Amanda? Melissa?" Jessica asks.

"No, Amanda must have done it."

The woman in the green top shakes her head. "Not me. Do you think…?"

Jessica clears her throat. "Spirit, do you have a name?"

A name? Do I have a name? I do, but it is not for these mortals…quick, make something up! I extend my tendril once more and guide the planchette around the board, spelling out the word "Geist," I know the Celts believed in spirits that they called *geists,* which they said were generally noisy and annoying.

*Hopefully, these people don't know about the Celts,* I think, suddenly aghast that I gave away such a declaration about myself.

They don't seem to find anything odd as they all seem more fascinated that the word is spelled and the pronunciation, not what it is.

"Geist? Is that your name?" Melissa asks, horribly mispronouncing it. I move the planchette suddenly to the word *yes*, causing the girls to shriek and laugh.

"Did that thing just move on its own?" Jessica asks, looking around the room. I flutter up behind her, wrapping a few tethers of my energy around her. She shivers as my cold cloak of death drifts over her. "Oh my god, it is freezing in here! Carlos, fix the fire, would you?"

"On it," the larger man says, crushing the can and dropping it to the ground.

And then it happens. Jessica removes her hands from the circle and she uses them to rub her shoulders, trying to bring herself warmth.

I coil around Jessica, my cloak still anchored to the board. I try to sink into her skin, wrapping tightly around her soul.

As Carlos moves towards the fire, I wave a hand dismissively and retract the chill I'd injected into the fire back, allowing it to roar to life once more. Carlos stumbles back, falling backwards and knocking his head on the table.

Everyone immediately gets up to see how he's doing, except for Jessica.

I latch onto her and sink into her with the speed of a falling arrow, cackling into her mind as she screams internally. I see her thoughts squirming like maggots on a dead thing, wriggling uncontrollably to assert dominance over her body. I feel her shaking, her tremors causing her to fall over to the side of the table. From within, she is even warmer than the room had been, a feeling that I hadn't experienced since the day I was murdered and was consigned to the void.

"I must thank you for pulling me from my miserable non-existence and giving me your body," I whisper, my voice deep and scratchy. "I was never going to escape on my own, and without your help I would have eventually faded from existence."

Jessica tries to fight me, but for her, it is too late. She is doomed to roam in the void as I take her place in the world once I can get the group to say goodbye on the Ouija board to seal Jessica's fate. I cannot banish Jessica until that step is taken.

I open my eyes as her screams grow distant, my head pounding as I peer up at four sets of worried expressions looking down at me. I blink and smile. "Is Carlos okay?" I say, knowing they believe it is Jessica who is talking.

Carlos smiles. "Just a knock on the head, nothing more. How about you?"

"I'm fine. But we need to banish the spirit before it tries anything!" I exclaim.

"What?" Melissa asks, looking at me as if I'm mad.

I give her a pitiful glare. "We need to form our circle and say goodbye to the spirit, or it could haunt us. Hurry!"

"Oh!" Amanda says, clapping her hands. "Like, closure?"

"That's right," I reply, looking back at the board. I place my hands on the planchette and hold it down, to prevent Jessica from trying to interfere as a last effort to save herself.

They take their positions, and we all hold the planchette. We circle the board three times with the planchette, saying goodbye each time. On the final goodbye, the fire roars even brighter, sparks flying from the logs as the embers burn white hot. I watch as the flames die down, until the fireplace is now smoking and lifeless.

I order, "In the back room, there's a mirror. Grab it for me, would you?"

Marty is confused but compliant, turning and snuffing his cigarette out on the old wood of the doorframe before flicking the stub towards the corner of the room. He walks out as Amanda stands behind me.

"Um, what are we doing now, Jessica?" Amanda asks as Marty returns with the mirror.

"I'm going to sever the spirit's connection with our world," I answer, not bothering to look at her.

"Is it an evil spirit?" Melissa asks.

I smile, crossing my arms. "This entity that came from the mirror is an ancient spirit. He was a murderer in life, and killed dozens of people over the course of his life. He was bound to dwell in mirrors in his death so that he would have to forever look into the eyes of those that he would wrong."

"You learned this all from just this one session?" Melissa asks.

I look at her askance. "I did."

Looking back as Carlos fishes out the small mirror, I frown at it. The square mirror is the size of a dinner plate and houses a dirty, but still reflective, sheet of glass. The Greek lettering at the bottom reads off that it belonged to the Daedalus family, with a special marking notating the year I was born.

*I used that mirror for so long,* I think to myself, watching as Melissa walks up to examine it. *I killed people because it was my nature. And then I was murdered myself and trapped in my own reflection.*

"So, the bound spirit is in here?" Melissa asks, looking at the mirror with hesitance. "Is it safe to hold?"

"So long as we don't use a spirit board in front of it, we'll be fine," I give her a smile. Turning to regard Carlos, I give him a nod. "Now, if you would be so kind, break it."

"What?" Carlos asks.

"If we break it, the spirit will never be able to return to our world through this doorway," I explain. "It'll be safer if it is broken. Trust me."

*Shatter!*

I look at Carlos's feet, where the frame of the mirror lay, smoke rising from the shattered glass, the glittering shards releasing a greasy residue and a keening wail that seems to float on the sighs of the group.

*They should never have played with a spirit board if they didn't know what they were doing.*

I tell them, "Thank you. The threat is over."

"Good," Carlos says, walking up and scooping me into an unexpected hug. He pulls back after a moment. "Jessica, are you okay? You're kind of hot, like you have a fever."

"I'm fine, really," I say, pushing away from him with a smile.

And I'm not lying, as I am free from the cold, and have a new chance at life.

I'm finally warm. I can see light.

But I want to bring darkness to the rest of the world.

## THE PALE MAN

Theresa Jacobs

Something wasn't right. Standing in the hall, her arms laden with miscellaneous linens, Leanne paused before the narrow door. A thought flashed through her mind that someone was in the closet. A chill ran up the back of her legs to her spine. Goosebumps stood the fine hairs on her arms. She took a step back, bumping into the wall.

*What is wrong with you?* She straightened and forced her hand around the small silver knob. She hesitated for a moment, gathering her courage, then threw open the closet door.

Twelve empty white shelves stared back at her and she let out a low chuckle.

*See, dummy. Besides, not even a child could fit in there,* she told herself as she set a pile of towels on a shelf. *There's nothing wrong with this house.*

*****

"It's quite a view, isn't it?"

Leanne started. "Oh." She tilted her head back and smiled. "You snuck up on me."

Mark wrapped his arms around her shoulders. "Sorry, didn't mean to. Look at this view. The realtor did right by us," he said.

Outside of the picture window, Holstein cows grazed on thick grass. A dense forest of pine trees encroached the lawn, and snowcapped mountain peaks lorded over it all. The sunset peeked over the trees; the wispy clouds brought pink and orange to the sky.

Leanne rested back against her husband. "I suppose so."

"I understand leaving our friends and family was hard. But this will be a good move, I promise."

Still facing the window, she pressed her lips together. She was stressed from moving thousands of miles away from her life. Turning into Mark's arms, she rested her face against his chest. "I know it will, honey. Once we're settled, we can bring all our friends and family in and show them our new town. In the meantime, why don't you go to the store and bring home something to cook for dinner."

As Mark shut the front door on his way out, the radio played at a low level from the kitchen and Leanne clicked on a few lights to push back the creeping autumn darkness. The house was a standard two-bedroom bungalow. The rooms were set at opposite ends of the hallway, with the linen closet between the bathroom and master bedroom. Passing from room to room, her eyes would dart to the closet and she'd recall the sallow boney form of her imagination.

A cold draft whistled through the hall and shadows from the living room shifted. Her skin tightened and her knees tensed. Standing still, moving only her head, she tried to see around the corner.

"Stop it, Leanne," she berated herself.

Her sphincter tightened, she forced her legs to step out of the bedroom and into the hall. Rounding the corner to the cluttered living room, she noted the picture window was still curtain-less and emitting weak light across the hardwood. The spectacular sunset was finished and darkness was coming on.

With no overhead light to turn on, and all their lamps still tucked safely away, Leanne opted to get a candle from the kitchen. She lit it with a match, then decided to tack some sheets over the window for the night. Moving through the living room, she bent to the box of linens.

A loud crack echoed through the house.

Her knees buckled, she shrieked, and bumped into a pile of boxes, still holding the candle safely upright. Somehow the flame didn't go out.

The boxes toppled, creating more raucous noise and her heart felt like it was sitting her throat. Uncertain what to think, she looked around for a weapon. The first thing she spotted was a broom. Feeling braver with something in her hand, she tiptoed back into the kitchen.

No one was there. If someone had made that noise, they were gone now. She concluded that no one but her was in the house.

The clock on the stove told her that Mark should be home within twenty minutes give or take. The house was giving her the heebie-jeebies like she'd never felt before.

Looking through the doorway into the shadow-infested living room, the light from her candle shined across the dark room, illuminating shapes into reality. In a split second she saw a mound of boxes, the sofa, recliner, filing cabinet and a tall pale man standing in the corner.

She screamed and fell backwards into the kitchen. She gasped for breath and felt like she was going to pass out from fright. She knew she needed to get out of the house, and tried to right herself so she could stand and run for the back door. She couldn't make her legs strong enough to obey her will. Her thoughts were jumbled in her mind but the idea that she would be killed by that pale man made it to the forefront. She scrabbled like a crab towards the back door.

Just as she reached the door, it opened. "I'm home," Mark called.

Before she could even get up, Mark stood above her in the kitchen with paper bags filling his arms. Immediately he said, "Leanne, what happened? Why are you on the floor?"

"I think there's someone in the house," she spoke in his ear as he bent to lift her off the floor.

"Where?"

Her eyes darted towards the living room.

Mark reached into his jacket and brought out his cell phone. In a swift motion, he flicked on the phone's flashlight and spun it around the dark room. "Who's in here?" he shouted.

Leanne watched the darkness light up, once again seeing boxes, the couch, recliner and filing cabinet—but no pale man.

Mark stomped in and checked the entire room. "There's no one here."

"A loud bang scared me, so I was coming to check it out when I swear—*I swear*—I saw a man standing over there. That's when I slipped and fell."

"I was coming up the driveway. I bet it was just the way the shadows moved when my headlights hit the wall." He demonstrated by scanning his flashlight across their jumbled possessions. "Here, let's get some curtains up and one of the floor lamps out. It'll feel homier."

Leanne rubbed her bare arms. "I could have sworn I saw a man. But maybe you're right. It sure scared me, I'll tell you that."

"Come on, we'll get settled a bit so we can enjoy our dinner."

*****

After a surprisingly uneventful night, Leanne woke feeling herself again. There was never a man in the house. She knew that now. No one would break into a house just to stand somewhere and not do anything else. Logic reasoned that there was never anyone in the first place. Tricks of light could do funny things.

"I'm sorry I have to rush out on you already," Mark said, leaning in for a goodbye kiss. "I have to be on time for my first day at the new job."

"It's fine, Hon. I knew I'd be home alone for a while."

"Okay babe, be safe. I love you."

"Love you too," she replied.

Leanne leaned on the living room window-frame, inhaling the fresh exhaust-free air and smiled for Mark's benefit. She would definitely have to get a car of her own and a job, or she'd go stir-crazy with nothing but nature surrounding her. She'd always been a city girl, so this was beautiful but uncomfortable for her. She felt vulnerable. Closing the front door, she took in the mess of fallen boxes around her. "Woo-hoo, what a fun day I get to have."

After hours of non-stop unpacking, breaking down boxes, and finding new homes for their possessions, she decided to pause for a late lunch. Reheating leftovers from dinner, she slid into the overstuffed recliner, popped the foot rest up and clicked on the television. They did not yet have cable or satellite, but they had screwed in the coaxial antenna cable in and a few static stations came through. She stopped at *I Love Lucy*.

Leanne was scooping chow mien into her mouth when she caught a movement out of the corner of her eye from down the long, shadowed hallway that led to the bedrooms. "Shit!" She jumped out of her chair, looking past the recliner into the hallway. Plate still in hand, she stepped back and looked out the window. The driveway was empty. Mark had not come home yet, so it wasn't him.

Keeping her eyes on the hall, she set the plate on the coffee table and walked sideways across the living room. Images of the pale man standing in the corner flashed though her mind. Her heart was beating too fast and fear tickled her belly. Her skin crawled as though she was being watched.

Knowing the day was only half over, she decided to get out of house. There was probably nothing wrong inside, but going outside into the beautiful yard would calm her frayed nerves. Side-stepping into the kitchen, she hurried to the table, grabbed her phone and the house key, picked up her shoes and rushed out into the yard.

The moment her feet hit the grass she felt silly. Here she was a grown woman standing in the backyard in her socks. Looking up to the windows at the back of the house, she still felt eyes watching her. She pulled on her shoes and made a beeline around to the front.

The afternoon sun warmed away her chills. She was glad for it as in her haste to flee the house, she didn't think to grab a coat. The grass in the back had been freshly mowed, she assumed by the management company who arranged the house sale. A cement path led her around to the driveway and for the first time since arriving, Leanne walked around the property.

A pile of something black in the grass below the picture window caught her eye. She went closer to inspect it and found a dead crow.

"So *that's* what caused that bang last night. Poor guy must have hit the window." While she hated to think the bird died because they hadn't put up curtains yet, she was relieved knowing the noise had not come from inside the house. Not wanting to touch the dead bird, she toed it across the lawn and into the shallow ditch near the road. The main road leading into town was on her right, and having arrived from that direction, she knew there was only one other house up that way. She began walking the roadside, but she took the left-hand route. She wasn't ready to meet new neighbors.

Dense low brush covered the spaces on each side of the road. After walking for about ten minutes pavement abruptly changed to gravel and curved to the left. Straight ahead it entered the forest, but was cordoned off with a heavy metal barrier. A sign bolted to the center of the barrier read: *Wild boar territory. Enter at own risk.*

She approached the barrier. The woods beyond harbored larger trees and dense brush.

"I wouldn't go in there alone, Miss," a voice said.

Leanne squealed and spun to find a paunchy older man leaning on a post, staring at her. "Uh, I wasn't going to." Her eyes darted around and she wondered where he came from; he must have picked up on her thoughts as he thumbed over his shoulder.

"I live in the last house, there, saw you meander by and thought I'd best warn ya. Many people have ignored that sign and didn't live to regret it—if ya get my drift."

"I didn't know there was any house way out here in the woods.

"Some house," the old man said. "It's more of a shack. Still, it makes for a good home. Real peaceful-like."

"Good to know. Well my husband and I moved in last night, so I was only checking out the land."

The man's eyes narrowed. "Lots of wildlife around here, some none too friendly. The cows attract the coyotes, so you'll hear them mostly. If you have cats or dogs, best keep 'em in at night."

"What about the boars? Do they come through the forest to the yards?"

"Nope. They won't go into your territory, but you need to stay out of theirs."

Leanne nodded, relieved to know a bit about where they lived now. "Did you know the people who lived in our house before?"

"That house been empty for years in my recollect. Though I'm not surprised the house finally went up for sale now. Heard through the grapevine the owner needs the money. But no one's actually lived there for…" his eyes rolled up in thought. "I've been here twenty-three years and no one. A caretaker kept it up, inside and out, would come once a month."

"We wanted to move to these parts and our realtor showed us this property," she said, flustered by the man's noncommittal attitude. She felt she hadn't really gotten her question answered. "My husband likes the country, and his new job is here."

"Huh. New folks use realtors, huh? Now *that's* some fancy-dancy. But sure, we've talked. Mostly the folks around here meet at the grange on Thursday nights. Word is, been some trouble there once."

"Trouble?"

"Was a long time ago. Now thing's are right as rain. Nothin' to worry about. Probably just grange gossip anyway. Are you continuing on?"

"What's up the road?"

"A pig farm about three miles in and more forest."

"Oh," Leanne said, disappointed that there wasn't more to see. Though not particularly excited about returning to the house, she was left with no options. "I'm Leanne, and my husband's name is Mark."

"Bill Sheckley," he replied and turned up his own driveway. "Can you get back by yourself all right? My arthritis is acting up or else I'd walk you home like a pure gentleman."

"It's not dark yet. I know the way. I'll be fine. Nice meeting you."

"Okay then. Night."

Leanne watched the man return home. Not once did he look back, and she felt he knew more than he was letting on. And if he knew more, why would he warn her about the wild boars, but not about strange events going on at the house? Living in the boonies wasn't as fun as she hoped.

Rounding the bushes near her driveway, she halted and held her breath. An image through the front picture window stopped her in her tracks. She felt her heart pound in her ears.

Even though the window was yards away, she could see him clearly. The pale man stood, slack-jawed, staring at her through the window. Even under the heat of the sun, chills broke over her entire body. Her fingers twitched, and she realized her cell phone was in her hand. She wanted desperately to look away but his black, soulless eyes held her mesmerized. She raised the phone enough to see the camera, thumbed it on and began talking to narrate the video.

"I have never in my life believed in ghosts, but ever since we came here last night weird things happened. I chalked it up to stress from the move and it's not. This is our window in our house and it's locked up tight, yet there is a man standing inside staring out at me. It's the same man I swear was standing in our living room corner last night. I am freaking the hell out here."

Her gaze never left the man in the window and as far as she could tell, his never left her either. He didn't move, or blink, or twitch. In contrast, she shook, shivered and shuffled backwards. When she felt her shoes slide from gravel to pavement, she stopped and contemplated going to Bill Sheckley's house. Maybe he hadn't been honest, but he was the only one out here. She stopped the recording and pressed the green phone icon.

The pale man stared on.

Pulling her eyes away for one second, Leanne hit Mark's contact information, and when she looked back to the window, the man was gone. The phone rang faintly before Mark's voicemail kicked in: "At the beep, you know what to do."

"Oh my god, Mark! This is insane—or you'll think I'm insane—but there's a ghost in the house! I told you there was someone there and you didn't believe me! But now I have a video on my phone to prove it to you. I'm outside in the yard. I need you to call me…hurry, please!"

Uncomfortable even standing near her apparently haunted house, she turned and walked towards the main road, heading to town. The familiar headlights of Mark's truck brought Leanne running to meet him.

He hadn't been able to receive her messages until he was ready to leave for the day, which upset them both, for had there been a real emergency (and she insisted this was), he never would have known. When she climbed into the truck and cranked the heat, he said, "Why didn't you call the office?"

Leanne held up the phone, "It's your new job, Mark; I figured I could wait out the time until you came back. But I won't go back there again."

"What! We spent all our savings on the down payment for this house." Mark rarely got angry, but she could see he was angry now. "This house and my new job are our future. I'm not going to have a hysterical wife ruin our future with an overly active imagination."

"Hysterical wife!" she yelled back at him. "How dare you! Didn't you listen to the message? There's a ghost in that house and I have proof!"

"Why didn't you go to one of the neighbors? There may not be many but there still are some."

"I met the guy in the last house, Bill Sheckley."

"I didn't even know there was a house past ours. Why didn't you stay with him until I came home?"

"He was friendly, yet not friendly at the same time. I can't explain it."

Swinging into the driveway, Mark parked, but left the engine running to give Leanne heat. "Show me the video."

Not wanting to see it again herself, she opened the gallery and passed him the phone. Leanne watched his expression, and felt scrutinized because every so often threw glances at the empty window. She waited for his reaction. When none came, she asked, "Well?"

"There is nothing in window." His eyebrows rose. "Leanne, have you been feeling okay? I understand this move has been hard…"

"No!" She snatched the phone and restarted the video. Mark was right; there was nothing in the window. Her memory showed the deep, dark-socketed eyes, the flabby skin around the man's midsection, the way he stared into her soul. "It…he was there. I swear it. I will not go back into that house."

With a heavy sigh, Mark leaned against the headrest. "What are we supposed to do? We drove for three days, unpacked, slept what—seven hours? I worked all day Leanne, I need to go in, eat, shower, and rest."

She began to cry. "I know. I'm tired, too. I spent half the day standing on the road. How do you think I feel? Am I going crazy, Mark?"

The driver's door popped open and Mark climbed out. "Just come inside. We'll talk over dinner, you won't be alone, and we'll figure it out." He met her around the front of the truck, wrapped an arm over her shoulder and they went through the front door. Icy air hit them. Their breath came out in foggy puffs.

"Mark?" Leanne said, shaking against his side.

"Whoa, it's freezing in here."

"See, let's grab some items quick and get out of here."

He directed her to the couch, clicked on the floor lamp and drew out his cell phone. "Hang on; let me check out the heater. Maybe it's not even on."

Mark walked to the thermostat in the hallway. Shadows shifted in the corners behind him.

"Mark?" Leanne straightened. Her stomach knotted and her teeth chattered.

His mouth opened to say something, and a strangled gurgle came out. He staggered back, dropped the phone to the floor and grasped at an invisible tightness around his throat. He rocked from side to side, still flailing his hands at his neck.

She stood rooted in her fear as her husband collapsed in a heap upon the floor. Whatever had attacked him let him go.

She fell beside him, taking his face into her hands. She shook his face. Behind Mark's head, a pair of pale legs appeared, naked, hairy, and translucent.

Leanne dropped her husband's head, and flipped herself onto her knees. A high-pitched keen escaped her mouth as she scrambled towards the front door. She anticipated icy fingers to grasp her ankle and pull her back in, but she kept going, throwing open the front door so that the cold air slapped her face. She bolted into the front yard.

She spun to look back at the house. All was quiet. Not even the crickets were singing in the cold evening. Her eyes darted back and forth from the shadowed ditch, to the pitch of night in the Holstein field. *Do boars only chase running prey? Are they near? Can they smell my fear?* She sniffled. *I sure can,* she thought as her entire body emitted a sour stench.

She desperately wished she had her cellphone, but she hadn't had time to grab it before she ran. She had to find help. She had to help

Mark. Leanne gasped, "Bill!" as she recalled his tale of the wildlife in the woods, and though earlier she wouldn't dream of going to him, now he was the closest person she knew.

She ran on, but the further away from her house she got, the more she doubted her decision. Thankful that the moon was out to aid her vision, she scanned the bushes for the opening to Bill's gravel drive. The night around her was oddly still, and the goosebumps of both fright and cold never left her arms. Reaching a gap in the bushes, an owl was startled by her presence. It hooted and took flight.

Cursing everything that transpired since their arrival, Leanne hustled towards Bill's dark, squat shack. Bill had been accurate in his description of the ramshackle home because it looked more like a large shed.

She rushed up the worn, wooden steps. No lights were visible in the house and knowing her knock would be too quiet, she gave the base of the door two fast kicks.

A wind picked up as she waited, rustling the leaves into a million whispering voices. The wolves bayed in unison and Leanne shivered. No sound came from the house.

She yelled, "*Bill!*" and began rapidly kicking the door.

She heard, "Wha-the-sum-bitch!" and Bill tore open the door so fast that Leanne's swinging foot almost caught him in the crotch.

Dancing on the step she said, "Hurry! You've got to come help! It's Mark!" The relief of being with another human released some of her tension and she broke down in tears.

"Ease up, Lassie. What are you saying?"

Taking a deep breath, she hitched a few times before being able to speak. "There was someone in our house! Mark's been hurt. We need help."

Bill squinted, glanced right towards the house even though it wasn't visible from his, and then eyed her. "Right then, my truck," he said, pointing at the tiny two-seat pickup. "You're gonna tell me what happened? Or am I supposed to guess?"

"Oh-uh," she stuttered. Now that she had to tell another person about the pale man, she felt foolish. "There's something, a ghost, or an entity, or something in the house and it attacked Mark."

Bill grunted a noncommittal noise. He got into the driver's side and she pulled herself up into the passenger's side. The truck backed down the drive and twenty seconds later they were swinging into Leanne's driveway.

Bill stopped the truck, but made no move to exit. He stared straight ahead. "And what do you expect me to do?"

Leanne jumped out of the passenger's side. "Help us!" she called back, her hand now on the rail at the steps. The front door stood open just as she'd left it. "Mark?"

Her knees began to shake and she braced the doorframe for support, sticking her head in the opening. Mark was still sprawled out, and she could see his chest rise and fall. She felt Bill come up behind her. She rushed to her husbands' side, lifting his head again, only this time he groaned and opened his eyes. "Can you stand?"

Mark rolled away from her, pushing himself up onto his elbows before sitting. "What happened?"

"Bill? Aren't you going to help?" Leanne asked as Bill stood at the threshold peering into the house. His eyes darted about the room and he waved at them, still not entering the house.

"Come on then, get outta there," Bill said.

Mark rubbed his neck. "Leanne?"

She stood and pulled at his arm as the temperature once again plummeted to below freezing. Both their breaths blew in visible fog and she began to shiver. "Hurry! I think the pale man is coming back!"

Bill called, "Come on, come on!"

Mark stood, swaying on his feet. Leanne clutched his side to steady him but before they could move, the pale man seemed to come from nowhere and launched himself at them. This time Leanne took the brunt of the hit. She flew back, hit the recliner and bounced into the wall. Mark stumbled to his knees and shouted at Bill, "Help us!"

"Sombitch!" Bill yelled and ran into the room. He grabbed Marks arm. "Get her and get out!" he shouted and then turned towards the pale man who was hovering over Leanne.

Leanne shouted, "What are you doing?"

Mark grabbed Leanne; she was frozen, watching what transpired. "Let's go," he said pulling her.

"But…Bill," she protested. "We can't leave him in there!"

"I said get out!" Bill yelled at her. "I told you this house had trouble. Now I got to deal with it after all these years."

She relented enough for Mark to pull her onto the front porch, but she refused to go farther and turned to look inside.

A growl emanated from walls. The foundation shook. The pale man solidified, the deep black pits in his eyes flashed white and his grin widened to show yellow pitted teeth. His fingers curled into clenched fists. He stared at the old man.

Bill spoke calmly, "It's me, Jason. It's me you want. I know I done you wrong all those years ago and I'm ready to face you now."

Bill braced himself, arms open as if to receive a hug, and the pale man flew into him, lifting him off his feet. The ghost threw Bill into the floor lamp and the wall behind. Glass shattered; the wooden coffee table cracked.

"Help him, Mark!" Leanne cried. "Pull him out of there."

"No!" Bill told them. "Take her away to safety. This is between me and Jason. I got to face the music. Go to the neighbor's and call for help for you and Leanne, not for me."

*****

The next neighbor was a quarter mile up the road. Leanne was happy to see cars in the driveway and she and Mark ran to the door.

Standing on the steps, Leanne whispered, "What are we going to tell them?"

"The truth I guess." He rang the bell.

The door opened a crack. They understood someone's unease at an unexpected visitor this far out in the woods. "Yes?" came a voice from inside.

Mark squeezed Leanne's hand and spoke, "Can you call the police and tell them a man is being attacked in our house?"

"*Henry*!" the woman shouted into the house. To them she asked, "Who are you?"

"I'm Mark and this is my wife Leanne…" He was cut off as the door opened wide and a man with a shotgun stood before them.

The woman standing behind Henry put her fingers to the gun and pointed it down. "You moved into *that* house?"

"Yes, literally yesterday," Leanne said.

"I'm sorry about the gun," said the man, "but I'm sure you understand. Please come inside."

"I'm Martha," the woman said, "and this is Henry. Please come in."

"Thanks. But Mr. Sheckley's hurt. He was attacked. Bill called the man Jason," Mark said as they cautiously entered the bright home.

As they stepped aside to allow Mark and Leanne in, the older couple exchanged glances. Leanne caught that and asked, "What? You know Jason? You do, don't you?"

Again, the older couple exchanged glances.

"You do know! What's wrong with our house?" Leanne asked.

Martha pointed Mark to the floral print sofa and motioned Leanne to follow her. "Henry, put coffee on."

"But we're in a hurry," Leanne protested.

"It'll take forty-five minutes for the police to get here, and if it's Bill that went in that house…" she paused and turned to Leanne. "It was Bill that went in, right?"

Leanne nodded.

"Then there is no rush. It's finally over and nothing to be done about it now. Godspeed to him."

"We can't just leave him there."

Henry and Martha exchanged glances once more. "You tell it Martha, you're better at the gossip."

"Oh hush," Martha waved him off. "It's not gossip if it's true." She directed her attention to Mark and Leanne. "First off, I'm sorry we didn't see you move in or we would have told you to get out."

"Why was it even for sale?" Mark felt angry at all the loss they were about to take. Then he felt guilty, thinking about Bill.

Martha shook her head. "Never should'a been. No one round these parts would ever dream of buying it. You must be from outta town?" They nodded and she resumed. "That is Bill Sheckley's house."

Leanne's jaw dropped; Marks clenched. "The old bastard."

"Aye, he knew better. Should'a tore that place down twenty-three years ago." Henry said.

Leanne leaned in. "Okay, he mentioned the house had been empty twenty-three years. What happened?"

"The Sheckley's were a normal couple like us," Martha said. "We bought up here when their boys were in their early teens. Johnathan and Jason. But there was always something off about Jason. Pale boy he was, even though he was outside all time."

"That's right," Henry agreed.

Martha went on, "People's pets would go missing and we'd chalk it up to the coyotes and aim to keep them in at night. Then they started to disappear during the day. And then two little girls went missing from the school. Well you can imagine the town went crazy trying to find them." Martha's eyes rolled and Leanne shuddered. "It hurts my heart to talk about all that. Let's just say the authorities looked at Jason. He went berserk, eh Henry?"

Henry nodded. "Uh huh."

"What'd he do?" Mark asked.

"He strangled Johnathan, even though John was older and stronger, somehow Jason's broken mind turned him into a monster. Then he strangled poor Mrs. Sheckley. Sweet woman she was too. Quiet and drawn. Anyway, Bill came in to find Jason in the midst of killing his wife and the only choice he had…" Martha shook her head again and tsked. "He shot Jason square in the head. Then he moved into his own shed and abandoned the house. The authorities cleaned it all away and Bill paid town folk to keep up the property. He never set foot in there again because of all the complaints about the ghost scaring folks. Appears Jason still can't rest. Probably wants revenge. Or who knows, maybe he was just so crazy that the insanity followed him into the netherworld."

"Bill knew the house was haunted?" Leanne asked. "But why did he suddenly decide to sell it?"

"Old Bill got the cancer," Martha said. "He's got medical bills."

Mark pushed back and stood up, pacing. "Shit, I've lost my shirt. You think insurance will cover a haunting?"

"God, Mark, we're not worrying about money here!" Leanne exclaimed.

Martha patted Leanne's hand. "I don't think Bill ever would have dreamed Jason could physically harm you, or he never would'a sold."

"It doesn't matter what he thought! He should have told us!"

Sirens and flashing lights interrupted.

"They're here. Let's go," Mark said.

Henry and Martha followed them out of the house and down the road.

*****

Bill Sheckley's back was broken, his neck snapped. The living room looked as though a tornado hit it and when Mark and Leanne explained the story to the police, they were taken into seclusion and questioned for hours.

They were released as the sun rose.

Leanne sat on the cement steps outside the police station and Mark put an arm around her. "Now what?" she asked.

"Maybe it's over. Jason got his revenge. He's probably moved on."

"I can't live there no matter what, Mark."

"Then we'll have to sell the house. We will be ruined otherwise."

"We'd have to disclose what happened."

"We'll see."

A year later when no one would buy the house, Mark sold the land to a developer who proposed it the perfect spot for a mobile home park.

A pale man stood in the forest, silently watching.

## THE BOY FROM EL SALVADOR

Bentley Little

Orientation was different than Tyler had expected.

He'd been told they'd have to endure some sort of presentation before being sent out to patrol the border, and he assumed it would be a generic do-this, don't-do-that video that reinforced the training he'd already received. But when he and the other new recruits sat down in the conference room, the first thing they were shown was a Power Point photograph of a very dark little boy scowling into the camera.

"This," Captain Stringfield said, "is the boy from El Salvador. You *will* see him. And when you do, *do not* engage."

There was no introduction, no preamble. No general overview, only those very specific instructions. The captain spoke like a drill sergeant, and Tyler could tell immediately that he was not going to like working for the man, but he needed this job, so he not only made sure he paid attention, he made sure the captain and the other new agents *knew* he was paying attention.

"When you see the boy," Captain Stringfield continued, "—and it's not *if,* but *when*—you are to immediately report the sighting. Do not talk to the boy or attempt to detain him. Note the location and immediately leave the premises."

The agent on Tyler's right raised his hand, asking his question before waiting to be called upon. "Isn't it our job to apprehend individuals crossing the border?"

Captain Stringfield frowned at him.

"Sir," the agent added quickly.

"The boy from El Salvador is already here. And despite what you might have heard on TV or read on the internet, border patrol agents are not tasked with detaining every minority child they meet."

"But if he's illegal—"

"Do not engage!" the captain roared. "Am I not being clear enough for you? Are you having a problem comprehending what I am saying?"

"No sir," the agent responded quickly.

"Any of the rest of you have difficulty following orders?"

"No sir!" they responded as one.

Stringfield nodded, and the rest of the orientation settled into a more routine description of duties and expectations. It was only at the end that the captain once again brought up the boy from El Salvador. The scowling photo once again appeared on the white wall, and Stringfield pointed randomly at the assembled recruits. His finger singled out Tyler. "What are you to do if you encounter this child?"

"Do not engage," Tyler said. "Note the time and location and report it to you."

"*Exactamente*," Stringfield said. "You are all dismissed. Pick up your assignments at the front desk."

"Weird," the agent who'd asked the question whispered to Tyler as they filed out of the conference room. His nametag identified him as Norris.

The agent next to them snorted. "Boy from El Salvador? Sounds like we have a captain chasing his own white whale."

Norris laughed. "I wasn't thinking Moby, but have to admit, the word 'dick' did occur to me as I was listening to him talk."

Tyler laughed as well, but there was an uneasiness beneath the shared humor, and the three of them followed the six other recruits to the front desk to get their assignments.

*****

They were all paired up with more experienced agents, and Gary, Tyler's partner, took him in a Jeep along a dirt road that cut through three of the biggest ranches on the border. At each property line was a cattleguard and a gate, and it was Tyler's job to hop out, open the gates, then close them behind the Jeep once Gary had driven through.

"This here used to be a main thoroughfare for smugglers," Gary said, pointing to the wide expanse in front of them. "It's calmed down since we got onto them, but part of our job is to make sure they know we're still patrolling here so they don't come back."

At one point, three men ran off the side of the road as they sped over a particularly rutted stretch of hardpan, and Tyler's adrenaline started pumping, thinking they were about to make an arrest, but it turned out to be a rancher and his sons out working on a stretch of fence, and Gary did not even slow down as he honked at them and passed by.

"So what's with this boy the captain told us about?" Tyler asked when they finally broke for lunch. The two of them were sitting on a flat rock at the edge of a low box canyon.

"The boy from El Salvador? I don't know why he has such a bug up his ass about that kid."

"He told us that if we saw him, we were just supposed to report where and when but not do anything."

"You'll definitely see him."

"That's what the captain said."

"That kid's a prankster. He's always up to something."

"Why don't you pick him up, then?"

"Oh, you can't catch that boy."

"Why? Because he's too fast?"

"No," Gary said, but he wouldn't say anymore.

*****

Norris didn't return to work the next day, and his partner, a fat curmudgeonly man everyone called Skeeve, had a closed-door meeting with Captain Stringfield and several administrative types. All of them seemed far more agitated than they should have been by a new recruit quitting, and it made Tyler wonder what had happened.

He and Gary stumbled onto a group of seven men that afternoon, all of them marching single file through a dusty arroyo adjacent to a power company easement. The men scattered at the sight of them. There was no way two agents could catch them all, so Gary kept his sights on the man in front, the coyote, and they apprehended him, and another man who had stuck with him, at the foot of a giant organ pipe cactus.

On the following day, Gary didn't show up for work. Tyler was afraid he'd be paired with Skeeve, but whether it was a reward for yesterday's bust or whether it was because he seemed competent and reliable, he was allowed to go out on his own. He didn't know the area well enough to go hot-dogging, so he stuck to the roads and trails Gary had shown him, at the appropriate points, putting the Jeep into Park and running out to open and close the gates himself.

Mid-morning, Tyler found himself in what the vehicle's GPS identified as National Forest land, although there wasn't a forest for hundreds of miles, only scrub brush, cactus and whatever else could grow out here in this hellscape. He'd taken a wrong turn at a fork a while back but was interested to see where the dirt road led, so he continued on. It had been an hour since he'd seen a building, a good twenty minutes since he'd seen a sign or fence, but all of a sudden someone was running across the road ahead of him, jumping over a tumbleweed, darting around a saguaro and disappearing. Pumped up by yesterday's success, he drove the Jeep off road, hoping to make a solo collar and cement his reputation. Two arrests in two days, after only three days on the job? He'd have his pick of assignments pretty soon.

Ahead, the hard dirt turned to soft sand, and he braked, hopping out. Movement in his peripheral vision showed him that the runner was off to his left, and he followed as fast as his feet would carry him.

"Stop!" he ordered. "*Parar*!"

He ran past ocotillos and paloverde trees, around boulders and behind hillocks, until Tyler found himself in a dry wash. There was no sign of the person he'd been chasing, but on the flat, solid ground on the opposite side of the wash was a small shack, an upright rectangular building barely bigger than an outhouse. It had once been white, but the elements had weathered it, the relentless desert peeling the paint, sandstorms and monsoons dirtying the color.

The dimensions of the shack seemed wrong, and Tyler felt an instinctive, almost physical revulsion toward the structure, but he pressed ahead anyway, his eye on the too-narrow door. He had no doubt that his quarry had taken refuge within the shack, and he drew his sidearm as he approached.

"Come out of there!" he shouted. "*Salir*!"

There was no response, and it was with an intensifying feeling of dread that Tyler moved forward. He did not know what it was about the shack that repulsed him, but certainly grew within him that the little building was just…*wrong*. It should not be here, it should not be this size, it should not be. Weapon in his right hand at the ready, he reached out and knocked on the narrow door with his left before immediately stepping back. He had the sudden urge to wipe off and wash the hand that had touched the door.

"Come out!" he called again. "*Ahora*! Now!"

A boy opened the door.

The boy from El Salvador.

Tyler recognized him immediately. He looked exactly as he had in the photograph, down to the belligerent scowl. Was this who he had been chasing? He thought it was someone bigger, an adult, but realized that he had not actually seen the person he'd been pursuing, had only peripherally perceived a fleeing form.

*What would Captain Stringfield do if he were here?* Tyler wondered. He imagined the older man breaking down the door rather than issuing a command, then pistol-whipping the child within. The scenario did not seem as far-fetched as it should have.

"Come out," Tyler ordered.

The boy said nothing but beckoned him into the shack. It was not a welcoming request. There seemed a distinct hostility to the subtle hand motion, a malevolent intent behind the ostensible invitation, and though Tyler was armed and was certain because of the size of the structure that the child was the only one in there, he found himself afraid to enter.

The scowl turned into a small smile, almost as though the kid could read his mind. Slowly, the boy closed the door, and Tyler stood there dumbly for several seconds before finally lowering his weapon. He turned away, not looking back as he retraced his steps back to the Jeep.

Returning to the office late in the afternoon, Tyler did not report the sighting as he'd been commanded, and he was not sure if that was because he feared for the boy's safety or because he feared for the captain's.

*****

He dreamed that night of the boy from El Salvador, who was pursuing *him* across the desert, and when he awoke shortly after two, having to go the bathroom, Tyler found that he was afraid to get out of bed.

What the hell was this? He was a grown man, for God's sake. Even as a child, he had not been scared by odd noises at night or fearful of shadows he could not identify. He had never in his life been frightened by the dark.

He was frightened now, though, and if he didn't have to go so badly, he would have waited out the night in bed, remaining safely under the covers until dawn. As it was, he pushed off the blanket and turned on the lamp next to the bedstand, then walked over to the door, where he turned on the room's overhead light. He stepped into the hall—

—and saw the scowling boy standing in the dark bathroom doorway.

Startled, Tyler nearly tripped over his feet. His hand found the switch for the hall light, but when he flipped it on, there was no one there. From this angle, he could see both the hamper and the toilet, and he told himself that refracted moonlight from the small bathroom window had backlit one of those two objects in such a way that, after his nightmare, he *thought* he'd seen a boy in the doorway.

But he did not shut the hall light off to test his theory.

And after quickly going to the bathroom, he left all of the lights on before crawling back to bed.

*****

Gary returned to work the next day, and Tyler was hesitant to tell his partner what he'd found on his day alone. But they had pretty much exhausted their personal histories, so there wasn't much conversation between the two of them, and after nearly of hour of silence, Tyler cleared his throat. "Something happened yesterday," he said.

"Yeah?"

"I saw the boy," he told Gary. "The boy from El Salvador. But I didn't tell Stringfield. Do you think I should have?"

"Not necessarily." The older man seemed only mildly interested. "What was he doing?"

"He was in this little shack—"

Gary braked to a halt, sending up a cloud of dust that briefly overwhelmed them. "You saw the shack?"

Tyler nodded.

"That's a different story," Gary muttered.

"Why? What's so important about the shack?"

The other agent looked around the empty landscape, as if afraid someone might overhear them.

"Because that's where the boy died. That's where Stringfield killed him."

Tyler wasn't as surprised as he should have been. He thought he might even have suspected it all along, though his mind had not allowed those suspicions to coalesce into a conscious thought.

Did he believe it?

He most definitely did.

Gary gave him no more details and forbade him to speak of the boy ever again, and the rest of the day was tense and silent. They parted without saying goodbye.

*****

His day off that week was Saturday, although that was not always going to be the case, and that morning, after an early breakfast, Tyler took his truck out to find the shack. He was not sure if it was legal to trespass across private land when he was not on duty, so he brought his ID with him, just in case.

And his gun.

The first time he had found the weathered building had been an accident, but he was able to retrace his route pretty easily and two hours later he found himself on foot headed for the dry wash. The small building was just where he had left it, although this time the door was open.

Once again, he experienced a feeling of revulsion upon looking at the structure, and he diverted his gaze downward as he approached across the wash, afraid of looking at it for too long. Before him, in the sand, something glinted in the sunlight, drawing his attention.

A nametag. And agent's nametag. He picked it up, turned it over, and dusted it off.

*Norris*.

The temperature was well into the nineties, but Tyler suddenly felt cold. Was this why Norris had not come back to the job? Had he…died here?

Tyler stopped, looking around for a body or bones or possibly a burial mound, but saw nothing out of the ordinary. His gaze moved up and ahead to the shack and its dark entrance. The open door, still unnervingly proportioned, was swinging lightly, hitting the front wall of the shack and making a rhythmic knocking sound though there was no wind to propel it.

Could Norris' body be inside?

Tyler knew he should leave immediately and get the hell out of here, but instead he drew his weapon and continued on. He stepped onto the solid ground on the other side of the wash and, gathering his courage, peeked into the doorway. Though the sun was out and bright, the lack of windows and slight overhang of the shack's roof rendered the interior to be almost completely dark.

He did not step in, but remained where he was, one hand on the doorjamb, the other on his service revolver. There were whispers in the gloom, accompanied by soft scuttlings in the sand that might have been small animals but weren't.

"Hello?" he called. He almost expected his voice to echo, despite the limited space within, but his shout sounded muffled.

He was not as brave as he thought he was, because instead of going in, he turned around to leave.

There, in the center of the wash, next to the spot where he'd found Norris' nametag, stood the boy from El Salvador.

Even in the open air in the light of day, there was something unsettling about the figure's unchanging appearance, the raggedy clothes, the fixed stare and scowl. He seemed awfully solid for a ghost, and Tyler thought that if he shot the boy, the bullet would tear though his body.

Only he could never do such a thing. Why would he ever shoot a child?

*Why had Stringfield killed the boy?*

That was the question that had been on his mind since Gary had first told him what had occurred, and Tyler's imagination had conjured up multiple scenarios in the meantime. None of them, however, had managed to justify the act, and even if the boy had somehow, for some reason, threatened the captain, a trained law enforcement officer—an *adult*—would have been able to resolve the situation with no recourse to deadly force.

So why had he killed the boy?

And why was he warning new recruits about the child?

Tyler couldn't face the boy any further. He turned to leave, but his thoughts continued. None of it made any sense. Maybe he'd get some answers if he asked Captain Stringfield, but there was no way he would ever do that. The man scared him, even more so now that he knew what the captain had done. Did everyone in the unit know what happened? Gary clearly did and hadn't seemed too perturbed by it, but what about higher-ups? Had there been an inquiry? Or did this kind of thing happen all the time?

Tyler made his way back to the truck. He felt anxious and uneasy as he drove through the desert toward home, feelings that only intensified when he found an unfamiliar car in his driveway and saw Captain Stringfield waiting for him on the front stoop. He got out of the pickup and approached the captain carefully.

Stringfield did not appear to have slept for several days. His normally clean-shaven face was rough with stubble, and his short hair was uncombed, giving him an aging punk look. He was wearing his uniform, but it was wrinkled and dirty, as though he'd been sleeping in it on the ground.

"Captain?" Tyler said tentatively.

Stringfield rushed toward him, grabbing the front of his shirt. "You found the shack?"

Tyler nodded, afraid to speak.

"Why didn't you report it? You know you were supposed to report it. I had to hear it from Gary!"

*Damn him*, Tyler thought.

"You know where it is?"

Tyler nodded again.

"You're going to take me there. Now."

There were a million questions he wanted to ask, but he didn't dare. He merely nodded and, taking out his keys, trudged back toward the truck, Stringfield following. His impression that the boy possessed mass and solidity may not have been far off, because while they were driving, the captain took out his service revolver to check that it was loaded.

The action left Tyler troubled. If Stringfield had killed the boy, the way Gary said he had, it would be impossible to kill him again. On the other hand, maybe Gary had been wrong and Stringfield *wanted* to kill the child. Tyler did not like the idea that he was bringing the captain out to commit murder.

He cleared his throat. "Excuse me, uh, Captain—"

"He's already dead," Stringfield said, as though Tyler had spoken his concerns aloud. "I just need to make sure."

The manner in which he spoke made it clear that there was to be no additional discussion, and Tyler nodded, shut up and kept driving, resigning himself to the fact that he might never learn what was really happening.

The sun was setting by the time they reached the section of dirt road where they had to stop. After telling the captain to get out, that they had to walk the rest of the way, Tyler opened the glove compartment and took out a flashlight. He hoped to be gone before it actually got dark, but just in case…

Stringfield let out an audible gasp when they finally reached the shack. It was not yet dark, but the shadows were lengthening, and it took both of them a moment to notice that the boy from El Salvador was standing in the open doorway. He smiled broadly, and his overlapping teeth were bright white in the fading light.

"Leave us," Stringfield ordered.

"Do you want me to wait—"

"Leave!"

Gun drawn, the captain advanced as the boy faded into the blackness within the small building. Stringfield stepped inside, and the door closed behind him.

*I still don't like that door*, Tyler thought.

From within the shack came a single gunshot.

Then silence.

He stood there for several moments, waiting to see if the door would open again, if one of them would come out, but there was no movement, no sound, as the sun continued to drop in the west. Even the surrounding environment was still, not a lizard or a bird or a bug revealing its presence. He considered going to the shack, opening the door and looking in, but in the end decided that he would rather not know.

Turning on the flashlight, not glancing behind him, Tyler walked back to the Jeep.

He was going to quit tomorrow, he decided, and find another job.

And he drove alone through the descending darkness back the way he had come.

## A STRANGE GIRL

Maureen O'Leary

Tess' mother tipped back in a plastic chair on the porch outside their motel room with her pedicured feet against the railing. She blew a stream of smoke like a dragon.

"Oh my God, Mom. Really?" The past twenty-four hours had been weird enough without the sight of her tidy suburban mother, who happened to be a medical doctor, smoking and squinting into the desert sun as if cancer wasn't a thing.

Her mother didn't answer, only gazed at the desert plain that stretched behind the motel. Tess considered the fact that maybe this woman who had taken her to a motel in the middle of nowhere wasn't really her mother at all. Maybe this woman with her mother's pedicure and her mother's voice was a desert doppelganger who did not mind ruining her lungs with smoke and wrinkling her skin with ultraviolet rays.

"I need this right now to settle my nerves," she said. "I smoked once in a while in med school when it got intense. Helped me to think. "

"Why are we here in the middle of nowhere?" Tess asked.

"I heard about this place in a dream." Her mother flicked ash over the railing. Her mother never talked about her dreams.

"What is that supposed to mean?"

"You don't need to know everything." She picked a piece of tobacco from her lip with a perfect red thumbnail.

The air conditioning unit was broken in the room. Otherwise, Tess would have gone inside to watch cable television and escape. Instead she was stuck outside with her mother who was smoking like a stranger and talking like one as well.

"How do those cuts feel?" Her mother ground the butt on the concrete pad in front of their door before wedging the nasty thing into the front pocket of her jeans.

"Fine." Tess stroked her own wrists through the gauze bracelets. She scanned the roof of the motel but there was no sign of the white blonde hair and watery green eyes of her ghost boyfriend anywhere.

"Tell me if they bother you," her mother said.

The heat rose in oily waves from the blacktop like a bad dream. Tess wasn't going to tell her mother anything.

*****

By dinnertime, the motel air conditioner was still out of commission and they drove until they found a chain family restaurant with a fake wagon wheel propped in front. There were other families around and Tess wondered at the term *family restaurant* and if she and her mother alone without her father could still be considered a family. They left him home all by himself and she worried about him. She wondered what he must be thinking.

She broke the yolks of her eggs into the field of fried potatoes and also wondered if her mother could be arrested for kidnapping when she was the mother and Tess was seventeen, almost not a kid.

Tess kept her questions—philosophical and practical—to herself while her mother sawed through a full turkey dinner complete with cranberry sauce, stuffing, and gravy. Her mother was normally a vegan. She ate kale and quinoa salads and went to yoga three times a week and advised her patients to do the same. Dr. Murphy did not eat turkey dinners in family restaurants.

"Who are you?" Tess asked.

Her mother just chewed.

On the way back to the motel they listened to the Spanish news station on the radio. Tess understood enough to hear that police had found the body of a missing girl buried in the desert. *Another* missing girl, implying others.

Her mother pulled over to the side of the highway where a short, rustic fence marked off a point of tourist interest at the base of a cliff. She got out of the car and Tess followed her to where the ground and the cliff met in an almost perfect forty-five degree angle.

Her mother placed a gentle hand under Tess' chin and tipped her gaze up. Bathed in the orange glow of the setting sun, ivory-hued spirals and crosses and swirling designs danced across the red rock. A sketch of a goat with a triangle face and long horns looked about to break out of the wall to scale the rest of the way to the top on its own. Impossibly high on the cliff face stretched a drawing of an enormous bird soaring above an ancient desert. The lines were simple, yet somehow as real as an actual eagle casting a moving shadow across the brush and sage.

"Petroglyphs." Tess' mother broke her silence. "Thousands of years old."

Tess watched as a nearly naked man—his age was hard to tell from the distances of both time and space—lowered himself down the cliff with a thick, braided leather rope. He pounded and scraped at the tip of the eagle's wing with a sharp horn, bracing himself against the cliff face with his bare and calloused feet.

He glanced at Tess and did a double take. He cocked his head to the side, a question in his sparkling eyes.

"Yes," Tess called out to him. "I see you."

"That's enough," her mother said.

The ghost artist grasping the rope went away like the dimming of a light. Tess turned toward the valley below the highway, the sunset now rendering the sky a searing red.

*****

Tess' ghost boyfriend was waiting back at the motel. Her stomach did flips of joy at the sight of him but she did not dare show her mother that he was there. She had already driven her mother to smoke cigarettes, sit in the sun without a hat, and eat meat. Who knew what Tess would drive her to do next?

Their room was open and a handyman wearing a tool belt knelt on the floor twisting a wrench on a bolt inside the air conditioner. The cover panel rested on a bed and on top of it stood a young woman with long black hair that hung down her back like a sheet of night rain.

"Nothing is broken," the young woman said. "He removed a part before you got here. He just wanted to come in here. That asshole has my favorite earrings in his trailer. A chunk of my hair, too."

The handyman smiled over his shoulder at Tess' mother who

smiled back. The dark-haired girl shimmered in the hot air and then disappeared.

"I'll get this up and running for you," the handyman said. He screwed the cover plate back on, his forearms rippling with hard muscle.

"It is pretty warm in there." Her mother talked in the voice she used with store clerks and Tess' teachers. If Tess did not know better, she would hear that voice and think her mother was an easy person to talk to.

The handyman finished with the wrench and got to his feet. He was only a few inches taller than Tess' mother but his chest was broad as a wall and his arms were long and cabled. Tess pictured him outside a low trailer lifting barbells above his chest while lying on a cracked vinyl bench.

Now as he stood before them, his tool belt hung with the glimmering heads of young women, tied to the strap by their hair. The one that dripped fresh blood from her neck was the girl who had been standing on the bed calling the handyman out on his bullshit. She whispered from where she hung. He had her earrings in his trailer. He'd murdered her for no reason.

Tess knew the heads were not there, at least, not on his tool belt.

"Watch what he does now," the ghost girl said, reappearing for a moment. The handyman closed and locked the window. He tipped an imaginary hat and gave Tess a wink.

"Thank you so much," her mother said.

Later when her mother was in the bathroom Tess checked the window and found a wad of chewing gum wedged in the lock, rendering it useless. She picked the gum out with her fingernail and tested the lock a few times to make sure the mechanism held secure.

Outside in the moonlight, the ghost boy stood, his nearly white hair like a halo glowing.

"Thank you for your help," Tess said out loud. Maybe the girl who had warned her could still hear. The air conditioner blasted and from deep inside the metal coils she heard the sound of women crying.

*****

One month before the trip to the desert, on the last night of Tess Murphy's normal pre-ghost boyfriend life, she drove away from the boring house party of a friend who lived on the levee in Walnut Grove.

On the road home, the moon lit the Sacramento River running along the two-lane Delta highway and it was beautiful as the wind blew through her hair and smelled like the promise of summer.

A deep voice from inside the car growled on the edge of laughter. Tess startled and the bumper shrieked against the rail as she jerked to the right. Sparks sprayed along the edge before she hooked into the empty oncoming lane.

The boy who suddenly appeared in the passenger seat was having a great time. He whooped and hollered while Tess struggled to keep from spinning over the levee. He arched his neck like a wild coyote, hung out the window and howled at the stars. He pounded the roof before falling into his seat, crackling sparks and fire. The radio switched on and the Rolling Stones exploded through the speakers. The boy beat the dashboard, singing along with the voice of an angel.

He smelled like sweet smoke, leather and fine perfume. He sang Mick Jagger's song about the devil as though he'd written it himself.

His eyes were green and they glowed in the dark.

She laughed because it was impossible not to even though she knew she should have been mad. She could have wrecked the car, killing both of them dead. Well, not both of them. One of them was already dead.

She could have picked him up anywhere along the levee road. The river roads were always haunted.

"I have certain rules." Tess turned down the music. "You can talk to me but I can't talk to you when my parents are around, especially my mother. I get in trouble for that."

He leaned forward and stroked his chin.

"I'm serious," she said, but she knew he'd never believe her if she couldn't stop smiling so she gave up trying and raised the volume on the radio. He sang along to one classic rock song after the other while she drove them through the California Delta where the highway and the water snaked together as if the road and river were more than friends.

And just as suddenly, he was gone. The ghost-boy's absence filled the car like the silence after a thunderclap.

"Where did you go?" she asked even though she knew that ghosts came and went as they pleased. She missed him already but there was nothing she could do to make him return.

When she got home, the damage to her bumper wasn't so bad that it couldn't wait until the morning to report.

That night at home, in bed, she lay blinking in the dark. A tree branch scraped against the window, or so she thought at first. She looked over and it was him floating as though on an elevator made of air.

She held her breath. He was serpentine and elegant with high cheekbones and a crooked front tooth in a sneaky half smile. He pressed his palms together like a penitent man and passed through the screen before bending before her on one knee. His eyes shone from beneath a sweep of his long, moonlight-colored hair.

She reached for his hand and the space between their bodies trembled and sparked. Her lips ached with the feather-light pressure and heat of his mouth on hers. She wanted more.

It wasn't right. He was dead. Tess was alive. There were rules of common decency and making out with a ghost broke several.

*My love.* When he whispered his deep voice vibrated in her ear. He ran his fingers down the side of her neck.

But then again lots of things were indecent in the world. There was poverty and war and other things. Besides, it wasn't exactly decent that she was a girl who saw dead people but she couldn't help that either.

*You are so beautiful,* he said. Her knees weakened. Falling in love with a ghost wasn't decent. In fact, it was all wrong.

But it felt so right.

*****

A few weeks later, Tess tried to do homework in her room. She was behind in every class because of the ghost-boy but she had to study biology or risk failing the class, which would bring more trouble from her parents than it was worth. She'd already overheard them talking about her and the news wasn't good. Maybe Tess was on drugs, they'd said. Maybe she was depressed.

The parts of a cat lay out in diagram in her textbook and the drawing was somehow even sadder than the real thing they'd dissected in class.

The page flipped as though someone blew on the book from below.

"I need to study," she whispered. He answered with a laugh. She covered her ears and tried to focus on the narrow feline esophagus as he appeared on the wall above her bed iridescent in his black leather jacket, his eyes green and narrow and glowing. The air closed in as she went to him. A sweet charge unfurled from her spine as she held his chiseled hips in the palms of her hands. She wanted to be in his world. The whine and promise of ancient rock gods hummed from her speakers and her heart beat along with their drums.

*Be with me, Tess. Die with me and we'll fly together.*

His desire filled the room with heavy heat. He would turn her will to steam. She breathed in his smell of smoke and cloves like it was a long drag on something she craved more than oxygen.

He pointed to the art supplies on her desk and an exacto knife rattled the can where she stored it upright with her colored pencils. Its razor was clean and silvery in the light of her desk lamp.

*I need to know that you want to be with me.* He said as he lowered his hand to hers, curling around the handle of the blade. *Prove it to me.*

The skin of her wrist opened in lines and the cuts stung. The ghost-boy loved what she was doing. It was just what he wanted and he was so pleased. Her whole body felt light from her head to her feet. She cut herself again and fell with a hard thud to the floor.

By the time her mother burst into the room, Tess' blood flowed in warm rivulets down her arms. Her mother snatched the exacto knife from Tess' slippery hand and shredded a sheet to wrap around her wrists in tight bonds.

"I'm sorry," Tess whispered. She was hollow in her bones. The only proof that she was still living was the throbbing of her veins.

*****

Her parents arranged that they would admit her to the hospital in the morning. She needed to go on suicide watch, her dad said through tears and her mother grimly agreed. Her father slept in the guest room that night while her mother made Tess sleep with her in her parents' bed. She brought Tess orange juice to drink and checked the wounds under the dressings.

They had reached her in time. The cuts weren't deep. Tess traced the fresh bandages her mother covered them with as if the moment she bore down on the blade had occurred in a dream.

Long before the sun rose, her mother whispered in her ear. "Get up," she said. "Don't wake up Dad. We're leaving."

*****

After the handyman left their motel room, Tess' mother was back to being silent. She didn't light another cigarette, thank God, but after her shower she turned out the lights and sat at the window staring into the desert night like a weird security guard. The moon was full and in its cold light her mother was beautiful but strange, her jaw tense and her eyes shining.

Tess considered mentioning that she had it on good authority from a ghost-girl that the handyman was a murderer, but she didn't have the energy to argue. She fell into bed and her mother didn't even say anything about the fact that she hadn't brushed her teeth.

When she woke in the dark night, the outside light caused the shadow of the handyman to fall across her eyes as he approached the window. Her mother was wide awake and stretched alongside her.

"Quiet," she said.

Tess had fixed the lock. She'd picked out the gum the handyman had lodged inside it, and she'd checked the latch twice while her mother was taking a shower.

"He's here," the girl with long black hair whispered from the corner. "Your mother put the gum back into the window so he could get in. Now he's coming for you both."

He would kill them and their heads would hang from the handyman's tool belt by their hair as they wept tears of blood that no one would see.

"Easy." Her mother's voice was less than a whisper, her forearm around Tess' waist an iron vise.

The window slid open and the man swung his leg over the sill and he was in. Tess flinched as he raised a hammer high over his head but her mother was quick as a bird in flight as she kicked him in his stomach. The hammer swung wide and hit the wall as the handyman folded over and Tess' mother leapt on him in the darkness.

Tess fumbled with the lamp and when she switched it on, the handyman lay on the floor curled into a human letter C. His hands were pressed to his own neck where blood flowed through his fingers in pulsing ribbons.

Her mother stepped over him as his hands fell away from the long red smile sliced across his jugular vein. The scalpel in her fingers dripped onto the floor.

"You killed him," the ghost-girl in the corner said.

"It was either him or us," Tess' mother told her.

"Good choice." The dark-haired ghost girl's laughter rose to the ceiling like bells.

Tess watched in shock as her mother bowed her head to the black haired girl as if in prayer to a goddess. The girl set off white sparks before she turned and walked through the window towards the desert plain. Tess' mother wiped her hands on her nightgown before reaching for her phone.

"You saw that girl?" Tess asked.

Her mother held up a finger and talked to dispatch. She'd killed a man, she said. He came into the room and tried to attack her with a hammer and now he was dead. When the call was done she pulled her jeans on under her bloody nightgown.

"Once they find the souvenirs of the missing girls in his trailer, they'll know what he was," she said.

"How do you know he has souvenirs in his trailer?" Tess asked.

The smell of metal steaming from the handyman's blood made her want to run screaming from the room but she had so many questions. Questions about her mother. Questions about herself.

"You know how I know. Same way you know. Same way you and I have always known what the dead have to say." She tossed Tess her duffel bag. "Get dressed. The cops will be here any minute. We'll tell them our story, then you and I are going home."

"Are you and Dad going to make me go to the hospital?"

Her mother rubbed the back of her hand against her face, smearing blood across her cheekbone. "I'll find a way to explain everything to Dad. You aren't going to any hospital. There is nothing wrong with you." Her voice had a new steel to it, a new certainty, and Tess believed her.

They stepped over the body of the handyman and waited for the police outside the room. The moon created long shadows across the desert floor where several yards away her ghost-boyfriend and the black-haired girl held hands.

Tess' eyes welled. Already he moved on to someone else. She had been willing to die for him, and now this.

Her mother's hand was strong on the back of her neck.

"If you let him go, he will stay here with her," she said softly. "And then neither of them would have to be alone out there."

"Is that how it works?" Tess' throat pinched against her words.

"You ignore them or you help them. You don't fall in love with them," her mother said. "Even if they have green eyes and a crooked smile."

"You could always see them." Tess accused, feeling as though her brain was slow; as if she'd been sleeping a long time and was having a hard time waking up.

"Yeah, I was a strange girl too as a kid, and I hated it. I thought if I could convince you the ghosts weren't real then you would lose interest and they'd leave you alone." Her voice dipped in sadness as her fingers twitched at the back pocket of her jeans. She pulled out the pack of cigarettes but instead of taking one out, she tossed the pack into the trashcan used for ashes. "I did the best I could," she said. "To be honest, I didn't know what to do."

The ghost-boy's eyes flickered like gas flames in the darkness. Tess' mother admitting that she hadn't known what to do was the strangest thing to happen that entire night, even beyond the handy-man's death. Tess didn't know what to say.

"He seems happy though, doesn't he?" Her mother wrapped her arm around her shoulders and the weight of it was steady. "She'll be a good girlfriend for him."

Tess' heart literally ached in her chest, yet somewhere under the pain she knew her mother was right and so as the sirens wailed in a long distance, Tess waved good-bye to her ghostly boyfriend. He reared back to let loose one last long howl at the moon as he and the black-haired girl shattered into a million particles of light, rising to the stars to take their place among them.

## PROOF OF AFTERLIFE

Derek Austin Johnson

It always ended badly. That was the lesson Sutter Luce learned after so many years of crawling through splintered fences and wading through hip-high reedy grass in his investigations. It was one he thought of now, as his tires splashed water against a curb and he parked his battered Camry a block away from the town. But that always was the lesson, he reminded himself. Regardless of our present moment, our fates remained the same: we were here, until we weren't.

His wife Cassie often warned him something bad would happen. "They're never safe, those old houses," she'd say. "At least, use the instruments."

She believed in the toys.

"You're playing at being a ghost hunter," Sutter once told her after an unsuccessful visit to an abandoned hotel in Shreveport, where Cassie had set up multiple EMF sensors. "It explains why you have so much stuff. You're not interested in finding ghosts; you're only interested in the chase. You don't even understand that there are different types of ghosts."

She hadn't liked that. And now, he was alone.

His stomach grumbled. Sutter had not eaten since breakfast, before he had made the journey from Houston to Shadow Hills. This was his ritual, stemming from a belief that physical hunger might manifest as some metaphysical need. It didn't stop the gurgling, however. No matter. If he found what he was looking for, he told himself, then he would treat himself to a large late-night meal at one of the chain restaurants dotting the freeways. His stomach croaked even louder in anticipation.

After circling the town square twice, he drove down several streets lined with houses dating from the early 1900s until he stood in front of the cottage: single story, graying white paint peeling from the wooden siding, the yellow tape wrapped around it seeming to hold everything together, as if it was a package that would fall apart if unstrung. It was sandwiched between two Victorian homes, both built in the early years of the last century, both of which dwarfed the smaller structure, yet the cottage appeared to loom over the other homes.

The setting sun cast long shadows that merged over the cottage's front lawn, a dark radiation that sapped the other structures of size and vitality—especially the house where a man murdered his family with a shotgun and then disappeared.

Sutter took another step toward it, then hesitated. This part always triggered his anxiety, regardless of where he went. He spent so much time looking for ghosts, finding the homes where their energy might still linger and hoping to capture one with a single, vibrant photograph, but always walked away with the usual errors: the halos that came from chromatic aberrations, the memory cards that blended past and present images, the rolling shutter smearing light from the flash. Things that got him excited for a second before he realized what they were.

He just needed one image, just one, to make his own hunting worthwhile. One image could provide concrete evidence of life beyond the phenomenal world. A proof of afterlife, he thought grimly.

And Sutter would get it here, in this place where murder occurred only a few short months ago. It was the violence that would manifest itself into energy—a psychic emergence of fear and anger that could break through any barriers with which the afterlife cloaked itself.

The spectral resonances should still be present. Ghosts, he reasoned, were like the background radiation: you find the strongest evidence for them the closer to death you looked. You didn't need gadgets to know this.

Closing his eyes, he breathed in the balmy late September air, the smell of dry grass mixed with rain, then looked in either direction. Seeing no one on the street (lack of onlookers made his investigations easier), he strode as casually as he could up to the cottage's enclosed porch. At the foot of the door sat open Styrofoam boxes overflowing with rotten food: browning leaves of romaine lettuce, shriveled carrots that made Sutter think of babies' fingers, white blobs of yogurt fuzzed with gray mold. Next to these were a small stack of shrunken apples, juice seeping from discolored spots in wrinkled green skin. Flies buzzed against the golden skin of a small roast chicken.

Sutter nudged an apple with his toe and it rolled away, leaving a streak of pungent liquid as it fell off the porch and disappeared behind a drying bush. He retched, but the sight of food, however rotten, made him even hungrier. His stomach growled again and he knew he was ready; the hunger always heightened his senses.

With a pocketknife, he sliced the strips of tape across the door, then turned the doorknob and pushed his shoulder against the door. Not only locked but also jammed. He wondered if the police forced it open, then remembered reading that a neighbor had seen the door ajar and gone inside to investigate, calling 911 immediately when she stepped into the living room and recoiled from the stench of decay.

At the thought, Sutter pulled a paper mask from his jacket pocket and fitted it over his nose. Death may have been his business, but the possibility of coming into contact with its putrefaction made him queasy. From his other pocket he removed the imitation leather case that contained his lock-picking set. He didn't think it would be too much trouble to get in; the locks from the old houses seldom fit the doors well, and entry proved simple.

He selected a torsion wrench and touched the doorknob with his index finger. The latch and deadbolt clicked, and the door swung open without a sound.

Sutter sniffed, then coughed and gagged. The air inside was cool, much cooler than the evening, causing sweat to bead across his forehead and drip down the bridge of his nose. And even through his paper mask there was the stench: acrid rotten meat mixed with the too-sweet citrusy fragrance of overripe fruit. His fingertips touched his mask. It was bad, but he thought he would be able to manage it.

He peered into the darkened cabin and checked his camera's battery again. Fully charged. Stepping through the door, he fished a small flashlight from his jacket pocket and allowed his eyes to adjust to the half-light. It should be fine, he told himself, as long as he kept the door open. Besides, windows surrounded many of these old homes; as long as he had sunlight, he shouldn't need manmade illumination.

Beyond a small foyer sat the living room. Dust furred a couch and two chairs that might have been purchased at a discount furniture store. On a glass-topped coffee table sat a ceramic planter where dried brown leaves curled against withered vines. Sutter set the flash and took several pictures in succession, then checked the screen. Each showed exactly the scene in front of him, nothing more. They didn't spend much time here, he thought, so of course their spiritual imprint wouldn't be found here.

Space flanked the living room. The pine floors creaked beneath his heavy boots as he made his way to what appeared to be a large office. A boxy computer monitor sat on a heavy oak desk, a thick spider web connecting it to the keyboard and mouse resting on an ink blotter. It surprised Sutter; according to the news reports, the father had worked at a tech company. Wouldn't he have purchased newer equipment? In addition, other than a couple of computer manuals and a few leather-bound books, nothing sat on the built-in bookshelves. No photos, no objets d'art. The utilitarianism seemed out of place for a home office.

Something moved against the spider web. It rose, as if a breeze pushed it to one side, though he felt nothing. Sutter snapped two pictures and examined the results. He saw nothing until he enlarged the capture. It was a spider with a round body that shone blue in the flash. The thick trichobothria made Sutter think of the fur of a black cat, though the spindly legs dispelled that image. Sutter shuddered. He wasn't afraid of spiders in general, and he hardly considered himself an arachnophobe, but this one did not look right: its body was too large, its legs too thin and too long.

He switched to the next image. The spider appeared even closer, the fine hairs on its body more discernable, its round black eyes slitted with amber.

On the digital camera, on a still frame, the spider suddenly turned to him and blinked.

His grip loosened and the camera tumbled from his hands, but he caught it before it hit the floor. He checked the screen again, but the image was the one from before, catching the spider's shape but not its detail. A glance at the settings confirmed that he had not turned on the camera's video recording. He had not imagined it; of that he was certain. He knew what he had seen.

Stepping closer to the desk, he examined the web but did not see the creature that had spun it. He waved his hand over the web, hoping that disturbed air would cause it to move, but the threads in the web remained taut.

He looked up, and realized that it was darker. Sunlight grew dimmer outside, deepening the shadows. He crossed the living room again to stand over a dark stain ruining the Oriental rug; so this was where the wife had been shot. He stood still for a moment, trying to feel anything amiss. He took his camera to focus on the stain, but it remained a stain and didn't manifest into something even more sinister than what it already was.

He peered through his camera, snapping a quick photo of the rug. Too dark, he realized, and turned on the flash for another photo. It caught the room, but nothing else, even as he adjusted the settings.

Sutter sighed, and wondered if his outing would be a bust. Maybe the spider had been his imagination after all. Maybe he should take another look at the spider web photos.

Frowning, he began to scroll through the images. He couldn't find the photos he had taken of the spider web. It should have been right before the photo of the rug, but now it was gone.

A shadow crossed over him.

He turned but saw nothing. Sutter started and backed away, pushing against a swinging door. It was a hallway sheathed in shadow, open doors illuminating decorated rugs on wooden floors. At the other end was another door with a glass knob. He reached behind him to push at the one through which he came but it wouldn't budge.

His footsteps clomped on the floor as he walked. The designs on the rug writhed in the dim light, reminding Sutter of snakes in a pit. As he passed one door, he stole a quick glance: a bathroom, its toilet stained, shower curtain as thin as cheesecloth tucked into a cracked tub, the slats of the wooden floor splintered and warped. He wondered how anybody would have been comfortable trying to use it.

The rotten smell grew stronger. *It's behind the door*, he thought. That's where the kitchen was. That's where the children died. He squeezed the knob and slowly twisted it. If his proof of afterlife was there, if it was still contained in this house, then surely it would be through this door.

He opened it.

It was indeed a kitchen, bare of appliances or cookware, the only furniture a small table of blonde wood. He tried a light, but the power had been shut off. Even in the dimming sunlight through the window the kitchen looked empty, as if nothing had ever lived here. Sutter's heart sank. To have come here, only to find something so mundane. It was nothing, nothing at all. Even the smell was gone, replaced by disinfectant and silence. He pulled his mask from his nose and sighed.

Still, he was here. He might as well take one more photo. He raised his camera, adjusted the lenses, and snapped a picture. The flash blinded him for a moment, causing him to rub his eyes.

And then it filled his nostrils. The overpowering stench. He leaned against the granite countertop and retched. Beneath it was a burning odor that Sutter associated with fireworks. Or gunfire. He heard music—powerful, thrumming through his body as if he were a guitar string. His camera banged against the counter and he saw the screen. It was video of three figures; white, eyes wide, mouths open and ravenous. And they were moving toward him.

Sutter realized he had it wrong. Completely wrong. He'd chided his wife about not understanding that there were different types of ghosts, but he had not considered something important. Some ghosts might dissipate, but others needed something to keep them here. He realized this as he felt their cold fingers slip through his clothes and taste his sweating flesh with their tongues.

He spun around and saw them. Three apparitions, one meeting him face to face, the other two coming to the top of his stomach.

The apparitions stared with empty sockets filled with black space like onyx that absorbed light. Ragged holes pierced their gaunt bodies, some the size of pebbles, others in their heads and chests large enough for Sutter to push his hands through without touching what appeared to be strips of flesh. And there were their mouths: open wide, with lips surrounded needle-like teeth that looked as sharp as the ivory nails tipping their slender fingers.

Through the gouges in the apparitions' bodies Sutter saw another apparition, a man sprawled next to the refrigerator, his hands roaming the wounds blossoming on its torso.

Sutter screamed and, without thinking, raised his camera and snapped off two quick shots. The flash illuminated a kitchen bare of any being but himself, but the figures returned along with the darkness.

He screamed again and ran from the kitchen, through the hallway. The front door. He could make it if he was fast.

As he ran to the living room a pain seared his stomach. He understood completely. The ghosts needed something to keep them here. That's why they seemed gaunt, why someone had left food on the front porch.

Some ghosts wanted vengeance. And some…some were hungry.

He tripped on the rug, his camera slipping from his hands and falling into the intricate oriental pattern. Sutter scrabbled for it while at the same time trying to stand, but it was too late. The ghosts were on him, their mouths extending to bite and feed.

This time, he wasn't the only hungry one.

## SCRATCHING

Katie Robinson

It's been six weeks since I last slept the night through.

Staring at myself in the bathroom mirror, I look like hell. There's sallow skin with dark circles under my eyes that no amount of rejuvenating and hydrating face cream will fix. My long, dark hair needs washing. No makeup. I look away from the mirror and reach for the box of pills the GP gave me. A low dose sedative. As I open the box, a small folded leaflet drops out. I pick it up and drop it in the bin without reading it, no doubt a long list of side effects. Popping a pill in my mouth, I wash it down with a glass of water.

"Right." I look at my reflection again. "We will sleep through the night, we will sleep through the night, we will sleep through the night." I try to sound confident, and I think I'm successful. I certainly sound more confident than I feel. Nodding to my reflection, I head out of the bathroom and into the bedroom.

I sigh at the pamphlets sitting on the bed. Mum must have put them there. She had dropped by this evening; I hadn't realized that she had come into the bedroom. I picked them up and flick through the collection. All the pamphlets were for new mattresses. If only she knew, it's not the mattress that's causing my insomnia. It has nothing to do with the bed.

Dropping the leaflets into the bin, I clamber into the bed, and I reach for a paperback. I've been reading this one for two weeks and can't remember anything about it. I've re-read the first chapter ten times now, more proof that lack of sleep is scrambling my brain. I open the book, read half a dozen words and close it again.

"What's the point?" I lift my phone off the charging pad and flick through the news. More political unrest, more death and tragedy; I take none of it in. I put the phone back on the charging pad and settle down. I'm hesitant to turn off the bedside lamp.

"For crying out loud! This is pathetic," I grunt, getting out of bed and walking to the door. I turn the hall light on and leave the door open a little, just enough to see outside the bedroom. I lift the cricket bat I took out of the cupboard weeks ago and peer into the hallway. There is nothing there. I stare out at the hallway for a moment, feeling anxiety tighten my stomach before I force myself to close the door and slide the recently purchased bolt across, locking myself in. I put the bat beside the bed and turn off the bedside lamp.

I'm not sure how long I lie awake, waiting for it to start.

Tonight it starts at 3 am, later than the last two nights. I roll over, facing away from the door and close my eyes tighter as the scratching starts and quickly gets louder. It gains in volume with each breath I take until I can't pretend I don't hear it. I turn over quickly, cursing as I do. I reach for the cricket bat and switch the lamp on.

The scratching stops immediately.

It takes me a few long moments sitting in the oppressive silence to gather my courage, pull back my blanket, and pad over to the door. My hand is shaking when I reach for the handle.

I've done this every night for the last six weeks, I know what's on the other side of the door, and still my hand shakes. I grip the bat tightly and wrench the door open.

There's nothing in the hallway.

I knew nothing would be there, but every night my heart hammers and my chest draws tight. Every night I tell myself that there will be something there. How could there be that much noise with nothing there? I don't understand.

Like all the times before, I stare at the hallway for a long time before locking the door and returning to bed. The scratching wakes me up twice more that night.

In the morning, I crawl out of bed and go into the bathroom. Checking myself in the mirror, I notice that I look terrible and feel worse. I head downstairs after a quick shower, picking up the post from the front mat and putter about in the kitchen making tea. There're still a few boxes in the kitchen, left over from when I moved in two months ago. Unpacking is a slow process, considering my lack of sleep.

I sit at the central island in the kitchen and try to figure out what I'm going to do with myself. The office still needs unpacking; it's a super-sized job which should keep me busy over the weekend and stop me from thinking too hard.

Decision made, I stand up…and freeze.

I spot movement in the doorway out of the corner of my eye and flinch. I drop my cup, but ignore the smash of broken china as it hits the floor.

There's a nothing in the doorway. Looking down, I see I've stepped on a broken piece of cup, a china shard is buried in my heel. I look back up but there's still nothing in the doorway.

"You're exhausted," I say, my voice cracking.

I hop across the kitchen to the first aid kit and work at getting the shards of the cup out of my foot. The shard isn't deep, and a wash and a plaster later, I find myself calming down. My heart slows and my hands stop shaking. By the time I've cleaned the mess, I feel almost normal.

I spend the rest of the day unpacking the 'office.' It's a box room really, barely big enough for my desk and a couple shelves. Prior to my moving in, this tiny room must have been a nursery, the wallpaper being the main give away, a soft pastel pink with a border of suitably adorable cartoon animals. It certainly doesn't scream sensible workspace, but I'll redecorate when I've got the time and energy.

It's late-afternoon before I stop for lunch. Back in the kitchen, munching on a sandwich, I absently go through the mail. Most of it is for the family that owned the house before me. I scrawl "Moved—not at this address" onto the front of the envelopes and put the mail into the pile to take out with me on Monday.

One of the letters catches my eye. It's a thick and battered envelope, the local supermarket logo emblazoned on the front, above the words "Printing your precious memories." As I lift the envelope, it splits, the photos falling free along with the receipt. Fortunately for the house's previous family, I've just unpacked all my stationary and have a replacement envelope. I plan to drop the photos with the estate agent on my way to work on Monday and ask them to forward the photos to the family.

I start picking the photos up from the floor and table and can't help but take a look at them. A man, woman, an old dog, a young boy, and a new baby. The family looks happy in every photo; it makes me smile to see them. But no wonder they moved; with the baby, this house is way too small.

I find myself imagining what their life must have been like in the house where I now live. I spot more photos that had slid under the central island. Reaching down to collect them, my breath catches. They must have been happy here, judging by their smiles. Maybe there were no scratching noises at night back then.

I continue to collect the fallen pictures, and stuff them all into the envelope.

I spend the rest of the afternoon and evening unpacking the office. The tiny room is now looking extra cozy with all my work stuff filling it. I'm secretly impressed that I managed to get it all in and am finishing off the last box when I hear the first *bang*.

It sounds like the metallic crash of a pot hitting the tiled floor of the kitchen. The sound makes me jump. I take a deep breath and try to slow my heart rate, which rocketed at the sudden noise.

Less than a minute later I hear something else fall, something bigger, followed by a clatter of objects skittering over the floor.

"Oh shit." My voice comes out as a whimper. I contemplate just staying put for a moment, the fear making me stupid. This won't go away if I ignore it. I stand, my legs weak and threatening to buckle under me. I steady myself and head out, but I slip into my bedroom to pick up the bat.

I clench my teeth as I start down the stairs. I can hear something. It's a sound I know from childhood, but not one that should be in my kitchen.

The sound stops the instant I flick the kitchen lights on, revealing nothing but pots, pans, and the washing up from lunch still soaking in the sink. The garbage pail's been knocked over; rubbish littering the floor, but there's nothing else out of place. There's no one here, yet somehow I know there is.

"I'm armed!" I shout, slightly impressed that my voice doesn't shake.

Something solid barrels into my legs, sending me to the ground. A brief but intense weight hits my stomach hard and I can't breathe.

I fight to get back on my feet, gasping to recover my breath. One of the tins suddenly spins across the floor. A yelp escapes me. The small central island shakes as something bumps it. One of the plates I had left there wobbles and falls. I expect it to hit the floor and smash, but it hits something else, something I can't see; something over two feet off the ground before it crashes to the floor.

I am back on my feet in an instant, tearing out of the kitchen and taking the stairs in the hallway two at a time. Each breath feels like burning sandpaper in my lungs. I reach my bedroom and spin, slamming the door behind me and sliding the small bolt across.

"The fuck!" I try to say but can't get the air in; I have to swallow a few times before my throat stops burning and the sudden intense nausea subsides.

I hear light steps in the hallway and I all but throw myself at the door just as something heavy, strong and very real pushes at the door. I'm jolted back an inch, the bolt gives and comes away from the doorframe but the door holds. I fight to get my feet under me, pushing back. The door shakes as the thing on the other side throws itself at the wood. I feel tears run down my cheeks.

I glance to the bedside table where my mobile phone usually sits only to see it bereft, it takes my brain a moment to register what my eyes were telling me. My phone is gone. I'd had it a moment ago, in the office.

My phone is in the office.

I tense as I hear the creature on the other side of the door back up to run against the door again. I brace myself for the thunderous blow. The door shakes again and I feel sweat break out across my entire body as the wood cracks.

"Go away!" I scream. The creature seems to hesitate. I hear it back away. It doesn't run at the door again. There's a whump as something heavy sits down and then silence. After several long heartbeats I risk edging back from the door; surely I have one of my old phones in here somewhere. There has to be something.

The sound that rises up on the other side of the door is a full blown howl. The sound swells and rolls like thunder until it is right above me, until it is impossibly loud. I slap my hands over my ears and squeeze my eyes closed. As loud as it is, it's so mournful that something in my chest loosens and grief fills me, drowning out the terror until all I can feel is a desperate despair and longing.

The sound stops as suddenly as it started; the silence heavy, filled by the sound of my breathing and…panting? The panting turns quickly into whining and the grief that sits on my chest swells. I'm crying, sniveling at the overwhelming feeling of loneliness. There's a gentle scratch at the door.

"You're the dog in the picture, aren't you?" I say aloud, not expecting an answer. The whining and scratching continue. "You belonged to the family and you were really loyal to them." I move back from the door a little. "You died; you were old." I turn to face the door. "But you stayed—you were a good boy." The whining continues. "Then they moved, and left you behind."

I reach for the door. I pull the handle down slowly and let the door crack open. The moment the door moves, the ghost outside pushes it forward. I over-balance and end up on my backside. I am shaking but the grief is still stronger than the fear. Something hot, moist and pretty rank-smelling touches my face. Dog breath.

Despite smelling the breath and hearing the whimpers, I can't see anything. There is nothing there, not really. Not anything as visible as a physical body, but there is something: a shimmer in the air, a sense of heaviness.

There is a *feeling*.

The apparition doesn't attack and I find myself reaching out despite everything. I flinch when my hand touches something entirely solid, covered in coarse fur.

There is a chuff of breath before the creature moves. It edges forwards until I can feel it pressed along my side, its hot breath disturbing my hair. We sit on the floor together for a long time, my hand resting on ghost-dog's back, absently petting something not really there. My legs start to ache, as does my back. But I don't move.

I can hear the steady whump-whump of a wagging tail striking the carpeted floor. "You just want some company, boy? Is that what all this fuss has been about? You miss your family?" I let out a slow sigh and close my eyes. "So *you're* the one who has been keeping me awake every night."

I know I can live here now, and make it my home.

For the first time in two months, I sleep through the night. The ghost-dog sleeps at the foot of my bed.

## FILLING STATION

Joe R. Lansdale

It was an old filling station. It was set off the road and the only reason I went there was because I really had to pee, and it was the only station I had seen signs for in a while. The signs were old and hand painted, and they had big faded red arrows on them that directed me to the place.

The station had once been on a main highway, but they built the Interstate through, and that put it out of the way. But somehow, it had hung on.

The station was grimy, with dust and bugs that had blown against the outside glass, which was long and wide. You could see through all the grime, but not clearly. The light behind the glass was dim, as if seen from a distance, even though I was close.

There were two pumps outside, and they were really old. There wasn't any business about putting your charge card in them and running the gas yourself. I could tell that just by looking at them.

You had to go inside to pay before the gas was turned on. But I didn't want gas. I wanted to pee. I parked over by the restroom and when I got out I saw on the restroom door a sign that said you had to ask for the key.

I quick-walked to the station's front door, which was an old, wooden affair that creaked open with a rusty hinge sound. There was a stringy guy in a gray cap behind the cash register, and on the counter next to the register were large smudgy glass jars of pickled eggs, pickled pig's feet, some big dill pickles in brine, as well as something suspicious in a jar full of yellow liquid. There was a pair of tongs lying on a cracked saucer, in case you wanted to screw off the lid of one of the jars and pull something out.

There were the usual odds and ends elsewhere. Chips, beef jerky, air-fresheners, and the like. Some of it looked too old to still be for sale. Some of the candies and chips had names I hadn't seen in ages and thought were long out of business.

On the wall behind the man was a boar's head. It was moth-eaten and one of the tusks was missing.

I asked about the restroom key. He took his time to answer. He had one of those voices that sounded as if it weren't used often and had corroded.

"You got to buy something."

"All right," I said. "I'll have a pack of gum."

"Needs to be more than gum."

"All right, then, how about a bag of chips and a package of gum?"

I got those items and paid for them and he gave me the restroom key, which was attached by a chain to a narrow board a foot long and as thick as my wrist.

"Door locks behind you," he said. "You won't need it coming out, but bring it back."

I told him I'd return for my goods after I finished up, went out, and walked around to where the restroom was.

When I used the key and entered, I heard the door lock behind me. I flicked on the light, which was one bulb in the center of the ceiling. It hummed to life, but was hazy and gave off a urine-like color. I decided the station fellow might not think the restroom was public, but it looked as if it were quite public, because it stunk of urine and feces and the little white mint in the urinal had turned as yellow as a canary. The smell that rose up from it was stifling. Beneath the urinal was a crusty dark stain. The last time this place had been clean was when it was built.

I decided I ought to do more than pee. I ought to go the whole hog, as much as I hated to in a hole like that. I went into the toilet, closed the door, tried to lock it, but the lock was poor, so you were really on a kind of honor system. If someone pushed it from the outside, the stall door would easily fly open.

By this time, I was glad to see there was paper on a roller, and that the seat wasn't too nasty looking, though there was a dark stain inside the porcelain bowl that made me gag a little. And, like the urinal, it was odiferous.

I used some toilet paper to wipe the seat off, placed the board and key on the back of the toilet tank, let down my pants, managed to sit down on the toilet to do my business, and that's when I heard the door open and someone come in.

I couldn't see who it was, but I could hear them, and they were next to the toilet stall, at that horrid urinal. I could hear them peeing.

"I showed him," said a man's voice, and for a moment I thought he might be speaking to me.

I decided not to respond, but tried to do what I had come to do as quickly as I could.

"I showed him. I showed him all right. But, oh, so much blood. And the guts steaming. Nice. Real nice."

I wondered if he was talking about a deer. It was hunting season. But who was he talking to? Had someone come inside with him, and if so, why weren't they speaking back?

There was a long moment of silence, and then I heard, "I cut him a lot. I wanted to meet some place nice, not here. I sure cut him, though. I should never have picked him up. I should never have. Jesus, why do I keep coming back here?"

There was a pause, as if waiting for an answer.

"He was like all the others. Just wouldn't listen. And I had to cut him. I had to cook him. I had to eat him."

I was finished doing what I had come to do by this time. I used the toilet paper, stood, and quietly pulled up and fastened my pants.

My skin was cold and there were goosebumps on my arms and on the back of my neck.

"You would know how to act, wouldn't you?" said the voice.

I caught my breath. Was he speaking to me?

The man had moved. I couldn't see him, but I could hear a bit of shuffling from the urinal to the door of the stall. I looked at the crack between the door and the stall, but couldn't see anyone. The door was a partial door so you could see feet underneath it, if you bent down to look, but I wasn't about to bend down and look with him that close. I clenched my fist in case he should push the door and come through.

The stall door moved ever so slightly.

"Not everyone has to die. Sometimes, it's good."

There was movement again, and I had the distinct feeling the man had stepped away from the stall. I stood there with my fist clenched for a long time. I didn't hear the outside bathroom door open, but I didn't hear him roaming around in there anymore either.

I decided I couldn't just stay in this stinky stall and wait and see what he was up to. Maybe he had gone out, and I hadn't heard him leave.

I inched close to the stall door, and though my skin tingled with fear, I put my eye to the crack and looked out. I couldn't see anyone from that angle. I stepped back and bent down and looked under the stall, where the urinal was, but I couldn't see feet.

I remembered then I had put the key and board on the back of the toilet tank lid. I picked it up. It was heavy. It would make a good weapon.

I took a deep breath and came out of the stall with the board cocked over my shoulder. I didn't see anyone. Now I was too frightened to go outside. I had the board, but opening the door and finding someone waiting out there was a horrible thing to contemplate.

Eventually, I built up my courage enough to open the door and look out at the night.

No one was outside. As I was standing there, the water at the sink came on. It startled me. I glanced back. Water was running full force from the faucet. It didn't look like the sort of faucet that was set off by movement. It was one of those old turn it on and off with your hand affairs. But how had it come on?

I took a breath. Decided it was obvious. It was as flawed as this entire bathroom. Somehow the handle had slipped and the water came on. It wasn't an entirely satisfying solution, but I went with it.

A moment later, the water shut off. That really troubled me. I went out.

I let the door close behind me without bothering with cutting off the light. I walked away with the board still in my hand. I went out and stood by my car. There was no one around. It was warmer out there and the air was certainly fresher.

Had it been the station owner? And if so, what the hell was he talking about? Was he messing with me? Was it someone confessing something terrible to himself, someone who noticed I was in there, then asked me how I would act if I were with him?

And that's when I heard a noise behind the closed bathroom door, and then the voice.

"I need someone else. I really do."

The bathroom door cracked open slightly. I could feel cold air slipping out from inside, along with the stink.

"Come back in," the voice said.

I got in my car, started it, backed up, and rolled away from there. I looked in my rearview mirror.

The bathroom door was open wider now. I could see a shadow pinned against the light from inside. Then the door opened even more and the shadow slipped out and rushed toward the rear of my car.

A somewhat human shape grabbed at the back of the car, found purchase and clung there, crawling up to the rear windshield.

At that moment, behind the car, the wedge of light the open bathroom door had provided went away as the door closed by itself and the shadowy shape clinging to the rear windshield blended with the night.

The light that had been on inside the main section of the grimy filling station was dark. My view of the station in my rearview mirror receded as I pressed my foot on the accelerator.

I drove onto the Interstate. There were lots of street lights along the way and lots of cars, and they made me feel better.

Few hours later I had the urge to stop for another bathroom break, and even though there were now plenty of brightly lit and modern stations just off the four-lane highway, I didn't stop. I held it.

At some point I realized I hadn't picked up the items I had bought at the station, and the bathroom key on the chain fastened to the board was on the seat beside me. I also remembered the bathroom door had locked behind me when I entered, so how had someone come in?

I rolled down my window to throw out the board and key. The wind that blew in was dark and foul and icy cold.

## HOUDINI'S LAST SEANCE

JT Siems

Lawrence Brown had his ear to the door when it flew open—his wife exiting and running down the hall in a swish of skirts.

A middle-aged woman with tears streaking down her face followed out of the room. "Oh Mrs. Brown, you angel! You're heaven-sent! Are you all right?"

Lawrence grabbed his cane and hobbled to the woman before she could go further. They both jumped as the door slammed.

"Mr. Brown, she did it! I didn't believe it at first but I'm sure of it. We spoke to my son Danny!" the woman cried as she kissed Lawrence's hand.

"Oh, that's wonderful, Madam! My Dorothy has a gift, she does. Now I hope we'll see you back," he said pleasantly, trying to extricate his hand from the sobbing woman's clammy, tear-soaked grasp.

"Oh, you will Mr. Brown, and all my friends too!"

Lawrence leaned on his cane and led her to the front door, discrete in his attempt to show her out as gently as he could. But the woman spun around, and her tears and snot spattered onto his arm. He grimaced in disgust.

"May I please thank your dear wife?" the woman gushed, still sobbing with joy. "She ran out of the room before I could offer a proper gratitude. Nothing's made any sense since the war took Danny. She's saved me, Mr. Brown!"

Lawrence gently redirected her back toward the door and gave her a sad smile. "Dorothy is quite attached to our infant son as you can imagine. Being away from him causes her great distress. She's catering to him now, but when you visit again…"

The woman nodded and thanked him again before finally taking her leave. Lawrence breathed deep and locked up. He turned around slowly, a faint feeling of dread spreading through his mind. The dusty floorboards creaked beneath his feet as he made his way to the end of the darkened hall. He knocked lightly on a door with cracking white paint and a black door knob.

"Dorothy?"

The only answer was a rapid creaking. Lawrence closed his eyes and slowly turned the obsidian knob. He closed his eyes and stuck his head into the room.

He heard the coos of the baby and the rapid creaking of the rocking chair.

"Dorothy my love, rousing success as always! When you're, uh, finished in here please come sit with me; I have some rather exciting news." He received no reply and quickly retreated, shutting the door behind him.

Lawrence sat on a fraying velvet settee in the parlor room for a good hour before the creaking stopped and he heard her rise. He hated the parlor room—it was Dorothy's workspace and the ghosts she talked to lingered in the air even after she had gone. He wasn't a brave man and he could only tolerate the room with his eyes tightly shut.

The swishing of her long black skirts announced her arrival. Dorothy paused, staring at Lawrence from across the room. "What is it?" she asked.

He looked her up and down. Her black hair was pulled back so tight that it stretched her cheeks. Her long black dress was a severe cut, riding up her neck and covering every surface below her head. A white lace collar was the only accent of color. While he appreciated the money her new endeavor brought in, this dark transformation pained him to see.

"Mr. Houdini has come back to town," he smiled, holding up a letter and a newspaper clipping.

Dorothy flinched.

Lawrence swallowed. "And I've received this letter from Mr. Houdini's secretary that he is interested in observing your services, my dear," he paused, "You do know about the reward, don't you?"

She crossed the room and glared down at him—the black ruffles of her skirts swallowed his knees.

"Of course I know about the reward! How might he have known about *me*, Lawrence?"

He breathed heavily and looked at his hands. "I wrote to him. You've got scores of happy customers. They all call you an angel sent from Heaven. I've no doubt you can do this."

"He means to humiliate me like all the common spiritualists that 'cold read' in the street!"

He stood and grasped her hands affectionately. "How can he humiliate you if your gift is true?"

She snatched her hands back. "My gift *is* true, but he'll find some way to sully my name. This is my vocation, my calling, Lawrence. How can you let that man into my parlor?"

"We need the money, Dorothy! Mr. Houdini is offering it up himself. All you've got to do is speak to his dear departed mother and all of our troubles are solved!"

"We wouldn't have these troubles had it not been for you, Lawrence. I must go back to my child."

Lawrence took a deep breath. She hadn't said no.

*****

Days passed with nary a word from Houdini. Anxiety gripped Lawrence and he spent his time haunting the dark hallway. Despite her anger at the suggestion, Dorothy seemed entirely unperturbed by nerves. She carried on as before, performing readings and séances, then spending all her free time rocking in the chair with their baby.

Everyone knew Houdini detested spiritualists, thanks to a particularly egregious attempt to contact his deceased mother. The wife of his once-good friend Sir Arthur Conan Doyle, herself a medium, channeled fifteen pages of automatic writing proclaiming the spirit to be none other than Houdini's mother, Cecilia.

But Cecilia was Hungarian, and her English was terrible—Houdini doubted she would have given such a lengthy message outside of her native tongue.

The magician had been distraught and found a new calling by exposing psychics as frauds. He exposed all their elaborate tricks to move tables, fake moaning voices, and produce ectoplasm. So confident was he in his ability to detect fraudulent spiritualists that he had offered a very public reward for any medium who might sway his mind.

Many had taken on the challenge, but none as yet had succeeded. Lawrence believed in his wife but hoped her gifts were enough to impress the magician—the Browns were desperate for the money that such notoriety was sure to bring.

*****

Three loud raps on the front door startled Lawrence from a late afternoon nap. For a moment he wasn't sure if it actually was the door or Dorothy's spirits playing tricks on him again. With great effort, he stretched his arms, steadied himself with his cane, and limped toward the door.

Sunlight flooded the dark entryway and gave the short man standing before him an angelic glow. Lawrence had never been in the presence of a star before and Harry Houdini was one of the biggest in the world. His likeness on posters and in newspapers was true, albeit in the flesh, he looked his age with lines forming on his face and a spattering of gray flecking from his otherwise jet-black hair.

He smiled like a gentleman. "Mr. Brown, I presume? I'm Harry Houdini and am here at your request." He reached out his hand and Lawrence was so eager to shake it he dropped his cane.

"Yes sir, Mr. Houdini! The pleasure is all mine! Please come in." Lawrence trembled as he reached down to retrieve his cane, but the escape artist was quick and placed the cane in Lawrence's grip before he could embarrass himself further. "Let me show you to the parlor room, sir. My wife Dorothy won't be but a minute."

As he stepped aside to let Houdini enter, Lawrence watched the man closely. The magician's eyes darted over every nook and cranny of the house. His lips moved silently as though he was narrating to himself what he was seeing.

After a moment of silence, Houdini seemed to remember himself and smiled grandly, "Might I have a tour first, my good man? You've such a beautiful home and it would help me to see your wife's environment so that I may get the most accurate sense of her talents."

"Well, Mr. Houdini, we're not what you'd call well-off—the house is what you see, the parlor, a kitchen and our personal bedroom upstairs, of course."

Houdini pointed down the darkened hall to the door with chipped white paint and the black door knob. "What about that room?"

Lawrence felt his face flush and hoped Houdini wouldn't notice.

"Dorothy is in there now tending to our infant son. She's not decent, I'm afraid. I'll just take you to the parlor sir."

Houdini nodded, disappointment and irritation written all over his face. Lawrence turned. He was already perspiring.

He opened the door to the parlor and gestured for Houdini to enter. "Please sit, Mr. Houdini, I'll just be a moment." Lawrence closed the door behind him and made his way to his infant son's room.

He rapped lightly on the door, chipped paint falling to the floor. "Dorothy, Mr. Houdini is here." He could hear the furious creaking of the rocking chair. Lawrence gently opened the door, and closing his eyes, stuck his head into the room. "My love, it's time." His eyes were still closed but he could hear her rise and approach him. He led her out of the room and back to the parlor.

They entered the parlor to find Houdini on his hands and knees, assessing the wooden séance table. He shot up to his feet, "Ah, Mrs. Brown, I've heard so much about you. Lovely home you have! As you may have heard, I have taken a special interest in psychic activity and would be honored to have a reading and see you in action."

Dorothy said nothing—gliding regally to the table, she sat down and shook out her wrists. Houdini looked to Lawrence, his face a bit baffled. Watching Dorothy closely, the magician finally relaxed into a seat across from her.

"I'll just be in the next room, my love," Lawrence called as he pulled the door behind him.

"No, Lawrence, you stay," Dorothy spat at him with an ominous look.

Lawrence flushed again. Houdini was watching everything, and this was not how Dorothy usually liked things. She had never invited Lawrence in for one of her readings.

After a brief hesitation, he shut the door and made his way to the table. The shades were drawn and the room was impossibly dark for such an early hour. There was a whisper of a match and the brief smell of smoke as Dorothy lit a candle and placed it on the table between them.

The flickering of the candle cast shadows on their faces and Lawrence could feel his heart racing. "Our fingers must touch, like this, pinkies and thumbs," Dorothy commanded.

Lawrence had never seen her like this before—such self-confidence and authority. Once they had obliged, Dorothy closed her eyes and slumped her head. Her breathing was loud and ragged.

Houdini's face was unreadable. He watched in silence and his piercing eyes took in everything. Lawrence felt a light breeze on his cheek and thought he could hear the creaking of the rocking chair from down the hallway. He willed himself not to shudder.

After a few minutes, Dorothy's head shot up and her eyes opened. But they weren't her eyes—they were black saucers. Lawrence gasped, but Houdini remained impassive.

There was a low, guttural growl which at first Lawrence took to be an intruding animal before he realized the sound was emanating from Dorothy's throat.

The breeze grew stronger, the candle flickered out, and the table began to rise from the floor. Lawrence cried out and snatched his hands back to his side. Now it was just Houdini and his wife, seemingly possessed, staring daggers at each other from across a floating table.

"Psychic hunter, misses his mother! Let's see what it takes to frighten him away!" cackled a deep voice that was not Dorothy's.

Lawrence was so frightened he couldn't breathe. He reached for his cane and Dorothy's head turned in his direction. A white, eggy substance ran down her cheeks like tears. "And scared, crippled Lawrence. Houdini, did he tell you how he came to be crippled? How it came to be that his wife brings in the money because he can't work? How it came to be that he killed his son?"

Houdini still didn't react.

Lawrence, broken, cried out, "I didn't kill our son, Dorothy! It was a coach accident, Mr. Houdini. I was pushing his buggy and the coach…it was an accident! Dorothy, please, if you're in there come out. Communing with these devils won't bring him back!"

A swirling wind howled, and the table rose all the way to the ceiling before falling back to the floor. The walls creaked and papers fluttered. The cane was wrenched from Lawrence's grip and it crashed into the table, shattering it into splinters.

Just as suddenly as it had started, the wind ceased and the room was deathly still. Houdini was still impassive as he studied Dorothy. She looked from Houdini to Lawrence, her face anguished. She wiped the eggy substance from her cheeks and ran out of the room. Lawrence fell to the floor sobbing.

Houdini silently assessed the room again before exiting the parlor and shutting Lawrence in with his wife's ghosts.

Houdini made his way through the house down the hall where a door was ajar, and within, he could hear the coos of a baby and a rocking chair creaking at a furious pace.

He entered the room. "Mrs. Brown, I thank you for the show…" his voice trailed off as he tried to make sense of the macabre scene before him.

Dorothy sat in the rocker—her back turned to him. Amidst the ruffles of her black dress she delicately cradled the skeleton of an infant. The tiny bones were a faded yellow and looked held together by pins.

"What I'd give, Mr. Houdini, for them to take this power, this curse and just give me back my baby!" she wailed.

Houdini's face was pensive. "Mrs. Brown, I think I've seen all I need to. I shan't return for another reading. My secretary will contact you about the check."

Houdini shut the door behind him. The soft coos of the baby and the creaking of the rocker haunted him as he made his way out of the house.

## SAL'S REQUIEM

Sebastian Crow

Sal Mingus dreams while awake. He is a ghost-walker, drifting through a room filled with the walking dead. Ectoplasmic puppets are dancing on an invisible wire; their uncoordinated bodies move with the herky-jerky motions of wind-up toys.

A man in coat and tails races through the viewing room, his body covered in flames. The dead watch on, amused as the burning man makes a beeline for the exit.

"That Felix, such a card. He does that at every funeral," a very dead George Ausberger says to Sal, who nods knowingly.

*It's a funeral of the dead for the dead. They're welcoming their newest member,* Sal thinks.

Near the casket, Molly Pickett is weeping. Black blood, thick as oil, pours from the gaping bullet wound in her eye. She speaks in a low, spectral drone to Donald Bigelow, dressed to the nines for his death in an immaculate three-piece, pinstripe suit and solid gold cufflinks. Clods of mud cake his bare feet.

Sal always believed it was just a myth that they removed the shoes before burial. Doesn't matter, this is his dream and he'll imagine the dead anyway he chooses. So, he imagines Donald naked, and then he is. Sal can distinctly see the y-incision from Don's autopsy, the black stitches keeping the remains of what internal organs weren't harvested from spilling out onto the plush, burgundy carpet.

He continues his ghost-walk of the funeral parlor. He avoids the ash-covered casket, with its unspeakable contents hidden by an honor guard of cracked vases filled with wilted roses, withered wreaths of plastic flowers and charred, curling photographs of Aimee—his daughter, his only child as she was in life; smiling and vibrant, her ghost caught in celluloid, the girl next door with her long, blonde hair and electric blue eyes.

Sal turns away, the pain of his loss still too fresh. He heads toward the rear of the room where Marsha Rennicker, his old high school sweetheart, lurches toward him, her misshapen body twisted and broken from the fatal fall that claimed her at age nineteen. She drags one leg like a mummy from some old B-movie. He steps behind a large wreath of dead roses and pale carnations to avoid her clutching embrace.

He sees himself, dressed in a blue chambray shirt and jeans, stumbling across the room, one side of his head caved in. Fat, slick-bodied beetles scurry out of a hole where his left eye should be.

And then he's dream-screaming, tripping the night fantastic. He dances a grim fandango across the funeral parlor floor, coupling and uncoupling with the undead. A ghost orchestra appears in front of Aimee's coffin, the musicians in various stages of rot. Some appear recently dead; their pale skins splotched with grey patches, while others are no more than animated skeletons, their ancient bones yellowed with age. Their clothes are mere tattered rags draped over their desiccated remains like oversized hospital gowns.

The band strikes up a strident, discordant waltz that is more a howl from Hell than actual music. Sal is not at all surprised when a rotting Bing Crosby steps up to the microphone and begins to croon in a hollow, sepulchral voice. In his left hand, he holds a human femur. Strips of putrid meat dangle from the well-gnawed bone.

*I'll be screaming at you in all the old familiar places,* he croons.

He spots Aimee, standing near her casket and winces. The right side of her face is fine, she's just as he remembers her: tan and beautiful, shoulder-length blonde hair, perfectly coiffed. But the left side is a nightmare scratched in flesh; skin blistered and blackened, ribbons of scars twist her lovely smile into a leering, skeleton grin and where the crash split her skull, a gray mass of brain matter pulsates like the beat of a heart.

She raises a hand and motions for him.

*Come dance with me, Father.*

Sal closes his eyes and counts to ten. When he opens them
Aimee is gone, as are all the other ghosts. His wife, L

standing beside the casket—closed because the crash caused too much damage for Clyde Sayles, the mortician, to repair.

Mourners form a procession to offer condolences. Sal wants to go to her and offer what cold comfort he can but doesn't think he can bear one more expression of sympathy from the crowd, no matter how well meant. He abandons his wife to the grieving mob and escapes into the anonymity of the night for a cigarette.

Later, on the drive home, Leanne is behind the wheel, staring glaze-eyed at the slick-black asphalt, operating the vehicle on instinct. He thinks he sees Aimee standing in the middle of the road, still beckoning him to come dance. Sal leans his forehead against the passenger side window. The car is silent, except for the sound of his sobs.

*****

Dull moonlight pours through the bedroom window. Death is creeping about, stalking the quiet, predawn hours. Sal can hear it, moving like a stealthy burglar in the living room downstairs.

Sal isn't sure if he's still dreaming. That sense of reality slipping away still lingers, as does the horror from the evening's viewing. But Leanne lies beside him, her chest rising softly, deep in sleep. He can smell the ripe but not entirely unpleasant aroma of her bed-farts, as familiar and welcome as the scent of her sweat. It reassures him he is awake and sane.

Nevertheless, he feels they are not alone in the house. Someone is in the living room. Someone who's waiting for him. Maybe it really is Death.

He climbs out of bed, soft as a church mouse, and stands over the bed, waiting for his eyes to adjust to the dark. Once he is certain he can see enough to proceed, he slips out of the room. To keep from waking Leanne, Sal risks the stairs without turning on the hall light, his bare feet feeling for purchase on the cool wood floor like a blind man in unfamiliar territory.

He counts the steps as he descends. *One, two, buckle my shoe; three, four, someone's at the door; five, six, I'm going to be sick.*

On the seventh step, he is extra careful. That one creaks, and he prefers not to alert whatever's in the living room of his approach. *Nine, ten, you can't come in; eleven, twelve, go straight to Hell.*

He can hear static coming from the television and even before he reaches the landing, he knows what he'll see.

Aimee stands in the glow of the television screen. No, it's more like she radiates from the television screen; a holographic 3D image, flickering bluish white, fading in and out as if she's a bad signal. Sal can smell the electricity cooking the air, the burnt ozone.

A burial shroud covers her.

At first, she doesn't move but ever so gradually she raises her head and the shroud slips from her, like a snake shedding its skin. Her lovely face contorted by fear and despair into that of a hideous, ancient hag.

*Why didn't you dance with me, Daddy? I wanted you to dance with me.*

Sal wishes he could find it in him to scream, but all he can muster is a strangled, pitiful mewl.

She lifts one arm and points an accusing finger.

"*Daddy?*"

Horrified, Sal watches as her face melts away, running like hot wax down a flaming candle, leaving only a mocking, grimacing skull glaring back at him.

Sal finds his voice as a proper scream rips from his throat.

*****

A cold gray sky spits rain from tumultuous clouds. The cemetery is packed with both the living and the dead in attendance. Sal spots Molly Pickett and Donald Bigelow and Marsha Rennicker, even good old George Ausberger is here, standing near Reverend Disch, who is oblivious to the dead surrounding him.

The Burning Man failed to make the funeral—maybe old Felix was afraid the rain would douse his flames. He also sees his parents, both gone for the past ten years, having died within a few months of each other after forty years of marriage. Leanne is sitting beside her parents, both still alive and filled with loathing for each other.

Sal suspects they're only waiting for one of them to die, neither wanting the other to have the satisfaction of seeing them dead; today their mutual animosity is tempered by love for their daughter.

*A blinding flash, the sound of metal against metal, the crash of shattering glass. The odor of burnt rubber and copper in the air. Sal can taste the blood, an acrid, burning sensation in his throat.*

Aimee walks between the gravestones, idly reading the inscriptions and admiring the roses and wreaths. She is no longer the terrifying wraith that visited him in his sleep this morning. Her face is whole and healthy. She's dressed in the yellow silk dress Leanne picked out for her funeral. He catches her eye, relieved when she returns his smile. This is how he prefers to remember his daughter—happy, vital, and alive.

He knows she wouldn't blame him for the crash. The guy in the oncoming vehicle was drunk and he ran the stop sign. Sal did everything he could to avoid the collision, but the rain…the road was so slick.

Sal's little Subaru refused to obey his commands and the drunk's car just kept coming, deadly and vengeful, as if it were alive and hellbent on murder. And in mere seconds, his dear Aimee was no more. And the drunk? Not a scratch. That was when Sal decided the universe was an arbitrary, malignant cancer.

"You know, being dead isn't so bad," Carl Wiggins says, looking pretty hale and hearty for a dead guy. Strange, considering the last time Sal had seen Carl the cancer had pretty much reduced him to a withered husk of a man.

That was in the hospital, six months ago, just hours before Carl succumbed to the disease eating away his body. Mates since high school, Carl's was the last funeral Sal attended until today.

"But alive is better?" Sal replies.

Carl shrugs. "In some ways. But in others, death is good; there's no more pain, no more uncertainty. The question of what comes next is answered and you get to see all your old friends and family that passed before you."

"Still, it's hard on us who have been left behind."

"Life is short. Just a brief detour between birth and eternity. I still get to peep in on my kids and Agnes. Hey, did you know that damned Agnes was cheating on me the whole time I was sick? Believe me, we'll have us some words about that when it's her time to go." Carl gives a dry chuckle.

"So I heard. She took up with Tony Ames not a month after you were buried. I bet that hurt."

"Not really. Tony's a good man and he loves her. Lord knows I wasn't much of a husband. Spent too much time chasing the almighty dollar and not enough paying attention to those who needed me. But hey, at least you got a good one. Leanne adores you."

Sal puts a hand on Leanne's shoulder. He feels some of the tension drain out of her and he is pleased that his touch can offer some comfort.

"She's my everything," Sal says but when he looks up, Carl is gone, and Aimee is standing beside him.

She takes him by the hand and her touch is as warm and real as if she was really there.

The Reverend Disch motions everyone to gather under the tent, set up to protect the coffin and mourners alike from the inclement weather. The sermon is short and filled with the same, tired platitudes offered at every funeral. Sal pays no attention to the words. He merely bows his head when persuaded to join in prayer and rides the rhythm of the preacher's rich voice until the final amen.

He keeps one hand on Leanne's shoulder, the other gripping Aimee's hand.

The crowd disperses slowly, trotting off to their waiting vehicles, umbrellas held over their heads, coats pulled up against the bite of the wind, until only Sal is left, standing alone with no one but the dead for company.

*****

Sal Mingus ghost-walks through the boneyard. The addled dead gather around him, clutching at his clothes; their grasping hands are icy, vaporous against his skin. Overhead, the gray sky splinters. Sheets of cold rain pour down, drenching his clothes and washing away the last of his tears. The wailing and gnashing of the dead echo across this valley of perpetual misery.

He could turn away now and return to the land of the living. There, love and warmth await to wrap him in their arms and comfort him in a cocoon of breathing flesh.

He's in the hospital where he's been since the car crash, trapped in a coma between perdition and paradise.

Up ahead, Aimee beckons him to follow. Sal turns his back to the light and heads into the darkening horizon towards his deceased daughter. He has to go; he knows he should be with her.

Behind him, the legion of the dead walk in procession, their moans and whimpering coalesce into a mournful dirge. They are singing his requiem, happy he is joining them.

## THE INHERITANCE

Logan Fourie

It has been said that places have memories; that when a place has been around for long enough and has *experienced* enough, it begins to remember. It begins to feel.

A home that has only known love and kindness is warm and friendly and welcoming, while a house that has known only pain and suffering and torment is a cold and forbidding place that hungers and yearns to feel that pain and suffering over and over again, because it would rather feel that than nothing at all. There are also places that are so hungry that they cling onto any semblance of sentience just so that they can feel alive, even for a little while.

I never put much stock into this…that is, until that day when my whole outlook changed.

*****

It was a warm and sunny day. It started out like any other.

I was in my college dorm room, doing research for my thesis. I had hit a bit of a brick wall. I wanted to be different. I wanted to be controversial. I wanted to stand out. But all I got was a sub-par piece of work that was as common as dirt.

I let out a long sigh of exasperation as I flung my notes across the room. *To hell with this!* I have never been a great writer but I had hoped that this would give me the opportunity to be daring. Instead, all I got was the typical dog and pony show. It was rubbish. I rubbed my eyes, sore from staring at the flashing cursor on the blank white screen of my laptop.

And then I heard a knock at my door…the knock that changed my life. It should have been nothing unusual, but I remember feeling a chill on the back of my neck like a premonition. I thought of Edgar Allan Poe:

*Suddenly I heard a tapping*
*Like somebody gently rapping.*
*Rapping on my chamber door.*

I looked towards the door and even considered ignoring it and not answering. Then I shrugged, and decided that it couldn't be worse than the wasted time of a failed graduate. I got out of my chair and opened the door.

A scrawny, pasty-looking man with round glasses stood before me, clutching a very boring looking brown leather satchel in front of him. His face cracked open in a vulgar imitation of a smile as he spoke. "Are you Mitch? Mitchell Callaway?"

I cocked my head at him and said that I was. He nodded, seemingly very impressed with himself and handed me an A3 envelope. He told me that a relative of mine had recently passed away and I was the only one in his will that was still alive.

I frowned at him and tried to figure out who he was talking about. Most of my family had passed on and the ones that remained I had little or no contact with. I looked at the envelope and tore it open and spilled the contents out. There was a typical last will and testament that was addressed to me and seemed to be from a distant uncle. I frowned as I vaguely recalled the name: Sampson Callaway. I hadn't spoken to him since I was probably seven years old.

And there was a note enclosed that had something very odd written on it: "Don't make the same mistake I did. You will know what to do."

The last thing inside the envelope was a set of really old-looking keys hung on a heavy rusted wrought iron key-ring. I examined the keys with interest for a moment, turning them over in my hand.

I looked back up to question the man but he was already gone. I checked the hall for any sign of him. There was none, so I shrugged and stepped back inside my room, closing the door behind me. Laying on my bed, I pored over the document.

Sampson Callaway was an uncle I met once, maybe twice. He was a bit of an eccentric, never married. He was what one would call an adventurer who had traveled the world in search of oddities and artifacts. All he really did was squander the family fortune on his wild theories and ideas and adventures, which is why most of the family rejected him.

It turns out that, of the little he had left at the time of his death, he still had a manor out in the marshlands not far from my college. Odd, I didn't recall him having property out there, or anybody having much of anything out there as a matter of fact. It piqued my interest and I found that the more I pored over the scant details the more intrigued I became. By the end of reading, I convinced myself that visiting his old house would be a better way of spending my time than getting wasted at the local pub.

With my mind made up, I grabbed a few essentials like a flashlight and batteries and a sleeping bag (just in case I decided to stay the night) and made my way out to the old house.

It was a dull drive. Not much to see except marshland and bayous and sickly-looking trees that felt like they belonged in those old cheesy scary movies. Also, the side roads were pretty well hidden. If it was not for the GPS, I would have missed the turn-off. I wondered how my uncle had managed to live his daily life way out here…it would have been an ordeal to even get to the store for a carton of milk.

I swerved the car down the dirt road. It was clear that nobody had been down this road in decades. It was muddy and not at all smooth. It gave a whole new definition to a bumpy ride. There were a few times I did not think my small Toyota would make the journey but, finally, I arrived at the manor.

I stopped my car at a set of huge, curved iron gates, the rust clinging to the bars like scabs of old wounds. One could see that, at one time, these gates had been beautiful. Now they were something out of a horror movie: a warning to turn back while I still could.

Instead, I got out of my car and looked down the dilapidated driveway. In the distance, I could make out the main building. It looked large, which surprised me. How is it that nobody knew about this house?

I looked around for any caretakers or any sign of human life. I called out but the only reply I got was the haunting cry of a lonely loon. The woeful sound sent shivers up my spine.

I walked to the imposing gates. Despite their age, they still looked very sturdy. I gave one a tug. There was a thick, old chain and lock holding the gate shut. *Well, this sucks,* I thought. I stood, looking at the chain, almost willing it to jump loose from its imprisoning lock. Then it came to me. I had to give myself a face-palm when I recalled the set of keys that came with the document.

I hurried back to the car and fished out the set of keys. Only one could possibly be the right one. I tried the first but it didn't fit. The second, with a bit of effort, slid into the rusted lock and cracked open the lock. I wiggled it free and pulled the chain through the bars of the gate. It made a rattle which reminded me of those clichéd images of ghosts pulling lengths of chains around with them, rattling them to scare the living.

I pushed the gates apart. They whined on their corroded hinges and swung open. I got back in my car and drove up the driveway and stopped at the front porch.

The house was clearly one of opulence, once upon a time. Now it was a thing discarded and left to the ravages of time. The once-white paint had turned to a sickly grey. The wood had begun to rot in many places and it was unclear just how safe the building would be.

I pondered my options. I could sell it, but how much would I really get for it as-is? I could get a loan to renovate it and make it into a museum or an inn but who would come all the way out here? Or…I could move into it myself, but would I want to live in the middle of nowhere? No wonder my uncle went crazy if he tried to live here.

As I stood there considering my options, a lost wind howled up and passed through me. It was such a random gust of cold air that it seemed like a lost soul searching for its way to heaven.

I grabbed my gear and made my way up to the entrance into the mammoth house.

The wood creaked and complained under my feet as I mounted the first step of the front porch. I was worried that it would give way under me as I felt bits of wood disintegrate beneath me. I stood perfectly still, gauging the structural soundness of the steps before going on. The second step moaned too but not as loudly as its brother. And the third still less. Once I stepped onto the porch landing, I was certain of my safety.

The once magnificent doors hung in a sad disgrace of disrepair, the white paint peeled back to reveal the rotted wood beneath. It really was a shame how much damage the place had seen. I found myself imagining what it would have looked like back in its prime: garden parties held in the yard under the sycamores and willows, dinner parties with dignitaries and debutantes dressed in their finest. The idea brought a smile to my face. Such a simpler time. Such a nobler time.

I turned the verdigris-colored knob. It squeaked and protested at being forced to turn after decades of inactivity. The doors creaked open and the smell of rotten wood and stale air poured over me. It was like opening a tomb and I felt like an intrepid explorer delving into the past.

As I stepped beyond the threshold, I felt a little like an intruder, as if I was not actually welcome; as if the house was aware of my presence and was not all too pleased with me disturbing its slumber. There was also something else. Something cold and dark, almost like a malicious hunger stalking the corners of the house.

I felt cold again and rubbed my arms. Strange though, as there were no signs of a breeze within the house, in fact the house felt humid and sticky (as it should, being out here, closed up, in the bayou for so many years) in most places. It was as if the warmth was being sucked from those spots by an entity hungry for life. It felt cruel and insatiable, as if it would swallow the world's warmth and happiness if given the chance. I sniggered at my silliness again. This house was giving me some strange ideas.

I went to what must have been a living room or audience hall or something of the kind and placed my bag and gear down. There was a fireplace that seemed to be functional. The room felt like it could have been cozy back in its youth. Now it was just as empty as the rest of the house.

Again, I wondered why my uncle kept this house and never did anything with it. It looked like he was trying to keep it just the same, almost like a shrine to his parents. It was baffling. Surely he could have recovered some of the family fortune if he had sold the place instead of keeping it just as his parents had left it.

I began my exploration in the room I was in. It looked like a standard welcoming room with a few high back settees and sofas as well as a few side tables and coffee stands (most so rotten that I would not dare put a cup on it). There were also a few paintings, most of which were badly faded and eaten away by the moisture. I tried to make out the images but many were just too worn away.

One of the few I could make out was of a couple, a man and wife, it seemed. This was not my uncle, but probably his mother and father.

The man in the painting towered over his wife and his grip on her shoulder made me shiver. It looked so domineering and controlling, almost like he was claiming his possession over her.

She, on the other hand, was the epitome of femininity. She was lovely and genteel, and because of the times, probably submissive. A person had to respect women from that time. They had so little in the way of personal freedom but did what they could with what they had. Yet her eyes seemed to have a strange sort of power and I stared at them for a minute. Then I nodded my respect to the woman and went on with my exploration.

The dining room was of some interest. It was dominated by a large table which looked like it could seat an army, yet only two chairs were placed at either end of the table, which I found very sad and telling of the married couple's relationship. Probably my uncle, who never married, simply left the seating arrangement of his parents.

One unique thing in the dining room was the huge floor-to-ceiling mirror. I stood before the gaudy, gilded thing. It seemed to serve no function beyond that of clear narcissism. I stood before the silvered reflection of myself. It was slightly distorted in places where the carved wood had warped from time and moisture. I giggled at the odd shapes it was making on its near perfect surface. Almost a reflection of what reality is and what people were like.

As I was watching my reflection warp and reform, I noticed something behind me in the mirror. I stopped and stood dead still as I gawked in fear.

There, behind me, stood a shadow. It was a woman, standing just beyond the pale light of the setting sun. It looked like the woman from the painting.

I screamed in surprise. I could hear my heart pound in my ears and I felt faint. I quickly turned around, away from the mirror, to confront the woman in the room.

I was shocked to see no one there. There was no woman standing behind me in the room. I turned again towards the mirror, but all I saw was my reflection looking back at me.

Had I really seen what I thought I'd seen?

It seemed like the house was giving me the creeps and I was seeing things that were not there. I walked out of the room but stopped dead at the painting I was looking at earlier. I felt the color drain from my face.

The painting of the couple was now missing the woman. Only the man was there, unchanged. My jaw dropped as I stared blankly at the painting. I felt sweat drip off me in torrents as I backed away from the painting. *Where had she gone? Am I going mad like my uncle?*

I made my way to the front of the house to get my sleeping bag. I was not spending another second in this place. To hell with it all. Tomorrow I would call in the wrecking ball and tear the house down to its foundations.

I turned around and yelped as I looked straight at a ghostly figure dressed in a stylish, yet worn black velvet dress from what looked like Victorian fashion. Her skin was pale and her blonde hair blew on a mysterious, ethereal wind. She stood in silent observation as if she was confused as to what I was doing there.

My jaw dropped and I tried to scream, but all that escaped was a futile whimper. I felt the blood drain from my face and my head began to swim and black stars danced in front of my eyes. My knees buckled and threatened to give out from under me. I was so frightened that I realized I was blacking out.

And then…my eyes slowly fluttered open and a dim light filtered me back into my world. I felt my head pound as I slowly rose to my elbows to sit up. I rubbed my aching head and neck and shook the butterflies free. I blinked, trying to gather my thoughts. *Did I see what I saw? Was she really there?* I felt nauseated and for a moment I wondered if I would vomit on the dusty, parquet floor.

And then I saw her again. She was sitting at one of the high-back settees nearest to the fireplace. She sat in silence, as if contemplating some deep thought. She slowly turned her gaze to me.

I was horrified to be noticed. Could she see me? Was this an aware entity? This was a ghost; I knew that. Could she harm me? Was she here to do evil?

She was definitely the woman from the painting.

She looked at me in a sort of bewildered wonderment as a smile slowly crept over her face. Her hands were folded on her lap demurely. I could see she was as beautiful in afterlife as she was in her life. We regarded each other for what felt like an eternity before one of us uttered a sound.

Oddly it was her who spoke first, her voice sounding like a gust of wind whistling around the corners of a vacant building. "Where is Sampson? Where is my lovely Sampson?"

I did my best to calm her by explaining that my uncle, her son, had died.

"Dead? You mean he will no longer visit this house?" She sobbed quietly as she dropped her head into her hands, her flaxen hair swirling around her like a melting halo.

I felt the air grow cold and the light dim as her alabaster-pale skin seemed to change hue to an icy-blue. The change of temperament terrified me. I was afraid that she could have some sort of power, to do what, I didn't know. That was what made it so frightening: I didn't know what to expect.

I remembered the note my uncle had written: "Don't make the same mistake I did. You will know what to do."

But I didn't know what to do! What mistake had my uncle made? Why didn't he specify? Why did he choose to be so cryptic?

My nerves felt raw and were sparking with energy. My mind swam. On the one hand, I felt a growing sense of terror as the ghostly form before me swirled and ebbed as if it was losing control over its shape. On the other hand, I felt a sense of sympathy. She didn't seem like she wanted to hurt me, but something in the air felt wrong. The air felt like it was growing thick and cold. There was an odor that wafted softly on the cold air currents; a smell of death and anger and vicious malignancy.

I had to get away. I had to leave this place. Something in my head screamed for me to get out. My uncle's mother looked off into the distance, black tears burning cracks into her otherwise flawless skin.

Even though she looked passive and seemed to be ignoring my presence, there was the feeling of impending doom rising up within me. A feeling of dread began to freeze the blood in my veins. Something was very wrong. Something was…coming.

I rose to my feet as quickly as my brain allowed. She was still looking off into the distance as I fumbled and stumbled to my leaden feet. Her head slowly began to turn to regard me. It was now a featureless mask, her beauty melted away like a wax doll held to a flame. Her lipless mouth opened into a grimace of pain and suffering. A blood-curdling scream sounded and she pointed an accusing finger in my direction.

I thought: *This is it. She's going to destroy me.*

But as the scream faded, I realized she wasn't pointing at me. It didn't seem like she was even looking at me. She was motioning to something behind me.

I felt the hairs on the back of my neck stand on end. My skin prickled because there was something behind me; I was certain of it. I felt the cold malignant presence edge closer and closer to my back. I felt it reach out to me and the warmth drain from my body again. My breath froze in wisps of ghostly mist as the air around me chilled.

I had to look behind me. I had to know.

I turned to see a towering, masculine figure loom over me. It was darkness manifest. It felt like its shadow swallowed all the light and warmth around it.

I began to back away from it as it reached out its hand towards me. No, not towards me…towards *her.* I dodged out of the way as the thing prowled past me towards the woman as she sat, still and expectant. It looked like her edges were fading, like something was sucking her essence towards it.

The ghost behind me swallowed up the last of her before turning around and gliding back towards the empty painting that hung pitifully from the wall.

The ghost began to flake away like a burnt-out stump turning to ash in the wind. The flakes of shadow flowed towards and into the painting, becoming two, reforming the figures within. The two resumed their respective positions in the painting as if they had never left.

I stared at the painting of the couple and slowly began to put together the pieces of the final message. I started to decipher my uncle's coded message. I finally figured out his mistake.

He'd said I'd know what to do.

I dusted myself off. I grabbed my discarded stuff as I made my hurried exit out of that dreaded place. I stepped outside, and saw that the full moon and stars lit the sky in ethereal beauty. Somewhere, during my ordeal, the meaning behind the message was revealed to me. I finally figured out what mistake my uncle warned me about.

By keeping the house as a shrine, it welcomed his mother back inside. She had no reason to leave.

I turned back to the house and nodded. *Yes, my uncle was right. I know what I need to do. Instead of keeping the house the same, I will remake it. I will get a loan to fix it up and make it into a place of joy and happiness. I will make it new and beautiful so that the spirits of my uncle's parents will not recognize the house anymore, so they won't know how to come back.*

I would not live in the past. I would not repeat my uncle's mistake.

## TRESPASS

D.J. Tyrer

It is strange how noises sound louder in empty rooms and corridors, as if they expand to fill the void, trying to breathe life back into spaces once filled with people.

As he walked along the dark hallway, following in the wake of a flashlight's beam that left corners in shadow, it seemed as if a second pair of footsteps accompanied Jack, but it was just the echo of his own.

He was one of the guards of the closed and musty building. He jiggled the handle of a classroom door to make sure it was locked. The door rattled against its frame in the otherwise silent building. He could understand why people might think the place was home to ghosts—the empty old schoolhouse was pretty spooky, if you were inclined to let your mind wander—and he could read more into the shadows than was really there.

Sometimes, just sometimes, he thought he could sense a sort of sadness in the air. If there was a ghost here, it would be a melancholy one.

He moved on, checking the doors as he passed them, ensuring they were locked, and shining his beam through their small glass panels to check nothing was amiss inside the classrooms. Most were empty, their furniture taken away for use elsewhere on the campus, years before. A few still looked as if they were merely waiting for students to arrive in the morning, chairs tucked neatly under tables.

Keys jangled on his belt that would've let him into any of the locked rooms, but having checked the ground floor windows were still securely boarded over before beginning his rounds, there was no need.

The echoing sound of footsteps accompanied his own as he continued on his rounds. He paused and shone the beam of his flashlight into an annex where a person might hide. Nothing, save a few motes of dust floating in the light.

He paused, breath held. Was that movement ahead? A shadowy figure?

Sometimes, he saw them. Thought he saw them…

Jack shone the flashlight down the corridor. Yes, movement. Then, it was gone.

There was nowhere for anyone to hide. Nobody there.

Moving the beam of the flashlight, he laughed as the shadows shifted at its edges. He'd created his own ghost out of shadows.

He walked on slowly. There was a faint mustiness in the air, the smell of a place that had been sealed up too long.

He paused.

The lock of the door marked 'Director of Art' was broken; it had been smashed long before Jack even took this job. He eased the door open. Without furniture or books on the shelves to absorb it, the noise seemed especially unnerving in the empty office, like a sound effect from a horror film. He shone his flashlight into the room, revealing a patch of damp on the wall; the place was beginning to decay. Looking down, he saw a couple of scraps of paper on the floor in exactly the same position as they were every time he checked—the same, doubtless, as when they were dropped years before.

Sometimes, Jack thought of picking them up, but couldn't bring himself to do so. It was as if the scraps belonged to the room exactly as they were.

He moved on, headed for the toilets down the corridor.

There was a loud echoing *plip-plip* of water splashing into a cistern or sink as he opened the door. The water was supposed to be turned off at the mains, none would spray from the taps if you turned them on, but there was always the sound of dripping from somewhere and a strong smell of damp. Dark shadows of mold crept from the corners of the room, making them seem gloomy even when he directed his light at them.

It was silly, but this was the only part of the building that made him feel nervous. Not the dripping sound— there could be any number of explanations for that—but there was a bucket and mop in the corner, as if a cleaner had just stepped away for a moment, and he hated to walk past the cracked mirrors, as if glancing into them would reveal something he didn't want to see. Then there were the doors of the stalls, which were always shut, as if they were in use.

He doubted the other guards were to blame, playing some stupid practical joke. No matter what their contracts might say about patrolling the Tate Building during their rounds, most just checked the exterior and maybe stepped inside for a moment to shine their flashlights' beams up and down the main corridor in a cursory check, before locking up and leaving. Perhaps it was just the way the doors of the stalls were hung that caused them to slowly swing back of their own accord, no matter how many times he pushed them open and checked inside.

The first cubicle door swung open easily, while the second creaked a little. The third was half-hanging off its hinges and he was glad it didn't fall off when he pushed it open. But, the fourth…

He pushed against it. The fourth didn't want to open.

The unidentified drip came again. *Plip-plip.*

He muttered a curse to himself and gave it a good shove. It was jammed.

"Is there somebody in there?" he asked, his voice sounding like a shout as it broke the silence.

There was no reply.

If there was someone hiding inside the stall, he was certain they must be able to hear the hammering of his heart. He took a deep, raspy breath and tried to slow it, pushed the door again. It still wouldn't open.

Was it a student messing about? The place seemed locked up tight, but he hadn't checked the fire escapes upstairs…

He stood, flashlight held in both hands like a club, as he tried to decide what to do. Leave it? Give it a kick? Look over the top of the door?

"Look, I'm going—" he started to say, voice a whisper, as he placed a hand on the door. He jumped back in surprise as it swung slowly open to reveal another empty stall.

He could hear his heart pounding in his ears as primal instincts fought against the evidence of his eyes. He tried to calm his rattled nerves. There was nothing. Not a thing.

Running his hand down the rough wood of the door, he checked for the bolt; it was missing. Couldn't have been locked, then. Must have been the damp making the wood swell, that was it. Always a logical answer, if you took the trouble to think about it. Ghosts indeed!

The other guards were lazy. Their lackluster approach to checking the building was quite unprofessional and the university was lucky the stories about the place seemed to act as an effective deterrent to the students; at least, he hadn't been told of any break-ins and had seen no evidence of any. He was a little surprised nobody had tried to hold a Hallowe'en party in the building or taken to daring one another to spend the night.

Well, there was definitely nobody there, hiding beneath the cistern or, he swung his flashlight up, atop the cubicle walls. Time for him to continue on.

Carefully ignoring the mop and bucket, shivering as he passed them, he went back into the corridor, the echoing sound of one final drip following him out like a farewell.

He paused and shone his flashlight back down the corridor, making sure that the second set of footsteps really were just echoes of his own.

That was the end of the ground floor and he took the stairs up to the next floor, which was another collection of classrooms and offices. Most of the rooms were locked up, but the few that were unlocked were uninteresting.

Unlike the floors above.

The top two floors of the Tate Building had been used for storage and plenty of junk had been left behind when it was closed down.

As he headed for a door marked Staff Only, Jack reflected that he had never been given a clear reason why the building had been shut down and left abandoned. No wonder there were stories. Not that it had ever been a hall of residence, where tales of suicide and murder would be more plausible. It was just a schoolhouse, so how could it be haunted?

The door creaked a little as he opened it. He doubted any of the other guards ever went up here. In fact, he was probably the only person who had been up the metal steps since the place was abandoned and, given that he doubted the university would bother clearing the contents of the rooms out, he would probably be the last, too, if they went ahead with demolishing it as planned.

The clanging of his boots on the metal steps was almost deafening in the stairwell. If there were any ghosts hiding on the upper floors, they would surely be aware of his approach.

Opening the door to the next floor, he was struck by a stronger, musty smell. The air didn't seem to circulate at all up here, probably because he was the only person who ever visited.

He stepped out into a corridor narrower than the ones below. The beam of the flashlight filled its width, then flickered and dimmed.

Muttering, he smacked his palm against the flashlight and brought the beam back. Typical cheap garbage that the company supplied them all with.

Probably best not to linger, just in case the light gave out; he wouldn't want to make his way through the building in total darkness—he'd probably trip and break his neck up here. Sometimes, he liked to see what he could find – the cramped storerooms were like his own private world, a series of Aladdin's caves.

Accompanied by the echo of his footsteps, he began to walk with a quickened pace, following the corridor, which twisted about the storerooms like a maze, unlike the broad, straight ones of the lower floors.

The beam of light dimmed, again.

"Not tonight." He smacked his flashlight and hurried on, glancing into the rooms he passed, wild shadows drunkenly dancing as he shined the beam about.

He halted and shone the beam ahead, certain he'd heard a noise.

Again, the sound of movement. Somebody was moving about in one of the storerooms ahead of him. Someone, or something…

He glanced back the way he'd come. The others would run away. He wasn't like them. He thought of Steve, the cowardly little rat.

A rat! That was it—a rat. He'd never seen one, but he remembered Steve claiming he had once. He'd thought the guy was making it up, but maybe there was one living here.

Just a rat. He let out a long breath and slowly began to walk towards where he thought the sound came from, shining his flashlight into storerooms, looking for any signs of movement. He wished he had quieter shoes than these heavy boots, but went as silently as he could.

Suddenly, a figure stepped out into the passageway ahead of him.

Jack swore and fumbled with his flashlight, nearly dropping it. The figure shrieked.

He swore again.

Getting a grip on his flashlight, he shone the beam at the intruder.

"What the—? Who the hell are you?"

A young woman, maybe eighteen or nineteen, dressed in denim, with short, spiky blonde hair, blinked at him with wide eyes.

He lowered the beam and watched the fear drain from her face as she saw his uniform.

She swore, then laughed. “I thought you were the ghost.”

“I thought you were a rat.”

“Sorry?”

He quickly amended his comment. “I thought you were the ghost, as well.”

Jack looked at her; other than looking particularly pale and washed out in the harsh glare of the light, she appeared to be flesh and blood. He felt foolish. “What are you doing in here? You know you’re not supposed to be in here—didn’t you see the signs?”

She ran her hand over her hair and took a deep breath.

“I was looking for the ghost.” She held up a small camcorder with a mini-flashlight taped to its side. “Ghost hunting.” She glanced away and bit her lip. “I guess I didn’t really think I was going to find it, so when I saw you…”

Jack looked up at the ceiling, then back at her.

“What am I going to do with you?”

Her eyes widened. “I’m not in trouble, am I? I can’t get thrown off my course!”

“I ought to report you for trespassing.” She gasped, but he shook his head and said, “But if I escort you out, it’ll save us both a lot of hassle.”

She smiled. “Thanks. I’m Binky, by the way.”

“Binky? What kind of name is that?”

“It’s short for Bianca. My parents called me Binky as a child and it stuck.”

“Oh. I’m Jack, and I’ll be showing you out. Come on,” he gestured with his flashlight, “that way. I want to complete my rounds.” He looked at her. “You here with anyone else?”

They began to walk. Binky shook her head. “No, just me.”

“You should never have come here at all. You know, this place is mainly locked up for your safety.”

“Really? It doesn’t seem very dangerous to me. That’s why I came alone.”

Jack shone his flashlight into a storeroom, revealing a number of mannequins, mostly incomplete.

“Well, you could injure yourself on some of this junk or it could fall on you, trap you. Most of the guards don’t come up here—if you fell through the floor, you could be trapped for days. If anyone heard your cries, they’d probably think it was the ghost.”

“It seems solid enough to me.” Binky jumped up and down and

chuckled.

"I'm serious. Look, there's a hole through there. If you went through it, you could get lost." He shone the beam into the next storeroom, showed her the hole.

He shivered; for a moment he had been certain there was a mop and bucket in the corner of the room. Stupid! The corner was empty. He shivered again, it was chilly; the walls of the room were streaked with damp.

He added, "There are plenty more ways in which you could get hurt, if you're not careful. Look at all this junk. You could trip over something if you weren't looking where you're going."

He paused and shone the flashlight ahead of them.

"Something wrong?" she asked.

"Nothing. Just shadows."

"So, how did that hole happen?"

"No idea. It was like that when I started," he said as he led her towards the stairs. "Probably just the damp that's getting into the bones of this old place; maybe they stored something very heavy in there. In fact, I did hear somebody fell through the floor there once and was killed."

"Ouch."

"Exactly, you don't want to wind up joining the dead."

She gave a nervous smile and shook her head.

"So, just be careful and stick near me."

"Imagine if the ghost startled you and you ran in there… oof!"

"Nice." He shook his head. "Now, I need to check the floor above, okay?"

"Cool." She perked up. "This is a pretty freaky place."

"It is, I guess, but you get used to it, after you've been here a while."

He shone his flashlight into a room full of crates and boxes, Binky leaning around him.

"Those mannequins, what's the story with them? What was this place?"

"It housed the faculties of art, drama, and, er, fashion, or something like that. Hence the mannequins."

Nodding, she asked, "You worked here long?"

He shined the beam into a room filled with rusting filing cabinets. "Yep."

"You ever see the ghost, Jack?"

He turned to her. “I don’t believe in ghosts.”
“No? So, you haven’t seen anything?”
He shrugged. “I’ve seen shadowy figures, once or twice, probably students like you poking about. How did you get in here, anyway?”
“The fire escape on this floor.”
He snorted.
“So,” she prompted, “just shadows?”
“Just shadows. I mean, you hear sounds, but things echo and the building creaks, so they’re probably nothing either. And, I heard you, of course, but you’re no ghost.”
“No.”
“There’s a rational explanation for everything, and that’s why I don’t believe in ghosts. This old place creaks a lot; there’s tons of shadows, and somewhere a faucet drips. All explainable.”
He marched on, Binky trailing after him.
“My turn to ask a question,” he said as he shone the flashlight into a room filled with half-finished portraits.
Binky shuddered. “Don’t you think the faces look like they’ve melted?”
“I’m no art critic.”
She laughed and, as they turned away, said, “Okay, ask your question.”
“You’re here searching for the ghost, right?”
“That’s what I said.”
“Well, did you find one?”
They reached the far stairwell and he opened the door and led the way up the stairs, clanking heavily.
“Good question, Jack. There’s all kinds of stories—a student who killed himself, a lecturer who was killed for giving bad grades, somebody who died trapped in the fire that gutted this place—”
Jack shone the flashlight at the walls as they exited the stairwell. “What fire? I haven’t seen any signs of fire damage in here, have you?”
“No, I guess not.” Binky sighed. “There probably isn’t a ghost, is there?”
“Now, you’re—” He fell silent and stared at her. “Did you hear that?”
She nodded. It came again, the sound of something heavy being dragged about in one of the storerooms ahead of them.
“You sure you came in here alone?” he whispered.

Another nod. From her expression, he thought she was either genuinely scared or an excellent actress. "What is it?" she whispered back.

He shrugged, tried not to let his own fear show. Was it likely somebody else decided to break in on the same night as her?

The sound came again.

"Somebody is moving a box around or something," he said.

"Or, a body."

"Stop it. Nobody's dragging around a body, but I have to take a look."

Did he have to look? Did he really? Would anyone really care if he just walked away like all the others? He wished he could.

"Stay here."

"I'm not staying alone," she hissed.

"Why not? You came alone. Oh, whatever, fine, but stay behind me."

"Should I film this? I have my camcorder."

"Just stay back and be ready to run."

"Okay."

They could still hear the sound coming from one of the storerooms.

He took a deep breath and threw the door open. The sounds instantly ceased.

"Who's there?" he cried.

Jack shone his flashlight around the room. Boxes of paper were stacked in leaning piles and sheets were scattered loosely about the floor, as if they had been blown about by a breeze.

"Who's there?" he repeated.

There was no other exit from the room, nor any sign of what had been dragged.

"Well?" Binky asked, peering over his shoulder.

"I don't know." He stepped into the room and aimed his light behind each pile of boxes. "Nobody. Nothing."

Not even a rat. A chill ran across his back.

He pulled a sheet of paper out of one of the boxes. "Blank test papers."

The pile fell and the sudden crash made Binky shriek. Jack jumped back in surprise and swore. Paper swirled about him and settled upon the floor.

Then, he gave a fragile laugh. "It's just the boxes tipping over."

"I want to go. Can we go, please? Please?"

Jack nodded. "Sure. I think we're both a little jumpy."

Binky gave another shriek. "What was that?"

"What was what?" He tossed the exam paper away and stepped out of the room.

"I saw someone." She pointed. "Down there. A shadow."

"It was nothing," he said, wishing he believed himself. "Sometimes you see shadows. It's just the darkness shifting as the light moves about."

She glanced back in the direction she'd pointed. "We both heard that sound!"

"Who knows what it was? Maybe it was the wind getting in from somewhere."

"I'm cold." She breathed out a puff of faint steam. "See?"

He shivered, but tried to inject some bravado into his voice. "Like I told you, there's a breeze. It made that noise and, now, it's making us cold. The rest is our imaginations. Let's get going."

Her lips were tight as she nodded.

"Let's go back to the stairwell, it'll be quicker," he told her.

"What about finishing your round?"

"You don't want to be here and I can't have you here, potentially being in danger."

"You think I'm in danger from—?" She didn't finish, but glanced off again and bit her lip. He wondered what she'd seen, but didn't want to ask.

"I just meant, wandering around in here is dangerous. It might not have been gutted by a fire, but it is falling apart. I wouldn't want you to have an accident and wind up a ghost here…"

She gave him a weak smile.

"I can finish up once you're gone."

"Fine." She nodded and they began to retrace their steps, the echo of his footsteps following after them.

"It's two flights down, then it's not far to the west staircase, down to the ground floor and, then, you can leave by the side door. Okay?"

Binky nodded. "Okay."

They reached the stairwell and he was grateful that the clanging of his heavy boots on the stairs muffled out any other sounds they might hear.

"Just two floors. There you go, through there."

The door slammed shut behind them and they paused, breathing heavily.

"Right."

There was the sound of a door slamming shut somewhere below them.

"Jack?"

He swore. "These doors are supposed to be locked."

She stared at him. "What?"

Footsteps…

Binky shook her head, sobbing. "I'm scared!"

"You're safe, you're safe. Look, the stairs are just along here. It's not far. You'll be fine. Just follow me."

He glanced at her over his shoulder, shook his head. She looked so pale and scared.

"There."

A clang of metal echoed up from below them. Binky glanced at him, but all Jack could do was shrug.

They ran down the stairs, down to the ground floor.

"This way."

He stopped dead.

"What is it, Jack? What? It's just a mop and bucket…"

He shook his head. This was bad. Something nagged at him.

"You have to go, now." He pointed. "The exit's down there."

Past the bucket.

They ran past it, Binky glancing about, eyes wide with fear.

They reached the doors, halted. He could still hear the echo of footsteps. A door slammed.

Sobbing, she looked at him.

Fumbling with the keys on his belt, he found the one he wanted, slipped it into the lock. There was a click and he threw one of the doors open. It was raining outside, but Binky stepped out into it with an expression of relief.

"Come with me," she said, looking back at him, rain running down her cheeks like tears.

Jack shook his head. "I have to finish my rounds."

"Jack…" She held out a hand towards him. He didn't move.

"Go. I have to finish my rounds."

He closed the door and locked it, left her to return to her life. The Tate Building was silent again.

"I have to finish my rounds," he told the empty corridor as he walked back along it.

Only he never did, not ever.

## THE STORM

E. A. Black

High winds blew mud and tree branches against the side of the house. Rain pummeled the roof.

She didn't like storms but it was too late to leave. Amy Preston shuttered a bedroom window with some difficulty since the rusted hinges refused to cooperate. She moved a few steps to another window to shutter it when lightning split the sky and the power went out, plunging her into darkness.

The house, located near a remote beach on the island of Caleb's Woe off the northeastern coast of Massachusetts, knew no ambient light. No full moon. No street lamps. She stood alone in inky blackness, surrounded by wailing winds and a churning Atlantic.

She shuttered the second window and moved to the hallway, feeling the bumps along the papered wall so she could find her way to the staircase. A tremendous crash resounded from the living room. Great, just what she needed. Rocks hurling through the windows? Crockery falling from the shelves as the walls shook?

The stairs were hard to navigate in the dark. Maybe weathering out the storm was a bad idea. She should have listened to her parents and gone to stay with them on the mainland until the storm passed.

Once she found the living room, she got her hands on some matches and a candle. She struck a match, but a breeze blew it out. Where did the breeze come from? Fletcher's breath? *No, he's dead.*

She stuck another match and this one stayed ignited. She lighted the candle and saw that the living room windows were intact and unbroken. She was safe from the storm. Her crystal cabinet sat upright against the wall, giving her a secure feeling.

Until she heard the voice. "Amy."

She turned. No one stood behind her. This wasn't the first time she heard Fletcher's voice, but hearing it during a storm on the first anniversary of the day she murdered him gave her the shivers.

*Don't get spooked. He can't tell. And he can't hurt me because he's dead and buried. I got away with it, so stop hearing things that aren't real.*

Shaking off the creepy-crawly things that ran up and down her spine, she took a few steps towards the window and stubbed her foot on an ottoman. She cursed as shards of pain shot through her pinky toe. What was it doing in the middle of the floor? Had something moved it?

She shoved it beneath its chair with her other foot and hobbled her way to shutter the rest of the windows. Then, she moved her way around the living room, her arms straight out with the candle in her hand, and hobbled to a cabinet to retrieve a flashlight.

With a click of a button, her living room was bathed in the soft glow of the flashlight and she blew out the candle.

"Amy…"

The flashlight traveled around the room as she turned. Shadows moved in the corners, mocking her. She glanced into a mirror and saw a brief vision of Fletcher reflected in it, glaring at her. She turned to look behind her but no one was there. Goosebumps rose on her arms as the room chilled.

*No. Stop it. You're spooking yourself.*

Damn, the heat had gone off with the power and this house cooled fast. She decided that wine would ease the chill. She grasped the flashlight firmly and headed to the wine cellar. Might as well make a party of it.

She listened for the voice again, but heard nothing over the screaming of the wind and the crashing of waves. She had checked the tide tables earlier that day. It was high tide right now. A storm surge was big trouble during a Nor'easter. The storm wasn't due to pass until morning.

She brandished the flashlight like a gun and walked towards the basement door. What wine should she drink? She had inherited Fletcher's expensive wine collection along with the rest of his wealth. How about the 2008 *Didier Dageuneaux*? No, she knew the perfect wine—the *Veuve Clicquot La Grande Dame*. Champagne, to celebrate shoving the old coot down the stairs and ushering in her nouveau riche life.

She gripped the handrail and aimed the flashlight down the stairs into the darkness. She took a step, and then another. When she reached the middle of the rickety staircase, her flashlight sputtered. She banged it against her palm and then it brightened.

At the last step, she was on the concrete floor and she felt a brisk chill against her bare feet. Dammit, water. The sump pump wasn't working and the basement had flooded. Water covered her feet to her ankles. Luckily, she kept all her stored boxes on tables or kept her important items in plastic boxes. There would be little water damage, but she needed to do something about the pool of water. It would have to wait until after the storm when the sump pump was working again.

She rolled her jeans up so they wouldn't get wet and splashed her way to the wine rack. She found the bottle of *Clicquot* in seconds and then turned to make her way back up the stairs.

The flashlight sputtered and went out. The darkness was so thick that it appeared as if the room spun. Shivering from the cold with wet feet, she whimpered as she sloshed her way forward, fingers tapping on the wine bottles and boxes, trying to remember which ones were where so she could reach the staircase.

A *ching* sounded from one of the bottles as if someone tapped it with a metal spoon. She froze in place, terrified. A second *ching* sounded— this one closer to where she stood.

Heart racing, she gripped the champagne bottle in her fist with the intent to use it as a weapon, but a weapon against what? No one stood with her. No one she could see, but she smelled spicy cologne. It floated around her like a rancid cloud.

Three *chings* clanged from a bottle to her left as it swayed to touch its neighboring bottles. She shrieked and felt her way along the wall of bottles, splashing in the water as she walked. Her fingers touched spiderwebs that stuck to her skin. She rubbed her fingers against her sweatshirt but the strands clung.

Sloshing ahead of her forced her to shake the flashlight and it lit up briefly to reveal something long and slithery coasting through the water toward her. Her teeth chattered so hard her jaw hurt.

When the snakelike, oily thing brushed against her ankles she screamed and ran towards what she hoped were the stairs in the dark. She tripped over a box and fell onto her knees in the icy water. The chill forced its way through her jeans and stung her legs.

She could hear something in the water behind her, splashing as it made its way in her direction. Soaking wet, she crawled across the floor, whimpering until she scraped the bottom step with her knuckles.

Crying out in pain, she shoved her hand into her mouth, and found the stairs to the living room. She heard chimes ringing from the clock on the fireplace mantle. Six chimes, six 6 p. m.—the same hour she sent Fletcher into a swan dive down to the cellar floor. Police had ruled his death an accident.

*Don't lose it now*, she told herself. *Fletcher is no more effective as a ghost than he was in life. You're free and clear.*

A sigh floated in the air behind her as a slight breeze ruffled her hair. Lightning flashed twice, illuminating the room. Out of the corner of her eye, she saw what looked like a shadow standing in her kitchen.

"Who's there?"

No one responded.

She called out, "I'm not afraid of you. You can't hurt me. Go back to your grave."

The old house menaced her in the dark. She shuffled her bare feet across the cold wood floor to the basement door and then opened it. A sigh greeted her as stale air wafted from down below.

There was also a smell, a faint one but it was unmistakably tangy. Old Spice. Fletcher wore an old man's cologne. She had tried to get him to wear something more modern, but he insisted on Old Spice.

Wet, cold, and uncomfortable, she shivered. Despite her fear, she gripped the champagne bottle in her fist. It would make a good cudgel.

Lightning flashed through the skylights, illuminating the living room once again. She counted one, two, three and then thunder boomed.

The rattan couch had been shoved into the middle of the floor, a rug bunched up in front of it. Two rattan armchairs had been turned on their sides. A faint tinkling of the song *Let It Be* played from a small music box sitting on an end table.

She was aware that her teeth were chattering. She couldn't stand around soaked to the bone. She set the champagne bottle on the coffee table that miraculously hadn't been knocked on its side like the other furniture.

She felt her way to the end table next to a chair and opened the top drawer where she knew there was another flashlight. She took the stairs to her bedroom with the flashlight illuminating her way. It flickered as she walked, casting shadows in nooks and crannies she didn't know existed.

Once in her bedroom, she quickly slipped out of her wet clothes and dried off with a bath towel. Then she put on clean, dry socks, jeans, and another oversized sweatshirt. Satisfied, she made her way back to the staircase.

As she walked down the hallway, the smell of stale whisky floated around her. Fletcher had been a mean drunk. But how could a ghost drink whisky? Or was it a residue of the past, just like the Old Spice cologne?

Her new flashlight went out. Despite the shaking, it would not turn back on. She cursed herself for never checking the flashlights in the house. How old were the batteries in them? Pretty old, apparently.

Alone in the dark, her heart raced as something dragged across the floor from behind her. Damn, she wished she had brought that champagne bottle along with her so she had a weapon.

She turned as lightning flashed, illuminating a small, squat figure on all fours sliding towards her. It crept on its belly; its pale body glowing in the flashes from the lightning. So frightened her voice failed her, she turned and raced towards the stairs, feeling along the wall with both hands. In her terror she had dropped the useless flashlight.

*He's really back! Fletcher is coming for me! I have to get out of here.*

She grabbed her coat from a hook near the front door and shrugged into it. She grabbed her keys and headed for the door, but at the last second backtracked to grab the bottle of champagne with the hand that held the keys. She rushed out the door as a crack of thunder shuddered around her.

Rain fell in sheets so thick she could not see two feet in front of her. She was outside, so she was convinced that Fletcher couldn't get to her now. As she stepped off the porch, wind buffeted her coat and shoved her across the walkway. She slipped into mud and fell to one knee.

As she stood, a tall figure approached from the side of her car. That sickening smell of Old Spice assailed her again and she screamed, but she could not hear her own voice over the roaring of the wind. She would not allow Fletcher to win. Heart racing in terror and nerves on end, she raised the champagne bottle and struck him three times on the side of the head.

Hands grasped her by her shoulders but she refused to back down.

Fletcher fell to the ground, and she pummeled him with the bottle until her arm was sore. Above the crashing surf and wailing wind she heard a high-pitched scream. A second figure grasped her and wrestled the bottle from her hands.

"Amy!"

Her mother's voice. Her parents had come to get her out of the storm.

Amy looked down as lightning lit up the area.

Her father lay on his back in a fractal of blood, open eyes staring through her. With a wail, she dropped to her knees.

The cold air chilled her to the bone, but that cold was also from the realization that Fletcher had outwitted her after all.

## MR. POTATO HEAD

Elizabeth Massie

The farm looked to have been deserted for years, ten maybe? Twenty? Blaire didn't know, couldn't tell, but didn't care. The two-story farmhouse, with its faded, tattered "No Trespassing" sign nailed at a tilt on the front door, was still standing, and even though she was certain it had no electricity or running water, it could serve as shelter for a while.

And Blaire and her sixteen-year-old daughter, Judy, were in dire need of shelter.

They'd been on the road seventeen hours without stopping except for a single piss break in the bushes off a graveled road in Tazewell County, running away from Blaire's abusive husband, Robert. Away from the past. Away from the pain. They had zigzagged across the state, with Judy sitting quietly in the passenger's seat and Blaire smoking cigarette after cigarette, fighting a headache as options tumbled back and forth in her brain.

Which consisted first and foremost of finding a place to hide.

It had been difficult getting away with so little cash. Blaire had thought she'd be able to withdraw from the bank account but discovered Robert had taken all but thirty-two dollars for his "boys' vacation." That was so Robert, though, wasn't it? Pull the rug out from under her financially, mentally, emotionally. Even literally last week, causing her to fall and strike her chin on the bedroom dresser.

Robert had left the day before, heading out with his buddies for their monthly boys' weekend away. As he'd stepped out through the front door, he'd turned back to Blaire in the foyer, lowered his voice, and said, "You best watch yourself. Nanna will keep me updated on your behaviors. Don't forget that."

That had been the last straw, the final threat. Nanna was Robert's mother, a busybody with age spots and pursed lips. Robert had brought her in to "help out" back in March. Blaire hated the way Nanna patted after her like a watchdog, whispering in Robert's ear, making up nasty lies so Robert would love his mother more than he loved his wife.

*Damn her! Damn Robert!*

Once Blaire was certain Robert was gone and Nanna was asleep on the sofa, she'd packed Judy and Judy's wheelchair into her old Toyota. She threw some clothes, two blankets, and a box of canned goods and toiletries into the trunk and lit out as fast as the car would go.

"We're going to be safe at last," Blaire said as the car sped southwest, then east, then south. "Your father won't take his anger out on me anymore. You do understand, don't you, Judy?"

Judy didn't answer.

Blaire looked over at her daughter, at the sweet face, the dark red hair. She appeared exhausted. "Judy? Did you hear me? Do you understand?"

"Yes, Mom," said Judy softly. "I understand."

Blaire began to cry but shook her head to dislodge the tears. "And if we'd stayed, he'd have started coming after you, too. You understand, don't you, Judy?"

"Yes, Mom. I understand."

"I love you, Judy."

"Love you, too, Mom."

So on they traveled.

Then Blaire spied the abandoned farm.

As uninviting as it might have looked to most, to Blaire it seemed a godsend. Situated in the brutally rural, isolated Allegheny Mountains, it consisted of a two-story farmhouse with a sagging porch, dilapidated barn, two sheds, and several acres of dry, rocky field that had once produced "Pride-Perfect Potatoes," or so the sun-bleached sign nailed to the side of the barn boasted. The no trespassing warning looked to be as withered and forgotten as the house.

Blaire slowed the Toyota then steered the car off the road, onto the weed-riddled driveway, and around the back of the house where no one passing by would see it.

"Well," she said as she turned off the ignition and let out a heavy sigh. "Here we are. What do you think?

Judy was silent.

"Judy?"

"It looks pretty bad, Mom."

"But nobody lives here," said Blaire. "And they haven't for a while. Plus, there aren't any other homes nearby, I've been watching, so no one will realize we're hiding. This is best for now."

"What if there are rats?"

"What's a rat but a little dog with a naked tail?" said Blaire with a forced chuckle. She got out to unload the wheelchair and her daughter.

The first thing Blaire noticed was the size of the rooms. In a house as big as it appeared from the outside, she had expected fair-sized rooms, maybe a large dining room, expansive parlor or den. Yet each room was small and boxy, with low, water-stained ceilings, warped flooring that seemed to tilt this way and that. There were countless dark spots on the floor where it looked as though potatoes had rotted. Blaire felt woozy and had to hold onto to a kitchen chair for a minute to catch her breath.

Then, "I'm going to look around."

Blaire left Judy in the kitchen. She went about the downstairs, through the dining room, living room, front foyer, bathroom, opening as many windows as would budge. Dust and grit flew out into the air like gnats. Brittle shades crumbled at her touch. Most of the window screens were torn, and dead flies lay upside down on the sills, their legs splayed in an appeal to Heaven. The walls were decorated in filthy wallpaper with scrolling patterns that suggested coiling potato vines and tiny eyes hiding within leaves. Blaire shuddered when she saw the walls, and turned away. As she made her way back to the kitchen, she glanced again at the wallpaper. It looked as if the tiny eyes were watching her intently. And then one winked.

Back in the kitchen, Blaire wiped off a chair at the table, plopped down, and lit a cigarette with trembling hands. She leaned on her elbows. Wallpaper didn't wink. Only a crazy person would think so. She was overly tired, was all. Overly tired, angry, and scared.

"Mom," said Judy. "We don't have to stay here, do we?"

Smoke curled out through Blaire's nostrils. It burned just right. "A short while 'til I figure out what to do. Few days. Week at most."

"This place stinks."

"I have a scented candle in the box in the car. I'll light it in a bit. Okay?"

"Okay."

Blaire closed her eyes. In the darkness she saw Robert standing in their kitchen with his fists clenched, his lip hitched. "What the fuck is wrong with you, Blaire?" he shouted. Blaire looked from Robert to their little dog, Sandy, who lay on the floor, too afraid of Robert to even move. Poor thing. Poor little thing...!

"What do we do now?" asked Judy.

Blaire opened her eyes. She pushed the heel of her hand against her temple. "It's still early afternoon. I'll go see if I can find some bleach and water. I'll clean up some of this before it gets dark. We'll sleep in here." *Where there isn't any wallpaper.*

"You forgot pillows."

"Maybe I can buy some pillows, too."

"Okay."

"There's enough light in here for you to knit while I'm gone." Judy's knitting bag was hanging on the back of her wheelchair. Blaire handed it to her daughter. "You'll be fine."

Judy said nothing.

"Okay, Judy?"

"Okay."

For the second time since they'd left, Blaire began to cry. Her poor daughter, so gentle and agreeable.

Blaire drove to the nearest town seven miles up the road, a settlement consisting of an out-of-business antique store, a gas station/convenience store called "Bobby's Food Mart", a Baptist church, a railroad crossing, three houses, and a silent warehouse with "Allegheny Apples" stenciled on the roof.

Blaire parked beside one of the two gas pumps at the station, put $15 into the tank, and then entered the convenience store. It was dim and smelled like a sinus infection. A middle-aged woman stood behind the counter, scraping a strip of lottery tickets with a dime. Blaire selected two fresh-ish bananas, two apples, a small bottle of bleach, and two jugs of water.

"You campin'?" asked the woman behind the counter as she rang up the goods.

"What? Oh yes," said Blaire.

"Where at?"

"Back up the road a bit."

"Gotta be careful. Ain't got no actual campgrounds 'round here. Don't wanna be on no private property."

A boy of about twelve, with a face covered in festering whiteheads that looked like the eyes of a potato stood up from behind the counter. Blaire hadn't heard him back there, eating chips. He licked his lips and dug another chip from the bag.

"Well," said Blaire.

"Bad time of year for campin'," said the woman.

"What with ticks and all," said the boy. He squeezed one of his potato eyes and it popped.

"We'll be fine," said Blaire.

"We'll?" asked the woman.

"Me. I'll be fine."

"And don' go where you ain't supposed to," said the boy.

Blaire slipped her fingers through the bag handles, hoisted the jugs under her arms, and hurried out. She wanted the woman and boy to forget her, to not give her a second thought. But what if a news report came over the radio or television, carrying Robert's lies? That *she* was abusive, that *she* was dangerous, that she had, what, kidnapped her daughter and had run off just to make Robert suffer? Oh, but Robert could lie so smoothly! Such talent, that man! Would the woman and boy in the store remember her? Would they notice that she looked like the woman authorities were seeking? Would they call the cops on her? And if they did, what would happen to her and Judy?

*Damn you, Robert!*

*****

Judy was asleep in her wheelchair. The knitting was on the floor. Her face was slumped forward and she was chilly to the touch. Blaire went out to the car, got the blankets. She covered Judy up. If only she'd remembered the damned pillows.

With a broken-bristle broom and rags from the pantry, Blaire cleaned the kitchen as quietly as she could. Every so often she pulled out her cell phone and gave it a shake. But each time, it reminded her that there was no reception here. That was good. Robert could not call her. Nanna could not call her. They were safe.

For a while.

They couldn't stay in the farmhouse for long. The woman and boy at the gas station might start wondering, might find out who they were, might go snooping. The woman might call Robert and tell him where Blaire and Judy were hiding, Robert might give her his hateful version of what happened…

*What happened?*

...that led to Blaire's desperate departure. The blow, the pain, the blood...

*...the dark red blood.*

If the woman contacted Robert, he and Nanna would come after Blair and Judy. Best to spend just one night here then hit the road again.

Blaire left Judy and went to the bottom of the stairs. She looked up. Along the wall beside the stairs was the same hideous, eye-infested wallpaper – dark animal eyes, milky potato-like eyes. Staring. She should just rip that nasty the paper down off the wall. She decided she would, right after super and once Judy was busy with her knitting.

Dirty, afternoon sunlight stretched across the foyer floor. Yet the top of the stairs appeared as dark as a bottomless well. What was up there? Maybe money. Maybe treasures of some type. No, of course not. This place would have been stripped clean of anything valuable in all this time.

*Probably.*

*But maybe not. Maybe people obeyed that crumbling "no trespassing" sign. Old Mr. Potato Head, or whatever his name was who used to live here, might have a stash somewhere that others haven't found.*

*Wouldn't that be super?*

She squeezed her eyes; the headache was back and chewed beneath her skull. Behind her closed lids she saw Nanna on the sofa, shaking her head furiously. She looked like a witch. "Why the hell did Robert marry you? What's wrong with you?" She saw Robert standing next to Judy's wheelchair. "Unless you can get it together, I ought to have you put away for life!" he said, and then placed his hand atop Judy's soft brown hair.

"Damn you both!" Blaire shouted back.

*Damn you both!*

Blaire's eyes snapped open. She looked up the stairs again.

*If there is something valuable I could sell, then we could get away. Farther....so much farther away....*

She grasped the banister and climbed into the darkness. The wooden railing was cold as a corpse. The steps groaned under her weight. It sounded as if the wallpaper was hissing and chuckling softly. But of course, that would only be mice.

The hall upstairs was uneven and sticky as if covered in...

*...blood...*

...syrup. Blaire pulled her cigarette lighter from her pocket, flicked it on, and picked her way down the hall toward the far room. Thick chunks of dry, brittle potato vines and patches of old potatoes were scattered about and she tried to step around them, over them. She moved into the room, across to the window, tugged up the shade. It fell apart in her hands. Obstinate daylight oozed through the window and reached only a third of the way across the floor. Shadows, long and deep, settled on the wallpaper.

Blaire stood and waited until her vision adjusted. There was nothing in the room but a stained mattress, several molded shoes, dust balls the size of small tumbleweeds. The closet door stood open; it was empty. No treasure. No hidden money.

But not to worry; there were two more rooms upstairs.

She flicked on her lighter again and headed for the door. And there was movement in the corner of her eye. She spun about and saw the wallpaper.

The tiny eyes within the vines were unnaturally bright, and they were turned and trained on her. They widened, twitched. And then they winked in unison.

Blaire gasped.

A coiling vine morphed into a bony hand. It twisted and reached out from the wallpaper, fingers scrabbling.

Blaire slammed back into the doorjamb. She dropped her lighter. It hit the floor and bounced out of sight. "Judy!"

A leaf cracked opened to reveal a hideous mouth. It whispered, "I know what you did."

Blaire screamed. She staggered into the hall in the darkness. "Judy!"

"Judy!"

Judy didn't answer.

Blaire stumbled toward the stairs, tripping over the some of the dried potato vines and rotted potatoes. She almost fell and grabbed for the wall to right herself. The wallpaper was cold as ice and it squirmed beneath her touch.

"Judy! Help me!"

*Stop it, you know Judy can't help you...*

Blaire reached the head of the stairs, heart hammering.

"Judy, help!" she cried again, though of course her daughter was downstairs in her wheelchair. Of course Judy couldn't help because she was…

*…dead…*

…paralyzed and had been since the car wreck in November when Blaire, drunk yet again, had picked Judy up from school and drove headlong into a tree.

"Judy!"

Something enormous and shapeless oozed out from the wallpaper halfway down the stairs, blocking Blaire's escape. It was dark as pitch yet its hideous eyes and mouth glowed like a jack-o-lantern. No, not a pumpkin. Like a carved potato covered in stubby growths and ancient, wrinkly skin. The eyes were hollows; the mouth, slashed huge and wide and filled with glistening teeth.

Blaire shrieked, tottered backward. The specter laughed and stepped closer, up three steps.

"Who are you?" Blaire wailed. She continued to back away, then struck the wall and slid to the floor. Her hand fell upon several of the dried vine chunks. The glow from the potato face illuminated them, and Blaire saw the truth. They were not dried vines. They were human bones. "What are you?"

"This is my home," said the specter. Its bright eyes grew even larger. Its teeth chattered cheerfully. "You've invaded my home. I don't like people to invade my home."

"You have to let me go! You have to let *us* go! My daughter, my little girl, we're just trying to be safe, we…"

And then Judy was beside the specter, standing straight and tall, her body transparent and her eyes as bright and horrifying as those of the specter. "Mom," she said.

"Judy!" cried Blaire.

"You broke your daughter's back," said the specter. "Your husband blamed you and rightly so."

Blaire blubbered. "It was an accident, Judy!"

"You almost burned the house down by falling asleep with a lit cigarette in bed," the specter continued. "In a drunken rage, you came at Robert and he was only able to stop you by jerking the rug and knocking you down. When Robert threatened to divorce you, you killed the dog, Sandy, and left him on the kitchen floor for Robert to find when he came home from work."

"All lies!"

"You promised to stop drinking. Robert gave you another chance when he moved his mother in to help out. He said if anything else happened, you were finished as a couple and he'd take Judy and move away."

"Lies!"

"No, not lies," said Judy. "Mom, he tried so hard. He loved you. But he hated what you did."

"I didn't do anything!" Blaire put her hands over her eyes. And there on her palms she saw Nanna on the couch in their living room, reading a book. She saw Judy in her wheelchair, knitting. Nanna looked up as Blaire, came in with her glass of vodka, took a sip, then vomited all over the floor. Nanna closed her book, pointed a finger at Blaire, and said, "What's wrong with you?"

In her wheelchair, Judy put her head down and began to sob, her brown hair falling over her eyes. Blaire saw Robert hurry into the room and place his hand protectively on top of Judy's head. "No more booze in this house, ever!" he said. "Nanna will make sure of that while I'm gone and when I'm back, we need to have a serious talk about our living arrangements. For God's sake, Blaire, think of your daughter, even if you no longer love me." With that, Robert gathered his duffle bag and left for his Army reserve weekend.

Blaire opened her eyes. The specter of Mr. Potato Head was now standing directly over her, staring down. Judy floated next to him, her body undulating like a sheet in a gentle wind.

"Okay," Blaire said. "Maybe I did drink a little, maybe it affected my thinking a little…"

The specter's eyes flashed. He leaned down far enough that Blaire could smell him – rotted food, rotten flesh. "A little? A *little*? You killed Robert's mother once he left for the weekend. Then you killed your daughter. Bashed both of their heads in with a hammer. A bloody revenge, wasn't it? If you couldn't have Judy, no one could. You were going to punish them all, and then run."

"I wouldn't do that!"

"Yes," said Judy. "You would."

"I love my daughter! I would never hurt her!"

"Yes," said Judy. "You would."

"Good but thoughtless people trespass here, and I scare 'em but let 'em go. Bad people come in…" The specter nodded at the bones on the floor. "Got no reason to let 'em go."

"Judy, make him stop!"

"He released me, Mom," said Judy. "He found my spirit trapped in my body. I didn't know I was dead. He freed me."

Blaire wailed, "No, none of this is true!" she batted out with her hands, which felt nothing but icy cold as they passed through the specter before her. "You're lying! Everybody lies! I hate you!" She leapt up and darted toward the steps. She slipped on a spot of molded potato, fell, and struck her head on the sharp edge of the stair railing. On the floor amid the bones, she gurgled as blood poured from her mouth, nose. And with three violent shivers, she died.

A week later, a pimple-faced boy whose mother ran Bobby's Food Mart found a car behind the farmhouse on the abandoned potato farm. The keys were still in it, so he drove it to his friends' house and they stripped it for parts. They made a cool $256 for their efforts, so it was a good day.

## SOMETHING TO NIBBLE ON

Christian A. Larsen

Everything was still. Still and dark, like the man behind the wheel was under a few fathoms of amniotic fluid. There was no sensation of up or down—just a gentle floating, but there was a growing sense of buoyancy, of coming up and up toward the light, a dim, shapeless, bluish-white. When he broke the surface, he recognized it immediately: moonlight on snow, but it was like looking at a competent but anonymous oil painting. He had no sense of place or time, just an image of the snow-frosted woods, with a few fresh flakes drifting down, down, down onto the cracked windshield.

"Help!" he screamed before he even meant to, an order issued from somewhere deep in the lizard part of his brain, only it wasn't a scream. It was supposed to be, but it crawled out from between his lips, as cracked as the windshield. "Help," he repeated from between his split lips with a force so weak, he couldn't even see his own breath on the crisp air.

*What's going on?* he thought. It was his first full thought since emerging. Evan. *Your name is Evan—Evan Holcomb*, he told himself. It didn't quite feel like news, but it was the bedrock upon which everything else would rest. *How did I get here?* He tried to move, but something resisted.

And then it started coming back. His visit to his grandmother. How could something so innocent come to this?

"I gotta go, Grandma," he said. "This paper isn't going to write itself."

"Oh, Honey, you see to your studies," she said, kissing him on the cheek with wet and somehow prickly lips. "Just give me a second, though. I have a little something to help keep up your strength," she said, shuffling toward the kitchen in her housecoat and slippers.

Evan didn't have a paper due. Even if he did, it was Saturday night, and nothing academic ever happened on a Saturday night. He had some drinking to do, and maybe he'd hook up with a girl, but homework—if he had any—would wait until after the hangover.

"Here, I made this for you," said Evan's grandma, handing him a ceramic platter. It was shaped like a 'STOP' sign, with divided sections filled with different kinds of homemade cookies in each compartment—all Evan's favorite kinds: gingersnaps, peanut butter blossoms, oatmeal raisin, and more. It was all wrapped up in cellophane, which he didn't touch because he knew it would make a mess if he broke the seal before he got home. He could read the words, though—the bubbled block lettering at the top of the platter that his grandma had hand-painted as part of her ceramic hobby: 'Something to Nibble On'.

"Thanks, Grandma," he said. "I'm not sharing any of these."

"Well, don't eat them all at once or you'll give yourself a bellyache." She kissed him again and sent him on his way. "Drive safely!" she called out before the storm door snicked shut. Evan could see her waving behind the door as the glass frosted over until she faded to oblivion.

Evan went to the bar, met some friends, but didn't meet any girls, and all the while the tray of cookies stayed in the car, still cellophane-wrapped on the passenger seat. He had drinks to start the evening, enough drinks to knock him sideways, but he stayed late—past midnight, and by the time they closed the bar, he felt pretty much like himself again. Good enough to drive, as one does. And remembering that, he remembered the accident.

It might have been an animal. It might have been a shadow. It might have only been a smudge of black ice, but whatever the reason, the road gave way to trees as the car caromed off the road, cutting through the more slender trees with the sound of gunshots, before coming to a rest on its side against an oak near the river's edge. There was shattered glass everywhere. To Evan, it looked like the granulated sugar from his grandma's cookies that he did not want to be picking out of his upholstery for as long as he owned the car.

But it wasn't sugar, and the glass wasn't from his windshield which was merely cracked. It was from the driver's side window. A rock was poking through where the glass had been. The car wasn't right against the ground, but it was close. Part of the door was touching the ground, and the only reason Evan hadn't fallen was that he was still wearing his seat belt. He tried to turn his head to see how the rest of the car was, and he couldn't. That was the first inkling he had that he might be hurt pretty badly—that he might be in some fairly serious trouble.

The car had been running the last he remembered. The lights had been on. They weren't anymore. Car probably died while I was unconscious—idled to death, he thought. And that made him wonder what time it was. The dashboard wasn't giving up any secrets, but his phone might. He tried to reach into his back pocket, but he couldn't feel his pockets or his hands. Fear found the next gear as he considered hypothermia and frostbite.

It's got to be almost dawn, he eventually thought. I can't be that far from the road, and someone will see me in the daylight. He tried to feel confident as he thought that, but it felt like more of a wish. It was still snowing when he woke up, so tracks would be obscured, maybe even totally covered up by the time help happened by, and he could scream himself hoarse maybe just a few dozen yards from rescue. He had to keep up his strength, just in case.

The cookies.

He could see a few of them on his dashboard. Gingersnaps collected with an oatmeal raisin and a peanut butter blossom, mingling as if the platter hadn't meant to keep them separate at all. And there was sugar on the dash. It looked like a field of stars on the colorless, dark mass. The cookies were so close he could smell them. I need to eat those cookies, he thought, but his arms wouldn't reach for them. He looked toward either shoulder to see what was pinning them, but it was too dark to tell. Better to wait until morning. Morning would make it all better, he said to himself the way he did when he hid under his comforter from whatever monster *du jour* was tormenting him that night.

Evan didn't remember falling asleep, or waking up, for that matter, but he was sure that time had passed and he'd missed it. Maybe it's the angle of the moon, he thought, and he tried to reach for one of those cookies he'd seen earlier—but they were gone. He couldn't see the platter, but the ones that had been on his dashboard were gone, and most of the sugar, too. Evan tried to turn his head to see if he could find the rest of the platter, but he couldn't.

He couldn't even move his own head, and then he really started to worry.

That's when he saw the rat. It crawled in through the broken driver's side window, crouching and darting across Evan's lap, up and over his arm until it sat on his shoulder, just out of Evan's field of vision. He could hear it nibbling on something there. More cookies. Evan wanted nothing more than to squirm out of the car and run away, but he couldn't even squirm. He knew at last that he was paralyzed from the neck down, but he was not dead, and he still had his dignity, so he screamed from the side of his mouth: "Get away from me!" at the rat, which ran across the center console, sitting on the passenger side still munching on one of the cookies.

"Oh, Jesus, I thought rats lived in the sewer," he said, half sobbing. "Why couldn't you be a rabbit or a squirrel?" But Evan knew that life was not taking requests right now. He was in a world of hurt, and he was just along for the ride.

Another rat climbed into the car, pulling itself up onto the dashboard. Then another one clambered up Evan's shirt, followed by another, dragging its long, pink tail across his face. He promised himself that when he got out of the car, he would make rat-killing his life's work. If his paralysis were permanent (and we're a long way from knowing that, buddy, so don't worry yourself, he thought), he'd get a wheelchair and a helper monkey to help him do it. Nothing but arsenic and spring traps for as long as I live, he swore in the dark in that car, while the rats ate the cookies his grandma baked for him.

Why did she have to give me those cookies? thought Evan, wondering when he would start to feel hungry himself. The cookies brought the rats, and pretty quick. I couldn't have been here for more than a couple of hours, tops, or it would be daylight already.

He could hear them nibbling on the cookies, but he didn't know how many there were anymore. Could be a dozen. He looked as far to his right as he could, but it was too dark to see anything except the dark-blind rectangle of the rearview mirror, still dutifully clinging to the windshield. Bring 'em, Evan thought. The more there are, the quicker they'll finish up all those cookies and be on their way. Then daylight. Then rescue. It has to happen that way.

More time passed, but Evan missed it. He knew because the windshield had caved in from a tree branch falling on it—which seemed odd because that meant he'd slept through it. How he slept through something like that, he couldn't guess, but the rats were gone, or at least they were done eating. He couldn't hear them anymore, but he could hear the wind howling, and started to wonder how long it would be before he was truly frostbitten. He was wearing a winter coat and even had gloves on, but he wasn't wearing a hat or anything on his face. He didn't feel cold at all, but he took that as a bad sign.

First one rat came back. Then another. Evan tried to blow at them to make them leave, but it was as effective as he feared it would be. It made one or two scurry back a length or two, and then clamber back up toward his face, staring at him with their black, intelligent eyes.

Evan could see in the rearview mirror now that the windshield had changed shape. He could see the rats from behind. He could see his own eyes, bright with fear. What goddamn time is it? Thirteen o'clock? And is the sun ever coming up?

Time only goes this slow when you're miserable, he answered as more rats crawled into his car, smelling cookies that were no longer there. "Ha, joke's on you, you little shit," he said at a particularly fat rat, perched in the crook of his left elbow. It was staring up at Evan, rotating its nose in a tight circle like it was reading the air.

It stretched up, and Evan felt its whiskers on his chin. It tickled. Felt so innocent. It reminded him of how his friend's hamster used to feel when they took it out to play with when he was a kid, but this thing was no pet, and just as he thought that, the rat bit him. It felt like a handful of needles going into his flesh, and he screamed.

"No, no—go away," he said. He looked in the rearview to see how bad it was, but the wound was on the wrong side of his face.

Another bite. His head moved from the force of it, but the rat did not give up. He had to give it to the bugger: it was no quitter. But then, neither was Evan. He stretched his jaw to make himself look bigger, and it made the rat retreat toward the car door. It groomed itself, not particularly frightened at that vantage point.

Evan felt a tug at his right ear.

*Jesus!* he wheezed. There was a rat sitting on his head, nibbling at his ear. The worst part was the sound—like leather ripping. Just a tiny wound, but that close to his senses, it sounded catastrophic. "Go away!" he said, trying to sound brave, but he could hear himself crying.

The rat on his head tore away a strip of cartilage and scrambled up into the passenger side, but it was replaced with another, and another. Evan looked in the rearview as they jostled for position and saw that his ear was mostly gone. They were tearing at the edges of the wound and lapping at the blood.

"Get fucked!" he tried to say, but his bottom lip felt heavy, and it came out more like: "Get 'ucked!" while his bottom lip sagged with the weight of the rat attached to it. The tugging sensation was the worst. The rat was wrestling with Evan's flesh, and from the sound of it, the rodent would be the winner.

Blood oozed from the many wounds, dripping down Evan's cheek and splattering into the rat's matted fur. Another rat crawled onto Evan's head and reached down to take a bite of Evan's nose. It clipped the flesh out neatly and scampered away, making room for the next, and the next. Evan tried to close his eyes, but his left wouldn't shut. *Nerve damage from the cold?* he wondered. He wished. He looked hard to his right into the rearview, and he saw why: his eyelid was gone. The rats had nibbled it off, leaving a ring of meat and bone encircling a perfectly good, restless eye.

That was when Evan stopped wishing for dawn, and started wishing for death.

Meanwhile, the rats ate.

And ate.

Daylight finally came. Evan woke up to it, more or less, but he didn't think he'd been sleeping—it was more like a sudden awareness of remote blueness and shadows angling across the light. It was the end of the longest night he had ever endured, and relief washed over him as celebratory as a barrel of beer. It was a few minutes before he had the courage to look into the rearview mirror, and when he did, it was bad.

The rats had taken his left eyelid, his right ear, and most of his nose except for his right nostril, which was now just an archway leading to nowhere. His upper lip was mostly unzipped, hanging down from his face like a gorged leech, and his bottom lip was gone. Disappeared. He could see the roots of his front teeth as they plunged under the surface of his gums, which were now no longer pink, but a pinkish shade of white.

But it was over. Someone would find him, and he would get the help he needed. His nighttime wishes for death seemed foolish now that hope welled back up in him like blood in a wound. He tried to shake that image out of his mind, but his head wouldn't shake.

That's okay, he thought. That's okay.

There was a hole in the windshield. He could see it now that it was light. It was framed by a quilt of shattered glass that had not yet come apart, like a cloth woven out of diamonds that caught the sun. He could see something through the hole, between the windshield and the tree. A white something; or something that had once been painted white but had now faded to the color of bone. It was like a fencepost but smaller. Maybe the size of half a yardstick. It was driven into the ground, planted there deliberately, surrounded by the shed remains of dried up flowers. Evan followed the stick up from the ground to the crossbar, which had black, block letters etched into it, reading: EVAN HOLCOMB, YOU WILL BE MISSED.

The marker had been there months, maybe years by the look of it—almost as long as Evan himself had been gone. He let out a fierce, wailing moan from his lipless mouth, which sent the deer bounding away, but the rats came scurrying toward him to eat the invisible meat of his ghost-flesh all over again.

## HOTEL ETERNAL

Jeff Parsons

This was where it happened. A man had died right here in this hotel hallway. The bloodstains had been cleaned up, leaving no trace of the accident, as if the man's death never occurred. But it did, only a few weeks earlier.

Martin felt a solemn dread creep over him. He had never investigated a haunting involving the newly dead. All of his other investigations were of rumored hauntings of people who died long ago. A new death…it almost seemed…sacrilegious to intrude. What were they going to find?

In all of his ghost-hunting experience, he usually discovered a natural cause for almost everything. Still, beyond the endless progression of lies, trickery, and deceit, and physical influences such as electrical interference or thermal expansion, there were those few cases that couldn't be explained away by science.

This case—this place—was one of those anomalies. Martin was convinced it wasn't like the usual fake crap that scored hits on their notorious Paranormalists website. Unusual activities had occurred long before the recent renovations in the abandoned Wayfarer's Hotel, a Victorian-style derelict of over forty bedrooms, making this place something completely different: a gateway landmark of the supernatural.

And right now was a perfect opportunity for his pursuits. Following the latest death inside the hotel, it was closed to the public because of bankruptcy proceedings. The remodeling would never be finished.

Trish, his partner, seemed to sense it the moment they entered the stately building. She was good at her job; insightful, clever, and charming. Martin, however, was better suited to technical pursuits.

Checking the camcorder again, he made sure it captured Trish in her glorious white-witch mode, head bowed, hands extended like mystical antennae, lips moving with sub-vocalizations as she extended her senses outward to contact the ethereal. Around her, the hallway held eight closed bedroom doors, four to a side, and a set of leisure rooms on the ends. The wan yellow glow of new electric lights, disguised as candles in wall sconces, sucked the vibrant color from the oak wainscot paneling, and transformed the burgundy carpeting into pools of murky blood.

*Lighting's okay*, he thought. *One always needs a beautiful woman in a haunted building for a great scene.*

Finally, Trish turned to face a nearby bedroom door. "I feel something coming from this room. It's very…cold…" she said, "…menacing." With a quick intake of breath, she nudged the door open.

The bedroom light bulbs instantly flared and exploded, causing him to flinch from the sudden brightness. A resounding clatter of metal—pots and pans—rang from another part of the building.

"That's from the kitchen behind the dining hall! Let's go," Martin said.

Trish hesitated. "We have the place to ourselves, right?"

"Of course. Let's go," he repeated, vexed at her slowness. One had to be fast to capture ghosts!

He strode down the hallway filming what he hoped would be live action drama, passing through a leisure room of bookshelves, cluttered with dusty tomes, plush chairs, and low-set tables. Trish followed him through another hallway connecting the hotel entrance, its foyer, a dining hall entrance, and another leisure room at the far end.

Throughout the hotel, the gloomy feeling prevailed, just barely softened by the quaint use of slim tables holding blue-glass oil lamps and flower arrangements, and small oil paintings in ornately carved wooden frames on the paneled walls. The intent was to resurrect the atmosphere of the late-1800s when the hotel first opened.

Approaching the dining hall, he captured this background ambience, also making sure that the camcorder view swept past a shuttered dumbwaiter panel on the wall and the beautiful multicolored light projected by the stained-glass windows of the foyer's entrance doors.

*I can sell this footage*, he thought. *It's really good.*

After a quick setup check for the camcorder, they entered the dining hall. Double doors swished closed behind them. A narrow glowing rim of candle sconces illuminated the cavernous room, leaving the upper ceiling vaults clothed in darkness. White linen-covered round tables and elegant chairs filled the room. The tables had formal place settings and decorative vase centerpieces filled with silk flowers. Two doors, separate and placed near the far corners, led to the kitchen.

Trish raised her voice to call out, "Hello? Anyone here?" Her greeting didn't echo. Silence resumed.

A vase fell over with a jingle of metal somewhere ahead. One of the kitchen doors cycled open and closed.

Electric sweat charged Martin's skin.

"You see that?" he asked, voice shaky.

"Uh huh."

"Poltergeist activity or angry ghost?"

"Don't know," she said.

They weaved their way forward through the ornate tables and chairs. The overturned vase came into view. It had been knocked over and the tablecloth underneath was wrinkled. Behind the vase, there were keys…the keys the manager had given them.

Flustered, Martin reached into his pocket. Moved his hand around. Found nothing. Then, he searched his other pockets, looking sheepishly back at Trish. "Must've fallen out." Scooping up the keys, he shoved them into a pocket.

She huffed. "Well, someone found them."

"Let's find out who," he said, motioning to the still wobbling kitchen door.

The air inside the kitchen was thick with decay. A rotted sandwich buffet was laid out on a long stainless-steel table; various breads and meats, lettuce, and tomatoes, in moldy plastic containers. Pots and pans lay scattered on the floor—all of them, it seemed.

*No one's in here. No other exits.* The sheen of cold sweat on his body caused a shiver. *A ghost? Could this finally be the real thing? Boy, will this film sell!*

The lights went out. The kitchen's afterimage dissolved away in his vision. The darkness was impenetrable.

*Fuse blown.*

He looked at his camcorder. Battery dead. *What the hell?*

"Trish?" he called out.

"Over here," the voice said, ahead of him.

Feeling with his trembling hands, he loaded new batteries into his camcorder. He was shivering, and the hair on his neck, back, and arms tingled as if wisps of cold cobwebs alighted upon his skin.

"Careful. Something's on the floor. I think it's your blood…" the voice breathed, close to him.

"What?"

A small beam of light snapped on, far behind him. He turned to squint at the light. It was Trish, shining a penlight at him from the kitchen door. She reached for the wall switch and the kitchen was flooded with overhead lights once again.

"Who are you talking to?" Trish asked, frowning at him.

"To you!"

"No, I just came into the kitchen." Eyes bugging out, she tried to say more, but her voice cracked as she staggered backward. And then, she screamed.

The force that had moved the pots and pans hit Martin, punching into his chest. He was catapulted up into the air, arms and legs flailing wildly. The ceiling crunched against his body. Repeatedly, he was smashed nearly senseless, convulsing in pain, watching helplessly as the wobbling penlight below escaped the room. Then, freefall, cracking his head on something hard. As his consciousness slipped away, distant voices surrounded him.

*****

He put his hand to his head. *Ouch.* The sweaty pulsing knot on his forehead didn't like to be touched. His head ached.

Something had pushed him.

Standing up was a chore. He felt around and used a chair to hoist himself up. It felt like ants were crawling around inside his skull. Blood rushing, ears ringing, he stood still and rode out the waves of dizziness.

His first thought was his camcorder. He grabbed it off the floor and checked it carefully. Something had definitely happened here in the kitchen, something paranormal. Something had pushed him down and he wondered if he had caught it on the digital camera. The camcorder was the most important thing in his life at the moment.

But Trish was important, too. He took his camcorder and made his way out of the kitchen. He wove himself through the foyer and past the ornate carvings of the parlor lobby.

The hotel's entrance doors were padlocked closed. *When did that happen?* He fingered the outline of the keys in his pocket. *Trish must be looking for another way out. Why did she leave me?*

A quick patter of footsteps crossed the ceiling, not directly overhead, but nearby. And then something moved. Eyes wide, his reflexes responded to something that had darted across his line of vision. It was impossibly quick, but in the leisure room ahead...he thought he saw it again.

Behind him, in the hallway, a bedroom door creaked. Body suddenly quivering, he turned in time to see the door move inward, slowly grinding to a half-open position as he retraced his steps to stand in front of it.

He positioned his camcorder. He needed to record this.

He licked his lips in nervous anticipation and entered the room. Eying the door, he gently pushed it fully open, then entered the room. It had the typical hurricane oil lamp on a table, a full-length mirror, a wall light, a canopied four post bed, and an enclosed bathroom partition in the corner. The large window was cracked open, curtains pulled back, letting in the summer scent of fresh cut grass, flowers, and pine trees, along with the occasional chirps of birds. Outside, the view was of a lawn and rose garden within the encroaching mountain confines of the White River National Forest in remote Colorado.

No one was in the room. The door had opened by itself. Air currents. *No ghosts!*

Disappointed, he returned to the parlor leisure room. The plush chairs had been moved, lined up, facing towards him, as if he was being watched. A residual aroma of brandy and cigars wafted in the air.

A slight tremor started in his hands. Time was measured by his thumping heartbeats.

"Trish?" he called out. No answer.

One squeaking step at a time, he climbed the stairs to another leisure room. Two archways led off to more bedroom hallways. From the archway on his left, he heard a whispering noise that sounded like tree leaves rustling in a wind. If he let his imagination get the best of him, it could sound like muffled voices.

*She's got to be that way.* Probably behind the door at the far end of the hallway.

He began to feel angry at her. She was not following the rules. Hauntings were always supposed to be investigated in pairs. You couldn't get good help these days; too many were non-believers and therefore took unnecessary chances.

The lights flickered as he walked down the hallway. The hallway's paintings reflected the shifting light in an odd manner. It was if the familiar scenes depicted in the pictures melted together with the background, so a country barn, a mountainside, an apple orchard, and a hillside of grapevines had no boundaries anymore and blended colors, shapes, and textures bled out into each other, coexisting and merging with everything else in the depicted scenes.

His headache got worse, the kind he called the "icicle in the eye." He wasn't sure if the ringing in his ears was related to the scratching he heard beyond the bedroom doors, in the walls, in his mind. He opened the door at the hallway's end and quickly stepped through, slamming it closed.

The room was easily a hundred feet long by thirty deep with two doors at the opposite end, essentially an enclosed veranda that ran the width of the building's front, with an artfully arranged décor of comfortable lounging furniture and frost-rimmed bay windows, panes set side by side, providing a panoramic view of the front lawn, driveway, surrounding forest and mountainside. All a naturally beautiful sight, more stunning at this point because a thick layer of tufted snow covered the outdoor scenery, obscured within a veil of fat snowflakes swirling down from low hanging dark clouds. And, it was nighttime…

"Damn," he muttered, stunned. *It's winter? How did that happen?*

Something else had changed, too. Eyesight blurry, he blinked several times to be sure, W*hat the hell?* The distant mountaintops were no longer covered by a verdant forest—there were buildings, seemingly growing out of the mountainside, strange buildings, starkly monolithic in nature and lacking straight angles.

At a loss for understanding, shocked by the chilly air, he wondered if he was losing his mind.

The faint smell of wood smoke tickled his nose. The muted pop and crackle of a fire drew his attention to a stone-lined fireplace set within the middle of the room's inner wall.

Skin crawling, he had the sensation again that he wasn't alone, but he couldn't see anyone. Curiously impulsive, yet on edge, he crept closer to the fireplace.

Someone was slouched in a high-back chair facing the warm, glowing fire. It was Trish!

"Trish! We have to get out of here…"

She turned to him, blinking slowly as if she'd just noticed him. She said, "There you are."

"Trish. What happened? For god's sakes, you shouldn't have started the fire. We aren't supposed to touch anything in this house, just observe and film."

She sighed and returned her tired attention back to the sparking fire.

"We never should've come here. We disturbed something…something very dangerous."

A heavy thump of footsteps approached the door he'd come from—the sound was slow and ponderous.

Martin raised his camcorder and started shooting, despite the fresh sweat beading like a rash across his body. He made sure the sound feature was at its maximum.

The footsteps stopped at the door.

Trish spoke again, not making sense. "I saw it: life after death. Ghosts exist in an endless film loop, caught in a trap like wild, confused, and scared animals sinking into a tar pit. Now I finally believe. I saw it here in this hotel."

The footsteps continued. Inside the room. Approaching them. He swung the camcorder around, but there was nothing to be seen, only heard.

"Trish—" His tongue got in the way of talking as his throat choked up. He lowered his precious camcorder.

"We hit the mother lode," she continued. "In this hotel, every ghost exists, even from parallel universes, with everything laid bare. And we're not going to be able to tell anyone."

A swift whoosh of displaced air and she stopped talking with a wet gurgle. Her body, and the chair she sat on, were sliced apart cleanly from the top right to the lower left, the razor-sharp cut continuing with a thin arc into the carpeted floor. The chair split and fell apart in different directions, tossing her forward in a fountain spray of arterial blood that spattered the fireplace, the ceiling, and Martin as he stood frozen, mouth open.

The footsteps started towards him.

He dashed away, across the room. Chairs were knocked aside, coffee tables overturned, knees scraped. A door was before him, but it wouldn't open when he pushed and pushed on it.

He fumbled for frantic seconds, on the verge of wailing, before he realized that the door had a knob and he turned it. Still grasping his camcorder, he fled down a short dark hallway, tangled his legs on some rope and stanchions, and suddenly found himself falling into a hole, headfirst, smacking his left arm on something unyielding, tumbling before landing on a pile of various items, both hard and soft, flat and edged.

*Oh, damn...damn...damn...*

In his panicked flight, he'd taken the wrong door and fell into the open space that went from the second floor to the basement. They'd been told not to access this staff service area because it was dangerous. A rusted metal staircase had been removed during renovations, leaving a gaping hole, and a pile of unusable junk had been tossed down into the basement for cleanup later.

He lay sprawled on mattresses, broken furniture, and rank shreds of garbage.

The pain hit him. His left arm wasn't broken, but the skin was scraped on the back from tricep to forearm. Blood rolled into his armpit as he inched his arm aloft to slow the bleeding. His breathing came in stabs and hitches from his bruised ribs.

Some questionably stained bed sheets were within easy reach. He grabbed one. It tore apart easily, dust rising into the dank air as he fashioned a long, wide bandage strip and wrapped it around his bloodied arm. The blood flow was slowed to a near stop.

Looking about, he realized that he could see in this small windowless room because the huge foundation stones weren't perfectly fitted and mortared to the lower support beams, letting in slivers of sunlight.

*Daytime?* Again, the changing weather outside disturbed him.

*My camcorder! Where is it?* he frantically thought as he stood up.

There it was, lying on the floor two feet away.

He looked up. Nothing following him as far as he could tell. No footsteps.

*Trish...*tears fell down his cheeks as he considered what to do. He had convinced her to take on this haunting, so he was responsible for her. Ghosts were not supposed to harm anyone; everyone knew that. Ghosts could scare you but not hurt you. Ghost hunting was always harmless.

So what happened?

Again he picked up his camcorder. This would not be a fruitless effort. He would sell this digital film. The world would know.

And he'd be famous.

He couldn't reach the first floor from here, so he pushed open the door and ventured into the basement. Closing the door gently, he scanned the area around him in the half-light. Outlines of stacked furniture, sheets covering unknown bulky items, and at least a dozen doors to storage rooms surrounding a large central space. More was undoubtedly hidden in the darkness beyond the limit of his vision.

*I'm going to get out of here*, he thought, despite a sudden empty feeling of desolate helplessness. *Which door? One door must get me out!*

As he moved deeper into the stuffy room, his vision blurred momentarily. The room grew brighter as small, soft globes of light burst from the walls, taking shape into translucent apparitions, ghosts, people he knew, once knew, didn't know, some that shouldn't be dead but were....closing in on him from all sides.

He raised the camcorder to record the orbs. Here was proof. Finally, he had proof of the spirit world. He would make history...he'd be famous.

As he fell under the surface of the sea of ghosts, they glowed and surrounded him, absorbing him into their dimensions. They pulsated and undulated, ingesting the soul of the man who so desperately sought to prove their existence.

The camcorder fell from his grasp and rolled uselessly across the floor.

## GOODNIGHT ERIC

Bruce Memblatt

The war is never over for me. The war began with a ghost; a challenge from my imagination. Every night a phantasm tried to frighten me with whispers in the dark.

At the start it terrified me, but because it happened night after night, my fear turned to anger.

The oddest thing of all was that I knew the name of the ghost. I wasn't alone in this big house. It was me and Eric. Although I absolutely knew my house was haunted, I wanted the spirit out; and I considered an exorcism.

But how do you get rid of a ghost? How do you kill a ghost? You can't kill something that's already dead, can you?

I had to find a way. I wondered if any priest would believe my story.

Over the next few weeks, I pored over every ghost story, every novel, and every ghost movie I could find. Most of the films involved searching for the ghost… I didn't need to hunt down Eric. He was always whispering and flitting about in the corner of my eye. I wanted a confrontation to see him head-on.

My house is in far upstate New York, right near the Canadian border. It is so far from the city, you'd never know there was a town or even civilization there. There are cows up here, cows and bears and deer, not people.

There are woods around this house, thick and green and rich as the earth that supports them. It had belonged to my grandparents and they were rich, rich as thieves, but they weren't thieves.

Gramps was filthy stinking rotten rich and being the only child of their only child, I got this big old mansion with these beautiful oak paneled walls, and long marble hallways, and parquet everywhere, out in the out, out in the middle of nowhere.

And in this room, the main living room is where I like this house the most, with its big roaring fireplace, and its windows so tall they catch the entire sky. Like that view on that very first night which changed my life. The moon lit the sky, the stars not far behind, looking like they were just as much a part of this room as the furniture.

I sat in this room for hours that night, with the lights out with and nothing but the fire and the sky. I was staring into the fire, thinking of life, and he caught me off guard by coming to my house uninvited.

That was the first night Eric came. I felt his stare, and I leaped right out of the big black leather chair that I loved the most.

Shaking like a frightened mouse, I could almost see him that first night; a dark flicker, a wave in the air.

"Who are you?" My hands were shaking.

"You know exactly who I am," he said. I felt a breeze, and I saw him move across the room quickly, in a whoosh; a dark shadow climbing the paneled walls, rushing through the moonlight, floating through the walls then back into the air again like a misguided missile.

"I swear, I don't know you. You're scaring me. Are you real?" I couldn't believe how calm I sounded, when my heart thudded so hard, I thought I would keel over in fright.

He stopped in front of the mirror above the marble fireplace, the large high-arched antique mirror, and stared into it, and said, "The answer is behind this mirror."

Was there something behind the mirror, some dark place? Maybe the place all ghosts come from?

"Stare into the mirror. Look at the glass. Look at yourself."

I couldn't believe any of this. My fear overtook me once again and I had to get out of the house or suffer a heart attack. I ran out the back door. I trembled in the cool night air, breathed deeply, and inhaled the scent of the pine trees. *None of this is real*, I told myself. *There is no Eric.*

*****

That was the very first night I met Eric.

He's been haunting me ever since. If it is possible to get used to a ghost, I was beginning to learn to live with Eric. He no longer terrorized me, but scared me in a different way: is this what death was? A lingering abyss; an unending moment in time, never finding peace? A limbo state, with no place to go? It was too sad to consider.

One night I approached the mirror. I stared at it until I was lost. It was so dark in the room, only the glow from the fireplace behind us and that sliver of moonlight. But I stared into that dark mirror, and soon I saw eyes that were not mine, faces that were not mine.

I heard voices that were not mine. I saw my grandmother's eyes, my grandfather's head shaking, his gray brow, his steely-blue eyes. I saw my grandmother next to him, and soon my parents, and before I knew it there were eyes and hands and faces surrounding me, faces of people I knew, faces of people I never knew. I was lost in a sea…a sea of faces. Eyes, so many eyes, I was lost in the mirror.

Lost with the dead.

I screamed for him. "Eric! Where are you?" I screamed for the one who had started all this horror in the first place. I screamed for the one who had scared me into staring at the mirror.

And then I felt his hand, his cold hand that wasn't a hand, but something between life and death, something from the shadows. He pulled me away into a dark black mist.

Was this the beyond the mirror he meant? Was I past the mirror? Past myself? Past the world?

"Quite a family reunion you conjured up there," he said, still pulling me. I could hardly see his face. I could hardly see anything.

He pulled me harder and we began traveling faster through the mist, through the thick black fog that seemed to be everywhere.

"Stop it, Eric! Let me go."

"If I let you go, you will fall," he said. "But so be it."

And then Eric was gone. And I dropped so fast. I was going to die, to join the limbo of the other side.

The mist around me flew past my eyes, in patches, in stretches, streaming, swirling, with me falling through it like a bullet.

Everything inside me shook, except my stomach. My stomach felt like it was ten miles above me. I screamed as I careened down through the thick black air.

Suddenly I found myself on a road. Where was I? I was lost in a dream; a nightmare.

The sky was translucent, but steely gray and the mist still drifted past me. That awful black mist. Awful everything. I had to find my way back. Back, out of this place, back to the world I knew. The world I thought I knew; the world when I was alive.

In the distance, I heard the sound of a car. It sounded so far away. Where was Eric? Why was I here? Where did the road lead?

Trees started to appear on the side of the road, as if this was a natural place, and not some crazy image in my head.

I could smell the fresh air, and then a house appeared but it wasn't just any house. It was the house I grew up in before my grandfather gave me the mansion. It wasn't a large house. It was a white Cape Cod, but we loved it, and mom made it so…

"Pretty?"

Oh god, Eric's whisper. He was back. I felt intense dread since he would make things even crazier because he was haunting me.

"Take a look around your house. The road where it happened."

"Where what happened?" I cried.

Somewhere inside of me, I knew where this was all leading, but I could never face it. This is what the raging war in me was all about. This is where the road led.

"Let's go inside. Let's go inside your house," he said. He reached for me again, his shadowy arm on my shoulder, his breathless mouth still articulating, the hairs on the back of my neck still standing.

We walked through the doorway. I could hear Mom in the kitchen, stirring and singing. The low sounds of the TV in the living room, bullets and banjos, and I knew dad was sitting on the couch in front of it, watching a Western, unraveling from the terrible day he had. Soon, he was going to tell Mom about his horrid day over dinner.

And me? Where was I?

"Step closer into the house," Eric whispered like he knew what I was going to find.

What could I do, except whatever Eric wanted? I was helpless under the spell of the other side. The dark side. The death side.

As we stepped through the narrow foyer, with the same pictures of anonymous country landscapes that had always been there, I could see the sunlight filtering through the kitchen by the archway at the end of the foyer. To the right of the kitchen was the living room, to the left, a stairway lined with more pictures, not of landscapes but photos of us and photos of Grandpa and Grandma, leading to our bedrooms.

The house looked and felt like it always did, like it was carved in time, but as we stepped into the kitchen, my mother's singing ended abruptly, and the sounds of her cooking stopped.

I could feel Eric trying to nudge me. I could feel him like a wave across my back, and I wanted to scream, I wanted to run somewhere, anywhere.

I stared into the kitchen. The table. The chairs. The old Frigidaire. The green shade up over the sink. The brick linoleum, and the sunlight filling the empty room. Where was it coming from? Sunlight in all this dark mist? Then I remembered what Eric said about memories, and I knew the sunlight was coming from me.

"Let's try the living room," Eric told me, and as we stepped out of the kitchen the sounds of the TV vanished.

Then something inside me screamed, and I told Eric, "I don't want to go in there, Eric! I want to go home!"

"But you *are* home," he said. I wanted to scream again. I wanted to run. I wanted to do anything but see what was in the living room. The feeling of déjà vu was overwhelming.

But still, we traveled towards the room. Eric wouldn't let me do anything else.

My legs moved as if driven. I could see the sunlight as we came closer. There were bay windows in the room, surrounded by the greenest trees, and a view of the driveway.

I wondered if it would all still be there as we entered.

And then I saw my parents.

I froze inside.

They were standing still, still as statues and they were dressed in black. They didn't notice me. Didn't even flinch.

There were flowers everywhere. On the coffee table. On the bureau against the wall.

"Eric, I want to leave!"

"Don't you want to stay with your mother and father?"

"But they can't see me. They aren't recognizing me. They aren't moving…they're just standing there, in those awful black suits! This isn't happening because they're both dead!"

I waited for something. Some response, anything, but still, nothing.

The overwhelming scent of the flowers filled my nostrils, and I tried to put it together in my mind. Why the black suits? Why the flowers? Why couldn't they see me? Where was I?

"I want to leave this place. I want to leave this horrible place!"

"But you can't," he said, and I almost saw sadness in his faded, vacant eyes. There would be a tear there if Eric were alive and not a dead thing—a dead, hollow thing.

"You can't leave this place because this place is you," the ghost said.

"No! It's a just dream, a nightmare. I must have hit the booze tonight. That's what happened. We're not here. You're not here. This is just a drunken dream that I don't want to know about!" I cried.

The shiny black hearse was parked in the driveway.

I screamed and shook so hard because I knew. I couldn't say it but I knew who that hearse was for.

I panicked. Then I ran. I ran out of the house fast over the green grass.

At the end of the driveway was the hearse. I passed it, and just as I went by, I saw faces in the back seat. Mom and Dad. They were in the back seat of the hearse now.

I ran fast as I could, but I wasn't going anywhere. I was stuck in place! Stuck on the road. The long highway stretched into forever, but I seemed to be running in place.

And then I felt him again, Eric next to me.

And suddenly the dark mist began to filter into the translucent sky and it was back again, filling the air, blotting the sun.

Eric tried to put his hand on my back, but all I felt was a shift of empty air when he said, "Stand here and listen."

"Listen? Listen for what?" I said, and then in the distance, the car I heard before, but this time it was revving up. I could hear it, felt it gaining speed.

And I heard a crash, and I saw myself, fire all around my face, inside the broken car, broken glass, broken metal, smoke everywhere and me, *and me*!

"And then what happens? What happens?" Eric said.

But I still, I still wouldn't go near it, and I clutched at my chest, at the air. And my legs, I could feel my legs give way, and I began to cry, and as I cried and I stared at the luminescent gray sky, and that awful dark mist filling the horizon.

Suddenly I saw lights. There were beautiful lights, high on the ceiling of a beautiful hall. We were inside a magnificent hall and there was music—lovely, heavenly music—and we were dancing, me and Eric as if we were one.

I could barely make out his face, as we spun around, just the fading outline of a fading ghost. But I could hear him. Heard him clearly.

"What is happening?" I asked.

"It's almost complete," he whispered.

"What is almost complete?"

"We are," he said.

I couldn't really feel Eric anymore, but I knew he was close. And the music was so nice and everything was so dreamy.

"The car. Do you remember what happened next?"

"No, Eric, No, I won't remember!"

"Who died in the car?"

I didn't want to know. "No," I said.

But suddenly I did know. I was sure I was going to break apart into a million pieces of me. Both of us. I couldn't stand it. Those bright lights, flashing so fast before my eyes, my insides grinding, my mind exploding, I tried to hold Eric tighter but I couldn't feel him because you can't really feel a ghost.

"I've been searching for you all these years while you've hid, alone, in the isolated country. Then I found you so I could take you here. You need to see this," he told me.

There would be no comfort from Eric.

I could barely feel myself. I could barely feel anything. But then I could feel myself disappearing.

I screamed "Eric! Make it stop!"

And he said, "I can't make it stop. This is you. This is all you. Tell me now, who died in that accident...who died in that car crash?"

"I won't say it. I never will!"

We were in the car, moving so fast. And the music become so loud, I thought my ears would split. The heavenly music changed from lilting to a horrendous jarring noise as I crashed the car head-on into a tree. I realized I couldn't feel my feet, my hands, or my mouth. I couldn't feel myself at all!

But we still spun so fast.

And where was Eric? I couldn't see him anymore.

"Say it!" Eric whispered in my ear.

"No."

"Who is Eric?" he asked.

"You!"

"And who I am I?"

"You are Eric! You are the persistent ghost that assumes the right to torment me."

"No. I am in your mirror, when you look inside to see your soul."

"What?" I had a horrific, sinking feeling. I was confused and bewildered.

Then I heard him ask. “What’s your name?”

I began to answer when I realized I couldn’t remember my name. How can a person not remember his own name?

“When was the last time you heard someone call your name?” he asked. “Didn’t they call you Eric?”

At once, the music stopped. The lights went out. The spinning stopped. And I was alone. I was back in my favorite room, in my favorite chair staring at the mirror, staring into it just like when this all started, but I couldn't see my reflection in the mirror any more.

I still couldn’t feel myself at all.

But I could almost feel a tear fill my eye as if I could produce something real again.

And then I heard a whisper in my head, a voice saying, “You will find everything about yourself in the cemetery. Go there to accept reality so you don’t have to hide anymore.”

## CUTTING THE MUSTARD

Graham Masterton and Dawn G. Harris

The library door flew open with a bang and a chilly gust of wind blew in, so that the leaflets on the librarian's counter were blown up into the air like a flock of seagulls and were scattered all over the floor.

Terrance Coleman looked up from his computer as Mrs. Parker stamped over to slam the door shut again. That was the second time this afternoon that it had swung open by itself, and the second time that Mrs. Parker had been obliged to bend over, puffing in annoyance, to scoop up all of her leaflets.

Terrance hadn't gone across to help her. As far as he was concerned, he was in charge of the non-fiction section of Broadbent Community Library and his responsibilities were clearly demarcated. He kept a running inventory of all the non-fiction titles and their condition and ordered more when requested. Fiction, children's books, CDs and library administration—none of those were Terrance's department. As far as he was concerned, shutting the door and picking up scattered leaflets would have come under "library administration."

Apart from his computer, its screen clustered all around with post-it notes, there was nothing on Terrance's desk apart from a well-chewed ball pen, a notepad, and a half-eaten ham roll. There wasn't a photo of a loved one; there wasn't even a lucky mascot.

Terrance typed in: *The History of Double-Enveloping Worm Gears* by B.M. Truscott, B.Eng, B.Sc. The library needed a new copy because somebody had inexplicably stolen the last one, or forgotten to bring it back.

A noisy group of about fifteen schoolchildren passed his aisle, as they did almost every day at 3:40 after they had finished their reading circle, and almost every day they would poke fun at him. It was mostly because of his name, which was displayed in a plastic holder on his desk, but maybe it was the way he looked, too, with his gingery-grey hair that stuck up like a worn-out scrubbing-brush.

"Colman's must-*ard*! Colman's must-*ard*!" they would chant at him. But today one girl of about twelve or thirteen came right up close to his desk and whispered, "*Terrance Coleman doesn't cut the mustard*!"

He stared back at her, and she gave him an extraordinary smile, a *knowing* smile, as if she were privy to all of his innermost secrets. She had blonde hair plaited into a tight coronet and limpid blue eyes, and for a girl of her age she was almost unnervingly pretty.

"What?" he said.

"Terrance Coleman doesn't cut the mustard!" she repeated, but this time she shrieked it at the top of her voice, and all her school friends laughed and jeered and made raspberry noises.

"Doesn't cut the mustard!" they chanted. "Doesn't cut the mustard!"

They were still chanting it as they pushed their way out of the library, leaving the door open behind them. At the open door, the blonde girl with the blue eyes paused for a moment and turned around to look at Terrance and smile, and as she did so another cold gust of wind blew in, so that her dress flapped. Then she was gone, and more leaflets flew onto the floor.

Terrance sat, unresponsive, and stared at the computer screen in front of him. He was used to this daily taunting, even though it made him feel even more unworthy at work than he did at home, all alone without even a fish to care for. Today, though, that girl had unsettled him more than anybody had for a long time, and he didn't understand why.

"You still here? Doesn't your shift end at four?" said a sudden deep voice behind him. Terrance turned slowly to see a man in a black gabardine jacket staring directly at him. He looked back at his keyboard before answering.

"What do you want, Inspector Riley? Come to see what I'm up to, have you?"

"Whatever would give you *that* idea, Mr. Coleman?" replied the man, lifting himself slightly onto his toes in what was almost a parody of a police officer. "Working in a library, teenagers around, ex-school teacher—is there something I *need* to worry about? I can see I don't need to worry about your *dress* sense. No, no—benefit of the doubt I always said that I'd give you. Benefit of the doubt."

"If you must know, I'm awaiting information on the new book *For The Sake Of Reptiles,* Inspector. I'm the head of non-fiction as you well know and we have a customer order request."

"Reptiles? Ah, you mean like *snakes*? Deal with snakes too, do you, Mr. Coleman? Consider yourself something of a snake yourself, do you? Always thought you were a bit on the slithery side."

Terrance took in a deep breath and closed his eyes. *I wish he would leave me alone.*

"I'm simply misunderstood, Inspector," he replied. His patience was beginning to wear thin. "I'm no more of a snake than the next single middle-aged man. Just because I live on my own and like to keep myself to myself."

"If only I could believe that, Mr. Coleman. But—well—the jury believed it, didn't they, and I suppose that's all that matters as far as you're concerned."

The afternoon sun suddenly shone through the narrow library windows and lit up the dust particles that were floating above Terrance's desk. Strangely, they seemed to be drifting towards his blank computer screen, and as they reached it, it looked as if they were disappearing into the blackness like a swarm of tiny fireflies being drawn into a long dark tunnel. But then the sun went in again, and they vanished. Terrance ran his fingertips across the screen, but there was no dust on it.

"I'll leave you be, Mr. Coleman," said Inspector Riley. "The wife's cooking bangers and mash tonight and I love a bit of mustard with my bangers and mash, so I might well be eating your namesake. Be good, won't you, Mr. Coleman? Keep yourself to yourself."

He patted Terence on the shoulder and walked off. Terrance was so agitated that he slammed his fists down onto the desk, breaking the pencil that he was holding. *Why? Why me? I never hurt them—none of them. Some of them even called me Uncle Terrance. Some of them even came back for more.*

*****

It was dark by the time he left the library. He walked along the high street to the bus-stop so that he could catch the 57 to take him home. A strong headwind made the tails of his raincoat billow and snap and he gripped his lapels tightly together because it was so cold. He felt almost as if the wind was trying to blow him back towards the library.

At least a dozen people were already waiting at the bus-stop, and he joined the end of the queue. He stood there shivering and stamping his feet to keep warm, cupping one hand over his left ear to stop the wind blowing into it and giving him earache, and still clutching his lapels together. This morning's weather bulletin had said that it was going to be chilly, but he didn't remember a warning of strong winds. The Met Office never seemed to get their forecasts right.

After only a minute or two, he noticed something that puzzled him. The woman in front of him in the queue was wearing a broad-brimmed brown hat with a beige ostrich feather stuck in the hatband, but the feather wasn't ruffled by the wind at all.

Frowning, he looked further up the queue and saw that a man was reading the *Evening Standard*, holding it wide open. The pages of his newspaper weren't flapping, as he would have expected. And near the front of the queue, two young men were smoking. The smoke from their cigarettes drifted away across the road, but lazily, and in the opposite direction from the way the wind was blowing.

Terrance looked around. Sweet wrappers and discarded plastic bottles were lying in the gutter and cluttering a nearby shop doorway, but none of this rubbish was stirring, even though he would have expected the wind to be scattering it everywhere. The wind seemed to be blowing only for him.

When the bus arrived, he struggled to make his way to the doors, and the driver gave him a curious look as he clung onto the rail and held onto his hat at the same time. It was only when he managed to stumble inside the bus and the doors closed behind him that the wind stopped blowing.

"Hey man," he said, as Terrance started to climb the stairs to the upper deck. "You isn't *drunk*, is you? I can't let you on the bus if you're drunk."

"Do I *look* drunk?" Terrance retorted. "Do I smell of alcohol? Do you want to smell my breath?"

"No, you're all right, man. You was so unsteady on your feet, that's all."

The only seat left on the upper deck was right at the back, next to a skinny schoolgirl in a green gingham dress. She shifted uncomfortably away from Terrance when he sat down. He gave her a smile and said, "Hey…I like your friendship bracelets."

The girl stared at him, frowning, as if he had spoken to her in a foreign language.

"I said—I like your friendship bracelets."

"Oh, do you? But I don't want one from *you*, thanks, if that's what you're thinking." The girl spoke in a lisping voice, because she was missing her top two front teeth. "You don't cut the mustard."

Terrance stared back at her, feeling as if his entire insides were draining away, like bathwater.

"What did you say?"

"You heard," said the girl, and turned away to look out of the window.

"Do you *know* me?" Terrance insisted. "Have you seen me in the library?"

"No, and no," the girl replied. "And I don't *want* to know you, either."

Terrance hesitated for a moment, and then he stood up and rang the bell for the next request stop. He got off the bus even though he was still at least a mile-and-a-half away from his home. He started to walk along Streatham High Road, past brightly-lit launderettes and Chinese supermarkets.

At first he felt only the softest of breezes, but the further he walked, the stronger the wind started to blow. By the time he reached the Savada Bhojana Restaurant, the wind was so strong that he was leaning forward against it, and passers-by were staring at him as if he were some kind of street magician.

He pushed open the restaurant door and stumbled inside, and immediately the wind dropped. He stood there for a few moments, his mouth tightly closed, holding his breath, because he couldn't stand the smell of curry.

The door had a bell attached to it which jangled loudly every time a customer went in or out, and it jangled now, and seemed to go on jangling for longer than usual. He could hear that jangle from his bedsit upstairs and every time he heard it he sucked in saliva between his teeth in futile annoyance. Upstairs he could also smell fenugreek from the restaurant: it seemed to permeate everything from his clothes to his mattress. He could even smell it in his nostrils when he was sitting in the library, although that may have been imaginary.

If he could afford more than £125 a week, he would move tomorrow. He sorely missed the large ground-floor flat where he used to live in Polworth Road, when he was head of physics at St. Martin's Secondary School. He missed it to the point of grief. He missed the silence and the high ceilings and the morning sun that shone through the living-room windows. He missed the finches that flustered around the bird-table.

Terrance weaved his way between the restaurant tables to the door that led upstairs. The restaurant was wallpapered in dark crimson with bronze statuettes of the goddess Shiva on either side. It was early in the evening but two couples were already eating. Even the sound of them laughing irritated him, and he was sure when he died the pathologist would find that the fumes from *bhuna gosht* and chicken *dupiaza* had stained his airways irrevocably orange, like nicotine.

He tried to keep holding his breath but Ghulam the owner saluted him from behind the bar and called out, "*Roz bākhair*, Mr. Mustard-sir! A very good evening! How are you?" and he had to wave back half-heartedly and say, "Fine, thanks!"

As he opened the door to go up to his bedsit, Ghulam came around the bar and said, "You had a caller, Mr. Mustard-sir."

"A caller? What do you mean? Who was it? Not the Sky technician? I told him not to come till after seven-thirty."

Ghulam was stocky, with wavy grey hair and a grey moustache like a dirty nailbrush. His eyes always twinkled in a way that made Terrance feel that he might know more about him than he was letting on. He wore a brocade waistcoat the same crimson as the walls, with spatters of dried curry sauce on it.

"It was soon after we opened. A young girl. She asked if you had been able to come back from work. When I said no, not yet, she said, do not be surprised if he does not come back at all."

"Really? Did she explain what she meant by that?"

Ghulam shook his head. "No. But she said that if you *did* come back, I was to tell you a special word."

"Which was what?"

"I don't have a good memory, Mr. Mustard-sir, except for what my customers order. But here…I have written it down."

He went over to the till, picked up an order-pad, and tore off the top page. He handed it to Terrance and said, "This was all she said. But she gave me a big, big smile, as if she was happy about something. Perhaps your niece? She seemed to know you very well."

Terrance took the page from the order-pad. He stared at it for nearly a quarter of a minute, feeling as if a Tupperware box full of woodlice had been emptied down his back, inside his shirt. Normally he opened and closed the door to his bedsit as quickly as he could, to stop the smell rising upstairs, but this time he left it half-open. He held up the page with his hand trembling and he opened and closed his mouth several times before he was able to speak.

Scrawled across the page, almost illegibly, was *ushabati53Y.*

"Are you sure this what she said?" he asked Ghulam, at last.

"That is it exactly, Mr. Mustard-sir. She even spelled out the letters for me, one by one. *You-ess-h*—and so forth."

Terrance said nothing more, not even "thank you", but climbed the steep hessian-carpeted stairs to his bedsit, closing the door behind him. It was too late, though. The strong smell of jalfrezi had already risen to the landing and he knew that it would have leaked under his door.

*****

He had intended to heat up the fish pie that he had bought yesterday from Lidl, but now he had no appetite at all. He could do nothing but sit on his sofa-bed with his head bowed and his hands clenched together. His room was bare. There were no pictures on the walls, no ornaments, only a dead cactus in a pot on the windowsill and an empty budgerigar cage. The inside of his brain felt like a blizzard—not of snowflakes, but of ripped-up photographs, thousands of ripped-up photographs, each of them featuring a leg or an arm or a bare shoulder or a wide-eyed pleading face.

He should have deleted them. He should have used that software that blanks out pictures with zeroes, so that they can never be recovered from any hard drive or data bank or i-cloud, ever. But they were so precious to him. They meant so much. Every one of them told a story of gentle coaxing and soft encouragement; of laughter and tears.

He poured out the rest of the can of Carlsberg that he had opened last night. It was flat, but that suited his mood completely. Who in the name of God could have found out the password to his work computer? He had never told anyone what it was and he had never written it down. Who could have guessed that he had used the name of Ushabati Ghosh, the child bride of the 1920s Indian physicist Satyendra Nath Bose, who had married her when he was twenty and she was only eleven?

He didn't pull out his bed that night. The restaurant's doorbell kept on jangling, and the smell of curry seemed to be stronger than ever. He lay sideways on the sofa and dropped off to sleep at about two o'clock. He dreamed that he could hear the wind whistling sarcastically and children's voices taunting him.

"Cut the mustard!" they were singing. "Cut the mustard! You can't—cu-hut the mustard!"

At about five in the morning he was woken up by a refuse lorry banging and crashing in the street outside. He sat up, confused, and found that his trousers were soaked with urine.

*****

When he arrived at the library the next morning he found a stack of books waiting for him on his desk—seven or eight of them, even though he had ordered only *For The Sake Of Reptiles* and *The History of Double-Enveloping Worm Gears*. His name *Terrance Coleman* was scribbled on a Post-it note and stuck to the top book.

He laid his ham roll down beside his notebook and peered at the titles of the books with growing bewilderment. This was the non-fiction section but these books all appeared to be fiction, or poetry. *The Dance of the Nymphs. Children of the Lost Forest. The Day My Youth Was Stolen. Lolita.*

Terrance looked around, feeling increasingly unsettled. The library was deserted, except for Mrs. Parker and an elderly man sitting in the corner leafing through an encyclopedia and systematically wiping his nose with a large white handkerchief. There were no schoolchildren, teasing him about his name: too early for that. No Inspector Riley, standing behind him like Moros, the legendary Greek messenger of impending doom.

He turned back to his desk but even before he reached forward to switch on his computer, he heard the library door swing open behind him, and a soft, fluffing sound. He paused, not turning around, but alert and listening. The fluffing grew louder, and he heard a leaflet flutter from Mrs. Parker's counter and onto the floor.

It was that wind again, he was sure of it, that wind that had blown only for him. The titles of those books should have told him that this was something sinister. More sinister than a knock on the window on a dark night; or the scratching sound of steel in a bleak winter storm.

He didn't dare to look behind him, but as he sat there, a small figure glided to stand close beside him, on his left-hand side. He slowly turned his head, his heart beating so hard that it hurt his ribs. The figure was only two meters away, and yet it was in shadow, as if it were standing against the sun.

He leaned forward and adjusted his glasses, trying to see the figure's face. It was a girl—he knew by her long hair, which was stirred by the rising wind. But he couldn't make out her face.

"Who are you?" he demanded, trying to sound authoritative, as he did in school. "What do you want? This is a public library, I hope you know that! We don't allow any nonsense in here!"

Without warning, his computer monitor flicked on, fuzzed and settled. Words started to appear on the screen, typing quickly from line to line with the keyboard keys denting in accordingly, even though Terrance wasn't touching them. He shoved his chair away from his desk, a blinding pain swelling in his head.

"Who are you? Get away! Get away from me!" he shouted at the girl. He scrambled across his desk for his phone and frantically pressed Mrs. Parker's extension number on the front counter.

The girl came closer, although her face remained in darkness.

"Read the words, Terrance," she told him, pointing to his computer screen. "Read the words and weep."

"Mrs. Parker? Mrs. Parker, you must help me—something's happening! I can't explain—but it's happening now! Please come!" and with that he slammed the phone down. He looked back to the monitor. The lines of words were still climbing up the screen. There were hundreds of them, thousands, even. At first he found it impossible to focus on them, but then they stopped.

"Read them, Terrance," the girl repeated, and as she did so her face was gradually lit up, so that he realized it was the same girl who had challenged him yesterday.

Terrance squinted at the monitor. As far as he could make out, the words were all a list of names, and dates, and places. *Sandra Livingstone, 14th May, Tooting Graveney Common. Jessie Wilson, 18th June, Norwood Grove Recreation Ground. Asha Mabela, 12th August, Brockwell Park.*

He read the last lines aloud, but in a whisper. *You must come in and talk to us, Terrance. You must come in and pay the price for what you did. We will show you. We will show you your darkest thoughts, and make you live them for us.*

He turned back to the girl and said, "I don't understand."

She gave him a knowing smile, but she didn't answer. Instead, she raised both of her hands, and the library doors swung open again.

A wild gust of wind blew in, almost like a hurricane, so that the pages of books flipped furiously back and forth with a sound like hundreds of people clapping. The girl paused beside Terrance for a few moments more, her hair whipping across her face. Then she glided away towards the door, with books flying off the shelves on either side of her.

*****

"Terrance!" shrieked Mrs. Parker. "Terrance, what's happening?" She was struggling against the wind as she came around her counter and started to clamber over the fallen books towards his desk. More books tumbled off the shelves and a heavy dictionary hit her on the shoulder. "*Terrance*!"

Gradually the wind began to die down, and by the time she reached his desk the library was silent again, and still. A last book dropped off a shelf, like the last lump of ice after a thaw.

"Terrance?" said Mrs. Parker, cautiously. "Terrance, where are you? Terrance?"

There was no sign of Terrance anywhere. His corduroy jacket was still hanging over the back of his chair. His ham roll, wrapped in cellophane, was still lying on his desk. His computer was still switched on but the screen was blank. Mrs. Parker went to the back of the non-fiction section, wondering if he had sheltered from the wind in the U-shaped recess of the geography section, but he wasn't there, either.

She walked slowly all around the library, picking up fallen books as she went. She even half-opened the door to the gent's toilet, and called out, "Terrance?"

There was no reply. Terrance had disappeared. She could only imagine that he had been frightened by the wind and run out of the library, although she was sure that she would have seen him as he came past her counter. Perhaps he had simply had enough of being a librarian and walked out without giving her any notice. He had always been taciturn and never exchanged pleasantries, not even "good morning," or "miserable weather, isn't it?" or "did you see *Strictly Come Dancing* last night?"

But if he had simply had enough and quit, why had he left his jacket behind and not taken his lunch? Perhaps he would come back and explain where he had been. Meanwhile, she switched off his computer.

The hours went past, and borrowers came and borrowers went. Books were taken out and books were returned. The school reading circle came in, laughing and jostling as usual, and they seemed to be disappointed that Terrance wasn't there to be jeered at.

"Where's old Mustard, then? Hasn't cut it today! That's it! Hasn't cut the mustard!"

*****

Two hours after the library closed, the sound of shrill singing echoed through its corridors. It was Mavis the cleaner, singing to her heart's content, accompanied by the discordant squeak of trolley wheels. Her trolley was crowded with dusters, disinfectant sprays, a sponge-mop and a plastic bucket, as well as a fluffy blue mascot of a bear that her granddaughter had given her.

She swept the floor past the library doors and into the non-fiction section. As she entered it, a chilly draft blew around her ankles and fluttered her pinafore. She looked to see if any of the windows had been left open, but as far as she could make out they were all closed. She carried on, warbling her song: "*…ever…I couldn't see your heart, the love you held couldn't start, reach out to me…walk on...*"

She pushed her trolley to the middle of the room and then approached Terrance's desk, duster in one hand and Mr. Sheen furniture polish in the other. But then she stopped, and saw that Terrance's jacket was still draped over the back of his chair.

She looked at her watch, and said, "That's weird." It was past seven o'clock and the library closed at five. As scruffy as he was, she couldn't imagine Terrance leaving his jacket behind, especially not in this weather, and when she lifted it up off the chair, she could see that he had left his wallet in the inside pocket.

"Terrance, ya still 'ere somewhere?" she called out. She waited, but there was no reply. "Terrance?" she called again, but there was still no answer, so she carried on singing and spraying polish onto his desk.

"I dunno, this man is so mucky," she muttered to herself. She tugged on a pair of blue nitrile gloves before she picked up Terrance's half-eaten coleslaw sandwich and dropped it into her bin.

Now she picked up her glass cleaning spray, wiping underneath his computer keyboard and over its keys, with a soft rattling sound. She polished the monitor screen and after she had swiped her yellow duster over it, she peered into it to see her own reflection. Almost at once, though, her face began to change, as if it were made of melting wax. She stared at the screen with ever-increasing bewilderment and horror as her hair shrank shorter and her cheeks turned pale and she realised that she wasn't looking at herself any more but Terrance. His eyes were closed but his mouth was slightly open, as if he were finding it difficult to breathe.

Mavis turned around, sharply, expecting to see Terrance standing behind her, but there was no one there.

She turned back at the screen, expecting his face to have vanished, but it was still there, almost as if it was pressed up against the glass from the inside. Now, though, he opened his eyes and stared directly at her, and his lips moved as if he were trying to say something, and she was sure that she could hear a faint, tiny voice calling out to her. She felt a shivery tingle all the way down to her feet, and she rubbed hard at the screen with her duster, trying to wipe his image away. As furiously as she wiped, though, she couldn't erase him, and she could still hear that tiny, muted voice.

In all the time he had worked at the library, Terrance had never once said hello to her, even though he expected his desk to be clean every morning. Yet here he was, calling out to her, as if he desperately needed her to help him.

It was then that the temperature in the library suddenly dropped like a stone, and Mavis felt as if all the blood in her body had become so cold that it had become as thick as treacle. The bookshelves started to creak, and a freezing draft made her arms go prickly with goosebumps.

"What ya doin', ya horrible, horrible man!" she screamed at Terrance's face. "You ain't in there—this is some sort o' computer trick."

She wiped the monitor screen around and around, harder and harder. It was then that the duster began to squeak and slime, and before long she realized it was becoming soaked in red and that she was swirling wide red streaks all over it. The harder she pressed, the more red liquid seemed to swell from the seams of the monitor frame, and she knew from its metallic smell that it was blood. She had been a trainee nurse once, and she knew what blood smelled like.

Blood was not only oozing from the frame of the monitor but now it started to dribble from the ventilation holes underneath the screen and drip all over the keyboard. Within seconds it was pouring out, sliding across the desk and pattering in blobs and sticky glops onto the carpet.

Mavis flung her blood-soaked duster to one side and tried to take a step back, but the interior of the library was now so cold that the blood had coagulated and it stuck to the sole of her shoe. Her shoe came loose and her stockinged foot slipped sideways on the blood-soaked laminate floor. She fell to her knees, grabbing for support from her trolley, but that toppled over with a crash. She screamed in fright.

She had to get out of there. With her pinafore drenched in blood, she managed to climb to her feet and hobbled in a sort of lopsided run out of the non-fiction section to the library doors. She unlocked them and then she stumbled out onto the forecourt. The street was deserted so she reached into her wet pinafore pocket and took out her phone. Even though it was tacky with blood she managed to prod out 999.

"What's your emergency?" the operator asked her.

"Police! Help me! I'm at Broadbent Library. There's nobody here but it's like somebody got murdered!"

"I'm sorry. I don't understand you. There's nobody there but you think that someone's been murdered?"

"I seen Mr. Terrence's face, but he wasn't there! He wasn't there but there's *blood*! There's so much blood! It keeps on comin'! Blood, blood and more blood!"

*****

Two police cars arrived, their blue lights flashing, in less than ten minutes. When they climbed out, four uniformed officers found Mavis sitting on the library steps, shivering. She had been too frightened to go back inside to fetch her coat.

"What's your name, love?" asked a female officer, squatting down beside her.

"Mavis. I do the cleaning here."

"And you reported that you saw blood?"

"It's in there. In the library. So much blood! It's everywhere. All over the floor."

"Whose blood, Mavis?"

"I don't know. There's nobody there."

"Didn't you tell the emergency operator that you saw somebody's face?"

"I did. The Mustard man. I seen his face but not him. Only his face. I tried to wipe it away but it wouldn't be wiped. And then all that blood come pourin' out his computer! Blood, blood, blood, but nobody there!"

The female officer looked up at her fellow officer. She said nothing, but raised her eyebrows in that expression that meant "nutter."

"Are the library doors still open?" the male officer asked her. "We'll take a butchers' inside, okay? Just to see what's what."

At that moment, another car arrived and parked behind the police cars. Its door opened and out stepped Inspector Riley, wearing a thick sheepskin coat with the collar turned up. He came up the library steps and said, "What's the SP? I was just on my way to Morden nick and I heard the shout on the radio."

"This is Mavis, the cleaner," said the female officer, standing up straight. "She says that there's blood in the library but nobody's there."

"Mavis?" said Inspector Riley. "You mentioned somebody called Terrence. Did you mean Terrance Colman?"

Mavis nodded. "Terrance Colman. That's him. I seen his face in his computer but he wasn't there."

"*In* his computer?"

"Yes. Like he's inside it. Like a goldfish in a bowl. But then all that blood." She pressed her hand against her mouth and then she said, "I think I'm going to bring up me lunch."

Inspector Riley turned to the female officer. "Take care of Mavis, would you?" he told her, and then he beckoned to the other officers and said, "Come on. Let's go in and see what the bloody hell this blood is all about."

He pushed open the library doors, and they gave a high, soft groan, like a child having a nightmare. The library was brightly lit, but it was still so cold that the officers' breath smoked.

"Blimey," said one of them. "It's like a bleeding fridge in here."

Inspector Riley walked straight across to the non-fiction section. He saw the blood as soon as he entered the alcove. It had spread halfway across the floor, all around the upturned cleaning trolley, and Mavis" footprints were still clearly visible, as well as her abandoned shoe.

"Hold on," said one of the officers. "I'll go and get some overshoes."

Inspector Riley waited at the edge of the pool of blood while the officer went off to fetch some plastic forensic shoe covers. He noticed that it was still creeping across the floor, until it was almost touching the toes of his suede Hush Puppies.

He could see Terrance's blood-smeared PC on his desk, but apart from the crimson circles where Mavis had wiped it, the screen was black and blank.

Once they had all pulled on their blue plastic overshoes, Inspector Riley told two of the officers to make a thorough search of the library, including the book storeroom, the staff room, and the toilets.

"Somebody must have been killed to produce all this blood, unless it was brought in here in a bucket, and I don't think that's very likely. There's no footprints apart from the cleaner's, and no tracks to show that a body was dragged out of here, so presumably the deceased is still on the premises."

He went up to Terrance's desk, his shoe covers making a sticky-tape sound on the floor.

"It looks like the blood came from *inside* the computer. How weird is that?"

The sergeant standing beside him shook his head. "On a weirdness scale of one to ten, guv, I'd say about seventy-three."

At that moment—even though Inspector Riley hadn't touched the keyboard—the computer screen switched itself on. At first it lit up bright and blank, but then the scene of a local park appeared, with flowerbeds and thick bushes. A pretty young girl of about twelve appeared, with blonde plaits and a pink blouse and jeans. She was laughing as she ran into the bushes and disappeared, but the camera followed her. It looked as if she were playing hide-and-seek and whoever was holding the camera was trying to find her.

After two or three minutes, the camera found her crouching down behind a bush. The cameraman's hand appeared, seizing her arm. She laughed again, but then the camera was dropped onto the ground and she stopped laughing and said, "No— no— *no*!" Her voice became muffled and then her pink blouse fell onto the ground, in view of the camera, followed a few moments after by her jeans.

Inspector Riley and the sergeant watched in silence as they heard the crackling of leaves and twigs, and then grunts and cries and finally the thin, pathetic sound of sobbing. The camera was picked up and focused on the girl lying beside the bush, naked.

"*Emily Wilson, July the twelfth, Dulwich Park,*" said a clear, childlike voice of a girl.

"Jesus," said the sergeant. But the videos continued, showing one young girl after another, sometimes in parks, sometimes in alleyways, sometimes indoors. At the end of each video, the same childlike voice would announce the girl's name. There must have been well over forty in all, but at last the screen went blank.

"So *this* is where Terrance Colman hid all his images," said Inspector Riley. "Right here in his library computer. We searched his home PC and his laptop but we never found anything to incriminate him."

"But where is he?" asked the sergeant. "And what's all this blood?"

The other two officers came back. "We've searched the whole place, guv. Not a sausage. No dead bodies, either."

"Well at least we've got enough evidence to take him back to court, if we do find him. That's if this blood isn't his. I'll give forensics a bell so that they can get the DNA—"

Before he could finish, the computer screen cracked diagonally, from one side to the other, and then it shattered completely, with sparkling glass spraying across Terrance's desk.

Out of the broken screen, something greasy and pale and bloody came bulging out. There was a slopping noise, and yards and yards of this blood-streaked tubing came piling out of the computer and onto the floor. It smelled rich and fetid, like the inside of an abattoir when dead cows are disembowelled.

Inspector Riley gagged when he realized that it was human intestines.

As soon as the last of the intestines slithered out, a dark brownish liver dropped onto the desk, followed by a sagging stomach and deflated lungs, and then a heart, with all its arteries sprouting out of it. After that, there was a clattering sound, and a shower of bones came tumbling out, almost all of them broken into pieces. A pelvis, a ribcage, shoulder blades, and then a spinal column, which rattled out like a skeletal boa constrictor.

When the spine had collapsed onto the floor, a head appeared inside the screen. It was deathly pale, with gingery-grey hair clotted with blood. Its hazel eyes were open and it was staring blindly but accusingly at Inspector Riley as if it blamed him for its dismemberment.

Inspector Riley was shaken, and he could hardly find the breath to speak. As the head rolled onto the desk, though, and lay on its side, he managed to say, "Terrance Arthur Colman," as if he were arresting him.

"Is that really him?" asked the sergeant, in awe.

"That's him all right. We couldn't catch him, could we? But all those children he abused—it looks like they managed to cut the mustard."

## THE BASEMENT

Dan Allen

I'm not scared…I can do this. I just need to get myself psyched up for it.

*There's nothing down there, nothing to worry about.*

"That's right. It's all good," I say aloud, trying to build up courage. Still, I hesitate for a minute and my shoulders slump. Afraid or not, I still need to go to the basement. I clench my teeth and suck in through the corners of my mouth. I take a step and pray the old stairs won't creak and give me away. My legs wilt like an old piece of celery and I take another step. The furnace clunks and rumbles.

*What was that?*

I try to ignore the idea something lurks in the shadows. I need to be quiet, so I can listen for other sounds. My temples throb from my pulse and I count heartbeats. A loud splash breaks the silence.

"Shit!" I cover my mouth, holding back a scream. I certainly don't want to draw unwanted attention. My knees buckle and my body goes rigid. I clamp my thighs together, squeezing off my bladder. Friggin rats.

*How large is that one? Pretty big splash. Must've been huge.*

"Piss off," I whisper, fully expecting them to obey. I don't want rats leaping down on my head and I stare at the narrow space above the cistern wall. I don't move an inch, not even a blink, and I wait.

*Nice swimming pool for the rats.*

I shudder at the thought, black forms wiggling through the water with their wiry tails slithering behind. Soon as I can save up a little,

I'm going to move from this old dump, but for now I need to do some laundry and I don't have time to deal with my paranoias.

The furnace belches. Moisture inside the burning logs pops in small explosions and I flinch and step away. Even though no one sees me, I'm embarrassed and dash into the pitch-black laundry room. It's cooler in here and I feel a draft.

*Maybe that's a spirit. An evil spirit.*

I need to find the light.

*Something's in here, hiding in the dark. If it grabs me I'm going to piss myself.*

I squeeze my eyes closed, shutting off my thoughts, and swat blindly at the wall.

"Where's the damn switch?" I ask aloud, the sound of my voice emboldening me. My fingers make contact, the room fills with light, and the phantom hiding behind the door dissipates. I lean against the wall, put my hand on my chest, and wait for my heart rate to go down.

*I really need to get my shit together.*

Easier said than done. I was born afraid of the dark. No one taught me to fear the night, it came naturally. When I grew older, I did my best to rationalize away my childhood demons and I tied them up in a little box I keep buried in the back corner of my memories. No more monsters under my bed, nothing abnormal in my closet, but the basement is another story. There are ghosts in the basement.

*Momma said there are no such things as ghosts.*

"Bullshit." I speak into the empty room. I've tried to reach out to friends for help, but people can be so mean. They don't believe in ghosts, some claim they never did, not even as children. I see the way they look at me, noses in the air and faces scrunched up like I had stinky feet. They shake their heads at the sight of a grown woman afraid of the boogeyman. I'm sure some of them think I'm touched in the head. A little off my rocker. When I walk into a room people stop talking and gaze at the floor.

I get to work, loading the washing machine and folding the warm gifts coming from the dryer. The monotony keeps my imagination sedated. I finish and stroll out of the room. I have my head lowered and I'm daydreaming of back home, humming a rhyme we sang while skipping rope. I flick off the lights. The sudden darkness freezes me, and my foot stops in mid-stride.

*Shit, I forgot about this part.*

I shut my eyes and count to three. I smell the musty dampness competing with the scent of smoldering oak. The burning logs hoard the oxygen, leaving little for me.

*Ghosts aren't real. Say it again: ghosts aren't real.*

"Ghosts aren't real," I say aloud.

Denial is my best defense. I remember, when I was a kid, pulling the sheets over my head and pretending I wasn't afraid. This child-like behavior is the only tool I have. If I show no fear, the spirits will let me pass.

*It's not going to work.*

I ignore my own doubt. I believe nothing will hurt me as long as I'm not afraid and I entrust my life to this theory. I hold my head up and throw my shoulders back. I wear a cloak of invincibility and I don't hesitate between steps. My actions are brave, but my inner thoughts begin to betray me as I clear the furnace. Pin pricks nibble over the back of my shoulders like scurrying spiders. Eyes are on me, watching and taking measure.

*Rats?*

Holes start burning through my imaginary camouflage. I only have a few more steps to go when my pretend cloak, now nothing but a shredded rag, loses power, its magical protection burnt out.

*No point in being quiet now. Run.*

I try to stay focused and take the stairs two steps at a time. I've always ran up the basement stairs. Nobody wants to be the last one.

*If something grabs my ankle, I'm going to have a heart attack.*

My fear pushes me faster, but I must be cautious with every step. A stumble would be fatal. I take a gulp of air. It tastes stale, like an old ashtray. I make it to the top and burst into clean kitchen air.

I don't sleep at night.

*****

I wait for daylight before getting up. It's safer this way, less chance I will provoke the restless thoughts lingering in my head. I have an appointment with someone who can help me cope with my fears, especially those in the basement.

*This isn't a good idea. People will laugh.*

"They won't find out."

*They will make fun of me.*

"Enough! You're always making excuses." I yell my rant into my bedroom mirror, talking to myself with no one to hear me except the rats in the basement.

I'm already late and my keys aren't on the hook. I search everywhere, the front hall, kitchen, and my bedroom. I even check the floor by the toilet because they just might be there.

*The laundry room.*

Right. I set them on the dryer while I did the jean load.

*No big deal, I'll just run down real quick and get them.*

By the time I get to the kitchen, old fears are scratching at my confidence. I put one foot on the top step and slowly transfer my weight.

"Please no creaks." I speak in a whisper. I move the other foot and listen for any stirrings below.

*Eww, what's that smell? Wet rat?*

I sit on the third step. From here I can peek down into the basement and study the shadows. I look for movement and listen for sounds that don't belong.

Dust specks dance in a small beam of sunlight shining through the only window. I watch them spinning and swirling in a fantasy ballet and I forget about ghosts. Hypnotized by the normally invisible fairies, I creep down the stairs for a closer look. I put my hand into the warm beam and the tiny dancers move and twist out of the way. A cloud passes in front of the sun and the magic vanishes. A chill brushes over my skin and my body tightens.

*I am so screwed.*

My stomach flips and I taste bitter acid. I forgot to pay attention. Something is moving behind me, I'm sure of it, but I'm not turning around. I don't want to see.

*Stupid, stupid, I'm so stupid.*

Fear tickles the hairs on the back of my neck. A heaviness closes in behind me, pulling on those childhood bedsheets and threatening to make me look. Even the air has weight, pressing on my shoulders, trying to flatten me to the floor. I look for an escape and focus on the door to the laundry room.

*Get the keys.*

I silently count to three and prepare to bolt.

I feel a presence, something evil. It's the ghost I've always feared and it's right behind me. I run, hoping my sudden movement catches it off guard. I see black things scattering and they screech, or maybe it's me screaming,

Using my brief advantage, I make it into the room and pull the door closed. I slip and fall headfirst, and I instinctively put out my hands to break my fall. Too late. I hear a crunch and then feel the pain. Dizzy, I close my eyes and the room still spins.

My cheek is pressed to the floor and I taste my tears, thick, salty and warm. They are pooling on the floor under my ear.

*That's odd, a puddle of tears.*

My chest heaves and I breathe short bursts through my nose. I try to move a hand, only to push away a dirty sock, to no avail. I lie still, listening and waiting, my heart beating loudly enough to give my location away. A very distinct sniffing sound breaks the silence.

*It smells me.*

The laundry room door scratches over the cement. I keep my eyes squeezed shut and listen to heavy footsteps. The floor vibrates against my face and the noise morphs into a heartbeat.

*I hear my pulse pounding in my head.*

I fear something is hovering right above me and I want to turn to see but I can't. Small feet scurry over my legs and I hear more sniffing. I force one eye to open and I see whiskers and large yellow buck teeth. I shudder, and the willies make my sides twitch.

I'm fading and I feel like I am floating, allowing me to see myself on the floor. My hair is red, and I wonder were all the blood came from.

The air turns frosty and I can see my breath. At last the ghost presents itself.

*****

I wander in a thick fog, unable to piece together a clear thought. I have no memory, no purpose, and no needs. I hear a familiar sound breaking through the mist; a door scratching over cement and footsteps going upstairs. Sparks fly, illuminating my past. A blur of sights, sounds, and memories whip by me at light speed. I experience a flash of clarity like remembering the lyrics to a tune dangling just beyond your mind's grasp. The confusion haunting me evaporates and I am aware.

I can hear someone stomping around and yelling at the TV. A bottle smacks the floor and rumbles over the hardwood. I want to go see who it is, but I'm unable to leave the basement. When I approach the stairs, my essence dissipates like the dust fairies without sunlight.

I hang my head and shuffle around in circles. I grasp at ideas, but they shatter before I can think them through. Attempting to focus is loud and painful and I surrender to the quiet. I am trapped in this basement.

I am alone, yet I'm tormented by the sounds of humanity, bringing back flashes of emotions, pleasures and desires. People are near but why do they ignore me? This is my house. Why have I been abandoned? A thousand times I search for a reason and then, with a flicker of memory, I recall the ridicule.

"Don't be so silly."

"There's nothing to be afraid of."

"Stop acting so crazy."

The scoffing words come back to me, bouncing off the walls and ricocheting through the room, gaining speed until they collide and mix together. It's clear now, they all did it. They goaded and bullied me into putting myself in danger. They said nothing evil lurks in the basement, but they lied.

"I'm not afraid!" I shout aloud, but no sound penetrates the air beyond my lips. I'm not afraid of the basement and I'm not afraid of ghosts.

The stranger in my home comes down to the cellar but he doesn't acknowledge me.

"Hey you, bastard!" I jump in front of him and wave my arms in the air. He doesn't answer me. I try banging on the furnace, my anger growing into a rage. I pound on the metal and I'm rewarded with a single thud.

He looks up. He heard it! He damn well heard it! I move to the pile of firewood and topple it over and watch, unsatisfied, as he calmly re-stacks the logs. I start spinning and twisting myself into a boiling funnel cloud. I cause enough breeze to move the hair on his forehead. I've mastered the trick of energy transfer and I start throwing sticks of firewood by simply willing them to move. The stranger looks right at my face and I think he sees me, but I realize he only sees the projectiles coming his way. It's his turn to run for the stairs.

I don't hear his voice anymore. I can't feel his presence and the furnace remains cold.

"Where'd you go?" I ask, my words lost in the empty house. I need some revenge and I take my frustration out on the leftover firewood, hurling sticks around and smashing anything I can.

Unsatisfied, I return to the location of my demise, and I find solace burying myself under phantom sheets and towels. I rest in the only grave I know.

Time has no relevance. I don't consider it and I have no idea if I have waited days or years, but I do hear activity in the house. I can make out voices, laughter, and the sound of little footsteps. I am so hungry, absolutely starving for companionship. I want someone to talk to, some distraction from this monotony. I hear a little girl. She sounds delightful and I hope she'll come down to the basement.

My new housemates have settled in and, once again, there's fire in the furnace and stacks of clothes in the laundry. I hide in my favorite shadows and observe, waiting for an opportune moment.

After a period of time it comes, starting with a familiar creak from the top step. A child giggles and soft footsteps descend the stairs. She stops by the furnace, her head tilted to the side and her eyes squinted.

I can smell her skin. It's new and fresh, like a just-opened bag of jellybeans. I must have her, I really must. I emerge from the shadows and I'm surprised to see the child startle. Her eyes grow large and her little mouth hangs open, like she was frozen in the middle of a song.

She can see me and there is an awkward pause. Her eyes shift, taking in the room. Before I can grab her, she turns on her heels and bolts for the stairs.

"Mommy! Mommy! Mommy!"

I lunge for her, my arms unnaturally long, growing to match her speed. Her screams split my head, causing my mouth to stretch open like a snake swallowing a cow. The little urchin is faster and beats me to the steps. My pursuit ends in bitter stardust at the boundary of my existence. I see her shadow on the stairwell wall and I hear her.

"Mommy, there's a ghost in the basement."

"Don't be so silly, Pumpkin. There's no such things as ghosts."

## THE EXPECTANT ONE

Quinn Parker

People who commit suicide assume their pain will end. It doesn't.
Best-case scenario: That pain gets passed on to the people you love.
Worst-case scenario: They end up like my brother.

*****

Isaac stands at the end of the hall, but I don't have to open my bedroom door to look. I know he's there, waiting. Every passing day gets a little worse.

Right after his funeral, things were calm. As time went on, we heard bangs and odd groans, and doors would slam if we left them open, especially those that opened to outside.

A week later, I saw him from the corner of my eye. Mom and Dad saw him, too, but in little fleeting glimpses. Pictures began falling off the walls, electronics malfunctioning, footsteps stomping their way through rooms adjacent to us. All the warning signs of a coming storm, but I rationalized this: as someone who's studied the paranormal, and a bit of a self-taught expert in death and dying, I know most places aren't haunted. A few people grieving hard enough in one location could 'project' that person back into reality. We just needed to cope and accept.

Mom believed, oh, god, how she believed, and wept over the fact that her "darling boy" couldn't move on. Dad growled for her to shut up because ghosts aren't real. I knew he just didn't want to face that he'd failed Isaac, too.

Now, I hear the rasp of his uniform scraping over itself as he waits. I don't know what he wants, but I sit in my bed, shaking, unwilling and unable to open the door. Even approaching it makes me shake so bad my legs stop holding me up, so I stay in bed, covers drawn to my neck, because I want to watch the door, just in case.

I try to create a plan for what to do if "in case" happens. I don't get a chance to finish. Down the hall, a creak signals the master bedroom door opening. Soft footsteps scuff their way to the bathroom. Dad would've trudged, or thumped, or stomped. Not intentionally to wake anyone, just because he walked the way he lived: loud, blunt, and generally not concerned with how his actions affected others.

The toilet flushes. Water runs from the sink. Mom steps out into the hall and gasps.

"Isaac?" I can hear her whisper, soft and probing. "Isaac, it's really you, isn't it?"

She's silent for a minute, then I hear, "Wait! Please don't go, Isaac!"

Faint, greenish ectoplasmic mist creeps under my door, thin enough to be a trick of the light. It doesn't trick me, though. This isn't grief any more, not just a projection. This means Isaac really hasn't left our plane.

Mom's slipper-padded steps approach the nearer end of the hall. She takes only a few, putting her just shy of my door, when, going against all I knew of ghosts, Isaac talks.

"There is nothing after this." Five words, and I don't know which chills me more: their meaning, or their delivery.

He speaks in a hoarse whisper that I know could never come from a real human—a whisper that seems to come from punctured lungs, squeezing through ribs and out through flapping, decomposing skin. In each word, I see his body, rotting in the ground, trapped in a box until the worms finally got to him. His voice shudders with anger that he's been separated from life, yet denied a real death.

"Oh, my boy…" Mom starts to speak, but stops. Not like she doesn't know what to say, but like something draws her attention and causes her to stop speaking.

I figure out what when a roar explodes through our house. The artillery shell of his ethereal rage comes with the shattering of glass through the hallway. My door blows inward, splintering and splitting. Pulling the sheet fully over me, I manage not to get hurt, only because the door broke into so many pieces that none are large enough to do real damage.

Dad fumbles in the master bedroom, and by the sounds of it, falls out of bed. Mom's cries accompany this a moment later, more sadness than fear. No more time to hide. We have to get moving. We have to get out of the house that Isaac died in.

"What the holy hell is going on out here?" Dad's booming voice isn't louder than the explosion, yet carries enough for Mom to focus back in on him. Heavy wood scrapes against the floor as he kicks something out of the way and walks into the hallway.

My shoes sit beside the bed. I grab them, because you never know what situation you might get into. A home intruder, a fire, a violent poltergeist; whatever the case, escape goes smoother with shoes on.

Poltergeist isn't the right word, really—those are generally caused by teenagers and traumatized children, specifically girls, who manifest repressed emotion as psychic energy, and I'm a little too old to cause one—but it would have to do until I could get to a library, or Earth Wind Spirit, or some other psychic emporium, to check out more books. If I learn what Isaac's become, I can avoid beings like him better in the future.

Tipping my sneakers to shake the splinters out, I run my hands through one more time, then slip them on, ignoring Dad as he tries to calm Mom in the hall. I head straight for my window. It sits above the back-porch balcony, and I can easily hang down to step on the porch railing, or just jump off, tucking into a roll as I hit the ground. I can and have done both to practice getting out, except I can't do this tonight, as my window doesn't open. I grip the sill tight, yanking hard. I stop when I realize the window had been open when I went to sleep.

Isaac glowers in the reflection, standing just behind me. "Running away? Again?"

With a shriek, I whirl around, but he's already gone. My cry attracts my parents, and there's a slight scuffle as Mom stumbles and falls into the debris. Dad appears at my doorway, not bothering to help her up. His eyes focus on the remnants of my door, which I can only assume is worse than his, because shock crosses his face. He flicks on the light, and the ceiling fan glows to life, revealing huge cracks in the walls.

Isaac had been closer to my room. The epicenter of his anger might've killed me if not for these now-broken walls standing guard over me.

"What are you screaming about in here?" Dad asks, a perturbed undercurrent running in the normally still waters of his voice. That's how I know how bad the hall looks before I even set foot out there. Dad never gets nervous, but he sounds scared.

"The window won't open. And Isaac, he was behind me. Talked to me. Stood right there." I point at the center of the room, my arm skin paler than usual. I wonder if my face looks like—well—a ghost.

Dad nods, turning on his heel and walking back out. "Get up, Lynn. We gotta go."

Credit where credit is due: Dad might not view many things as dangerous, and he might not value safety like I do, but when the situation is bad enough to make him take action, he doesn't hesitate. I follow him and Mom down the stairs toward the front door. There's talk of them getting footwear. Dad makes it clear that as long as they have keys, shoes aren't important.

Get in the car, get out of here. That's the only goal.

Problem is, it's an obvious goal. Dad grabs his keys out of the bowl by the front entrance, but the door slams shut again. He tries yanking it with no result, then it flies open, striking him in the head. Cartilage crunches as he stumbles back, blood running from a gash that runs from his receding hairline to his chin, with a small gap where the protrusion of his nose kept his lips from being split open.

Dad hits the ground hard. Mom screams. Isaac appears over him. Though I can see through him, his back is to me, obscuring what I'm sure is a vicious snarl. "Get up, boy. Real men help themselves."

Then he's gone again, leaving Dad scrambling backward, wide eyes trying to see someone who is no longer here. The front door locks, then the deadbolt engages, and Dad doesn't dare reach for it again.

"We can't get out! We need to get somewhere safe." Mom's panicked gasps aren't helpful. She's always been Captain Obvious. Normally, such a statement would annoy me, but this isn't the time to be annoyed.

I say, "Entities are strongest in the dark! We only need to last until the sun comes up."

They might not listen, but at least I could give them some direction. The closest my parents ever came to dealing with a spirit was praying to the Father, Son, and Holy Ghost once every Sunday.

Mom nods to me and runs for the light switches, but as soon as she flips them, the hallway lights burst in a shower of glass and sparks. She wails, hitting more switches, causing more small explosions.

Isaac doesn't like this attempt to restrain him. In the living room, the glass of our still-hanging pictures shatter, and books fly from the shelves like frightened birds. The TV turns on, flipping rapidly from channel to channel, sound distorted by static electricity. Crashes and noises from upstairs make it clear that our lights, lamps, and ceiling fans are being thrown around the room, just in case we wanted to go back up.

"The basement!" Mom yells. "There are lanterns, and flashlights!"

I try to stop her, but she races to the basement door at the back of the house. Dad, stumbling and holding his head, gets close to her, reaching out to hold her back. He's not close enough, and Isaac appears behind her. With one hard, handless shove, my brother's ghost sends her flying down the stairs. Bones snap as she lands.

The apparition fades, and Dad goes down after her. Behind me, the back door opens.

"Well? Gonna run away? Leave 'em to die like the coward you are?" Isaac's voice is cold, coming from over my shoulder, filling my ears with ice water. For a moment, I'm as paralyzed by fear as I am by indecision. I want to leave. I know I should leave. Leaving is the safe choice, and I've always made safe choices, choices that protect me above everyone else.

But when Isaac returned from Iraq, he scared me. I made the choice to stay out of the house, avoiding his mood swings. I chose not to talk to him about his nightmares. His depression. I protected myself, and thought it'd be okay, until my parents found his body.

They found him in the basement.

I wouldn't make the same mistake twice.

Steeling my nerves, I walk slowly into the darkest part of our house, trying the basement light as I go. The bulb turns on and stays on. The door shuts behind me.

At the bottom of the steps, Dad looks up at me, tears mixing with blood on his split face. Mom's legs are definitely broken. No limb is supposed to bend that way. She cries quietly into Dad's chest, barely noticing as I reach the bottom.

"What's wrong?" Isaac growls, unseen, his voice echoing from every shadowy corner of the room. "Don't you know everything works out for the best? Try staying positive."

Our basement has no windows. It's an older style with cement walls. No leaks, no drains, no way in, and no way out, other than the door we'd come through. Shelves full of gardening tools and hardware gleam in the swaying light cast by the single bulb hanging over a round wooden table in the center of the room.

Dad used to have poker night down here. He hasn't had poker night in a few months. Tonight, there are three chairs, set perfectly at the same distance from each other.

The light makes all the metal in here shine, except for Isaac's gun. It sits dead center on the table, dark and heavy, as if drinking in the light rather than reflecting it. The darkest thing in what would've been the darkest room, if Isaac had blown out this light, too.

There'd be no moonlight or sunlight to aid us down here. In a room like this, with no exposure to the outside world, time stopped.

"Sit." The one word, half-garbled by his ethereal state, is still a clear enough command. Dad and I begrudgingly hoist Mom into one of the chairs, then take our own seats. I can't stop shaking, heart racing as I try to figure a way out of a room more secure than most modern bomb shelters.

Rooms like this, back in the older days, were designed as natural coolers. Pitch black, cold, and dry. A place you could store food for the long winter without fear of it going bad.

A feeling passes through me. It's the shudder of intuition I don't want to listen to, but down here, what choice do I have?

Reaching forward, I pick up the weapon, looking it over. Mom keeps whimpering with pain; Dad doesn't speak, just watches as I find the button to eject the cartridge. I've seen enough self-defense videos on YouTube to know how to take apart a weapon, or at least remove the bullets.

The only bullet in the gun sits in the chamber, ready for a target.

I put it back in the center. "There's just one bullet."

Mom and Dad exchange a look. They'd found Isaac with an empty gun. He'd bought the damn thing at Walmart, and the clerk didn't think it strange that he only needed a single round. That single round entered his mouth, and stopped in the ceiling.

We all look at each other, slow and scared. Light glints off the sweat on Mom's brow, and off the blood on Dad's skull. I imagine I'm shining too, in some way. My pupils, blown-out from adrenaline, no doubt show Mom in one eye, Dad in the other.

"One of you must shoot yourself, or I'll kill all of you." Isaac's voice howls through a graveyard as vast as the whole earth.

The light begins to flicker.

## ALL THAT SHE LEAVES BEHIND

S.J.Budd

There was no need to tell anyone from the University that I was going to be gone for a few days. None of them knew my name, and they still wouldn't when I got back.

Soon after my arrival in my dad's hometown, I remembered many things—like pigeons coming home to roost. The streets seemed alien, yet familiar. I had been here just once when I was six, but I still remembered.

Sitting in the back of the taxi, I knew exactly where I was going. And suddenly there it was: the house, exactly as my grandmother had left it…creepy and haunted-looking, except for the cars parked in front.

Once I entered the old place, I realized that it was creepy inside as well.

In the hallway, the large portrait set in a gold-painted frame depicting a man dressed in a hunting outfit still loomed, still staring at me with a shotgun hung over his right shoulder. It looked comical in a small, old house. It must have hung once in a grand house. Gran had said it was worth quite a bit. She had wanted us to know that, just in case. The man in the painting could be a relative; I just didn't know.

The carpet under my feet was still the one of yellow and blue flowers swirling in amongst the light brown. In most places it was threadbare underneath, and white flooring poked through. The pattern led up the staircase. In places, it frayed and hung loose. Was that why she had fallen?

I stopped still, looking outside the window to check nothing untoward had happened since I'd stepped over the stone steps. Why? Because the front room was completely untouched by time like it was waiting for me to return.

I heard a sudden gasp of shock as I walked in but it wasn't me making a noise.

A relative whose name I didn't quite remember was suddenly in front of me. He spoke in quiet words; I had to strain to hear. "We've been waiting for you."

"Let me rest a minute before I talk to the family," I told him, and found a spot on the sofa. I sat with my back straight and knees trembling. My hands fought to hold me together; they clenched and released, clenched and released. If only Gran could have stayed here amongst her things!

My father walked in. I stood up and let him hug me.

"So glad you could come to the funeral," he said. "We're dividing up some possessions, so you're right on time."

He led me into the living room.

Dad pointed out the antique clock perched high in the centre of the room, carved from dark wood with brass hands and cream face. It was very old and made no sound. Either it was broken or someone had stopped the hands from turning. No one objected to my dad having it, since it had been in the family too long to throw away. I've never liked the tick tock of clocks, that constant sound of time escaping, never being yours to own.

The living room had always been small but it was packed full of mourners and the corners were hard to find behind Gran's things. It was deep and endless and cluttered, and there was always something new for the eyes to find.

My memories reached out like floating tendrils to examine what I had found. They were the delicate figurines on the windowsill she used to collect. They looked so frail and delicate I was surprised there were still there and not chipped.

There had always been a budgie in a high-up cage, the one I remembered had been blue and speckled and always sang. There were still the same paintings, of dogs playing snooker, a toucan drinking Guinness. Yes, she had always loved animals. I remembered that now, bringing her ever so slightly closer to me.

Everyone waiting here with me for the hearse to arrive looked the same, just older. Everyone was here except for her, the person we had really come here to see.

The whole scene of us gathered in uneasy silence with no one to play host reminded me of dramas where the situation turns from dead to a hive of frantic activity.

Always in the aftermath of a murder, there are many custodians of the peace attending, the whole area cordoned off with tape and flashing lights, cameras to permanently preserve what happened and a court to consider their verdict. It comforts us to know people care but it's of no use to the dead. This doesn't protect them, we only serve those who are still here giving ourselves a purpose to fight off guilt. This was how I felt now.

Why hadn't Gran ever visited me? Why hadn't I visited her? I couldn't even remember if she had sent me cards on my birthdays. I think I would have remembered; I would have kept those with the others. Had there been a moment of swift decision of choosing to let me go, or had we been prey to a slow idling drift?

Looking down into my milky tea, I struggled to recall what she looked like. I couldn't remember the color of her eyes. Blue? Mine were threatening to cry and I swallowed it all down.

I remembered her as a warm and tiny person, even as a child I was almost as tall as her. It was strange to feel this broken over someone whom I'd only met a few times. Maybe we'd had a deeper connection I was too young to realize?

The hearse finally arrived, and the attendants took the body of my grandmother.

After watching the coffin disappear behind a red curtain inside the hearse, a few of us went to the pub and drank a few pints. They tasted bitter and were hard to swallow, my throat burning up from all the things I wasn't saying.

We came back to the empty house with our chip-shop dinners after sundown. As we approached the house, the glinting windows in the darkness looked like droopy, sorrowful eyes watching us return. I shuddered as I stood directly in front of them.

Inside we watched TV, except no one really watched it; we just stared at it sealed off in our own thoughts, heavy with ache and longing. There were so many things I had wanted to ask of her, but I knew this was not the time.

I really wanted answers—why had this separation occurred? Was it anyone's fault? Had Gran ever thought of me in the years in which she hadn't seen me? Had she ever thought about visiting when I was young? Had she completely forgotten I was her only grandchild?

Paternal grandmothers pass down thirty-one percent of their genes to their granddaughters. Was I a third of her? Since she had passed, I felt like a wave had washed over me, not washing me clean but taking something of me with it. There was a gap in my mind, a lost section. This void could never be fleshed out; it was a gap in a bookshelf, or a broken and empty chair.

*****

That night I slept in the back room, cold even with extra blankets, but the portable heater scared me, it was so old. I didn't use it and shivered instead. I thought of the University, I'd been there two months and was failing miserably. No one knew me. I hid either in my room or in the library. No one knocked on my door anymore. I had been too shy to open the only barrier that kept me safe.

As I lay awake, I caught her smile forming in my mind, warm and loving and I knew that was exactly how she had looked. I just knew. Eighty years she had lived in these walls, dreaming of what was to come until there was nothing.

She died here at the foot of the stairs. She had been alive for such a long time and yet I saw her so little. Though there was something of her still here, as long as she was remembered.

Once when we had stayed here as a family, just before mum had left, I had been standing at the top of the stairs with a toy hung loose in my grip. I had been throwing it down the stairs and listening to the rattles it made as it rolled and chipped down.

Dad had had enough. I didn't know why it displeased him so. All things broke eventually. He had warned me that if I did it again, he'd come up there and give me a smack. So I did it to see if he would, and he did. He was true to his word.

Afterwards I felt the hot pain rise to my skin. Gran appeared at the foot of the stairs with a look of shame and regret. She came up without making a noise and sat right down with her arm around me. She told me that it wasn't right what he did.

"It's not right," she kept saying as she rubbed my shoulders. My life could have been so much different if she had stayed in it.

I closed my eyes letting my mind run and run, pulling out memory after memory, hoping it was right. Soon I had a small collection; the way she scratched her forearms when she was thinking of something to say, the way her shoulders slouched slightly, her delicate springy way of walking, the stray cat she had taken in that refused to venture further from the kitchen…until I felt like I had her there in my mind, still impossibly far away but there was a buoy to cling to as I lay in darkness.

I didn't want her to be forgotten again. I wanted to truly connect with her, know what she knew, feel what she felt, and laugh at what she laughed at. Did she love the feel of sunlight on her face, the sound of rain coming down on the roof?

I'll never know now if she was like me, or I was like her. What, if anything, had I inherited from her? She had worn green to my parent's wedding, my favorite color, the only one that suited my skin. Was it hers also?

Did she ever think of me in the years in which I never saw her? Or was I just another forgotten thing, buried deep in the front room with the others? Had she resented me for never coming up? Had she gotten too old to visit me? Why hadn't I thought of popping up here?

What had made her smile and chuckle her chin up? Had she been a reader, what were her favorites—had we read the same things? Did she like a tipple? All these things I'll never know, all those memories of hers lost forever, all our shared moments we'll never get to have. Because you can never go back. Never.

*****

I must have fallen asleep but awoke again at the array of unfamiliar silence around me. At Uni, it was always so noisy, always loud groups of people either coming home or going out. But here it was so quiet, I felt so alone except for the ticking of the clock down in the front room.

Tick tock.

The clock scared me. It was a symbol of time ticking away until my own death.

I gathered myself into a small ball and heard only my soft breaths of terror and feeling the pulses of pain reaching into every part of me. Slowly I stretched out, unfurling my limbs back into place as best I could. I didn't feel quite right. When I was finally able to bring myself up into an upright position I noticed there was a wan source of light coming from the front room.

The bedroom door was ajar; just behind it I stood and waited, listening. I knew that everyone else was sleeping on the second floor. I also knew that the living room down the hall wasn't empty.

I felt a presence.

I wanted to go into the living room and see for myself. It was just like Christmas, making that choice to believe in the magic or become dead-headed like the adults.

The TV was on mute, just a mess of bright pictures. The chair in front of it was no longer empty. Poking out from the top was old, dyed-brown hair. I pushed open the door, but my movement felt like wading through water with heavy boots. I was afraid yet calm, and my body fought against this most unnatural action but I won.

My grandmother was here. I didn't know why I felt so calm; I should have been terrified to see something that wasn't possible. I felt the hair rise on my arms, but I went forward. I wanted to see her one more time.

She sat in her chair, her feet tucked under her, looking out beyond the four walls and deep into something I couldn't see. Her fingers rested under her chin. I knew she was thinking. Her pen placed on the crossword, either she'd given up or become stuck or it could be something else. I didn't know if she had noticed me. I saw now she looked like dad and I felt a sadness that I didn't much look like her. I had my mother's eyes.

Maybe she was looking at the photos above the heater. I didn't know. She wouldn't turn to face me and I was scared to touch her in case she caved in to dust and rot. Her heart no longer beat, there was no life inside. She appeared ethereal and fragile, but paradoxically I knew she was strong.

I cleared my throat, afraid I wouldn't be able to speak, but I did. "Gran?"

I knew she could hear me but she wouldn't look. I sensed from her a sadness entwined around layers of anger that had hardened to rock. She was as angry with others as she was with herself.

Suddenly the clock stopped ticking. I felt my breath being sucked back into my chest. Time had stopped, the TV had frozen. Gran sat so close but fading fast.

I hadn't been this near her for so long and I was scared to let her go again. I didn't know where she was heading. I just wanted her to stay here, with me. I wanted to bring her back, cherish her, atone for my absence and make her feel warm and loved again. I wanted to take her from this cold room to back home. I lingered by her side, unsure of how I could reach her. I bent over slightly so I could tap her lightly on the shoulder of her pale blue cardigan.

After a moment, she stopped fading. She held out a hand to me and I didn't know if I should take it. What would happen if you touch a ghost?

Finally I took her hand. At first, it felt cold but then warmed when it entered my grip, mixing with my skin. She looked right at me and there was a smile forming on her lips. She knew I had come back. I couldn't find the words to speak but I wanted her to know I'd been thinking of her.

I felt her take hold of my life and use it to show me hers. I let her flow into me, all of her old memories, walking on the moors picking yellow flowers to take home for ma, watching her pa come home from work until he didn't and the sirens that came, haunting her town at night when the bombs came down until finding the man that made all those hurts fade out.

Then in her memories, she stopped visiting me. She'd had grown old, it was a long trip across country to come visit. She wasn't sure if she was welcome after the divorce. Father kept himself very busy after that; he rarely saw me and when he did, he wanted to do exciting things like taking me to theme parks and on holidays abroad. He didn't want to bring me up here to visit her in case I found that dull and asked for Mum.

She spent years looking at the photo of me she kept close, the photo in which I stayed the same when all the while she knew I was getting older. Perhaps she recounted the many moments she had missed, and would continue to miss. Gran hadn't blamed me; I was young and pre-occupied with divorce and uprooting.

But she had always thought I would come looking for her eventually when I remembered the moments of us being together. She'd always thought that I'd walk down her garden path with a little suitcase in tow. I was her only granddaughter. Hers.

My footsteps never came. Her hand would often linger on the receiver; she'd dial a few numbers and then hang up. It had been too long, she thought.

Eventually it was a struggle for her to get up, and she really wanted some help with making tea, getting the shopping in, having someone read to her when her eyes felt tired. Her hair turned white and the world forgot her. Life goes on for those who can. Here in this room she stayed, afraid of the world changing around her. Of the noise outside. Completely forgotten.

Then her hand gripped me tighter, her anger towards the world at large now turned to me. She never spoke but I felt her thoughts.

*I waited for someone to come. I needed help, but I was left to die. You never came and yet here you are now, finally arriving on the day the hearse took my corpse away.*

She let go and her hand flicked me away in dismissal. The clock came back to life. It rang louder and louder with each strike. It was the song of her waiting, of hoping I would develop a heart and come back. The ticks and tocks had waited a long time and now they were angry and there was nothing I could do to quell her hurt.

I had always thought I was a good person but now I knew I wasn't. I hadn't even known her first name until the funeral. I was just like everyone else, monsters in human form.

Gran disappeared, but the room was angry and wanted me gone. I was too late. I tore away back upstairs where I hid under a mess of blankets. Peeling back the curtain, I saw light around the edges of the sky.

I knew my grandmother would keep coming back. She wanted to stay in the house where she had lived for eighty years. This house and her suffering…it was all she knew. She wanted to stay with her memories.

But soon it would be morning, and I would be gone from this haunted house.

*****

Back at the University, it is always cold, ever since I'd held her hand. I sit in my room and I never come out. Dad has gone back to work and Mother has remarried. I don't live with either of them. I wonder if they ever think of me, whether one of them will invite me to stay for Christmas but I imagine not. I'll be stuck here alone. Dad will be drinking and Mum will be going abroad to escape the winter sun.

I wrap myself in blankets, hating how tired and hungry I always feel now. I know everyone has forgotten me. My knees and hips ache tirelessly and no one has come so far to bring me food.

I daren't go outside; it's too noisy and boisterous and I don't belong to that world. So I can't go outside.

I just want familiarity; to feel loved in my world.

I'll just hide in my room until someone comes. I hope someone does come.

## SCARLET RIBBONS

Kitty Kane

I hear it again in my mother's house. The tune is old; it brings memories—painful, hurtful memories. I can never quite find where it's coming from. However close to it I think I am getting, it still seems to be the same distance away.

She's lonely, and has been that way for many years. I've shared that pain with her, and it's been worse to bear than my own. The pain I feel from her loneliness is so strong, it's physical.

I feel the pain she suffered, the pain she continues to suffer, but I'm here. I'm here and she isn't, but she's waiting, just across the void; she waits and waits, but I'm not ready. I love her, oh how I love her, but I'm not ready. She should understand that, but she doesn't. She is tired of waiting and I'm sure she now seeks to take from me that which keeps me here.

I have responsibilities here. I have love here. I'm scared of her; I don't like admitting it but I'm terrified. Now I hear the melody, the tune that speaks of the wishes of a child.

Her name was Ruby and she was not only my sister, but my best friend. Twins are special, you know. The bond between twins has many times been investigated, never scientifically understood, but I understand.

*****

The accident had been a pile-up. Dad's car had been the fifth car to smash into the one in front. That impact had shaken Ruby loose from the front seatbelt where she sat, but there was another impact from behind. This one had thrown Ruby through the car windscreen, and over the bridge that the motorway was on, and down into the frigid river below. Her body has never been found, but nobody could have survived such a fall.

They searched for days, but they never found Ruby. I know she is dead because her mind is no longer part of mine, but I can't believe that she is gone completely. I still felt her presence in a different sort of way, every time I hear the music.

What they found in the car was the gift Ruby had bought for me on that shopping trip with my father. Heaven knows how she knew I wanted it, but when the policeman handed it to me, there was my Ruby doll.

The doll came with me through my entire childhood and through college, still dressed in her pretty little satin dress, looking so very much like my Ruby, but there was one difference. The doll sported two scarlet ribbons in her hair.

I had bought the ribbons for Ruby, but never had the chance to give them to her. Instead, I put them on the doll.

*****

I like to think that my sister wouldn't harm me, but the lonesome years have made her angry, angrier than I ever knew her to be in life. I'm not certain it's me she wants, as I sit here, puzzling through this turmoil. I think maybe it's my babies she wants. I have twins of my own now, you see, one girl, one boy, and they are my world.

She's still here; she's always been here, waiting. I need to placate her, before she takes her revenge because she is gone and I have a life.

This evening, my mother is my babysitter. I go to my mother's house to pick up my children, Joey and Scarlett. The rooms are not the same anymore, but the house always makes me hear the sounds of Ruby playing a record, happy in life, unlike the terrible sadness she feels in death.

Except for Ruby's ghost, the house is empty. I can't find them. I call to my mother, but she is nowhere to be found, my children gone with her. Panic swells inside me. The night is cold, and snow has begun to fall. The roads were treacherous on the way here. If Mom had taken them out, where are they?

It's late and my panic is becoming blind now. I run upstairs, calling their names.

I don't want to, but I know I'm going to have to look in all the rooms. I try to avoid going in the upstairs rooms. The memories are tough on me. After Ruby died, I never ventured into her room, and my mom had it redecorated after the search for her body was called off indefinitely.

I go into Ruby's room. Gone are all the red and frills from her room, and it is done now in neutral colors; your typical guest bedroom, nothing special, but certainly nothing Ruby would have liked. I guess my mother wanted it to be as different as possible, to lessen the blow of going in and seeing her things.

My mother cleared everything out of the room except one item, the doll that is a perfect copy of Ruby. After college I gave the doll back to my mother, and here it is.

I shake my head. I grab the doll and suddenly I'm not in the room anymore, I'm in Dad's car, and I'm not me, I'm Ruby. There is fog all around. It's snowing and the car feels like its slipping. I'm strapped in but I wriggle out from the harness because I'm scared.

Dad tells me to sit still, but that moment he turns his head and we hit something in front…hard. I'm not in my seat anymore; I'm flying through the air. We are on the bridge, as my body propels forward towards the railing of the bridge and I sail straight over the top. I'm falling!

Down, down, down I go. I'm screaming my own name, Jamie! Jamie! I'm me but I'm her, I'm Ruby and Jamie at once. I'm afraid; I'm so very afraid.

I hit the water hard and I go under. I tumble over and over under the frigid river. Ice hits me and I lose which way is up. It's dark but somehow I can see. I can see it all. Suddenly I'm not Ruby and me anymore. I am me again, only me, and I spot her. She's dressed just as she was on that final day.

Somebody is with her, down here under the ice cold water, but I can't see who as I'm thrown up to the surface. I gasp for air and I hear a sound I know.

Something grabs my ankle, pulling me under.

And I wake up. I'm not in the river and I never have been. I'm in Ruby's room, holding her doll.

I know where my children are. My mother has taken them for a ride in her car, and now they are at the bridge. Ruby's bridge. I know where Ruby is. After all these years, I know where her body is. And I know my children are in danger.

I rush to my car. Just like so long ago, tonight is foggy with snow.

When I reach the bridge, I see my mother's car halfway down the river's banks. My mother is crying; she is holding Scarlett's hand, but where is Joey? I throw the car door open and race to the river.

I jump into the frigid water, the impact stealing my breath from the shocking cold. The cold is so intense that it is painful.

I dive to the crevice where my sister's ghost haunts. I see Ruby there and her flesh is bloated and gray. There is no light in her eyes, but it's what she is grasping that makes me swoon.

I'm swimming through the frigid river, and I realize I'm still clutching the doll. I brought it with me, still held in my hands from when I originally picked it up in Ruby's bedroom.

I see my sister again. She's just a skeleton now and she is wedged under a ridge in the water. My son is here! My son is not breathing. I must get to him. I force my arms and legs to move and I try to wrench him from the skeletal hand of my long-dead sister.

I shove the doll at her. She lets Joey go and clutches the doll. I pull my son to me but Ruby throws back her head and howls. Even under water I hear it; it chills me more than the water has done the whole time. Desperate for air, I propel my son and me up to the surface.

Would-be rescuers line the bank. A man grabs Joey from my grip but I can't keep myself up. I see once more my mother and my daughter up on the bridge.

With horror I see my daughter's face change. Her eyes squint and with a determination I've only ever seen in one child before. Scarlett's face merges with my sister's face. My daughter is clutching hair ribbons; the ribbons that I had bought for Ruby all those years ago and never had the chance to give her.

I watch in horror as my second twin throws herself into the dark, roiling, freezing water.

I'm losing my fight for breath; I can hear the tune of the record player again. A man on the record sings about seeing his child in prayer, praying for scarlet ribbons; scarlet ribbons for her hair.

Suddenly I realize what Ruby wants: she never got her gift, the ribbons I bought for her all those years ago that were supposed to adorn the hair of the doll that is now under the water with my sister.

I see Scarlett swimming towards Ruby. I must reach my child before my sister does.

I dive under and it's dark again. I dive deeper, aiming for the underwater ledge where I'd last seen my dead sister.

I can see again! She's there and she's back to looking normal as she grabs a hold of my child, my sweet girl. Oh, but they look so similar! They could be twins, one clutching a perfect miniature replica of the other—the only difference is the ribbons in Scarlett's hands as her long dead aunt clutches her.

I'm almost there. Ruby's flesh is once again becoming mottled and gray. It begins to fall away in the water, and Scarlett struggles against Ruby, batting at her with perfect little hands, hitting while still clutching the ribbons. Each time the ribbons come near to Ruby she reaches for it, but my Scarlett is a strong little thing and she struggles out of her aunt's bony grip, and begins to swim to me.

I reach for my daughter and grab the ribbons, pulling them out of Scarlett's hands.

Then I move quickly. I push my daughter away from me and she swims upwards, up towards the surface. I follow her, and as she breaks the surface I throw her towards the bank.

The rescuers are still there as lights flash and sirens wail. A woman grabs Scarlett and pulls her to safety. But I am exhausted; depleted, frozen and oxygen-starved.

I can see my son is sitting up now, breathing, thank God. Scarlett is wailing; she's certainly alive.

I must finish this, and it must be now. I dive once more down to the ledge where my sister waits. Waits for the gift she wanted so much, and never got because her life was cut short way too soon.

As I go farther down, I see her once more, and she is the Ruby I knew, the Ruby I loved, my friend, my sister, and very nearly the murderer of my children. I can't hate her; she's been here all this time, lonely, sad, lost. I give her the ribbons.

I can hear the melody, even under water. It sounds like it's being played on an old record player, a note misses every so often. I lose consciousness in the dark, freezing water. I am with my sister, who is no longer lost.

*****

I didn't die that night in the river. Two men dived after me and risked their own lives to save mine.

I was pulled from the water clutching the skeleton of a small girl. A small girl that had been dead in the river for many years, her body wedged under an underwater ledge that was near impossible to see. DNA tests confirmed that it was Ruby, but I knew that before the results came back, because the melody no longer haunts me when I go to my mother's house.

## THE WHITE ROAD

Tim Waggoner

It didn't happen the way the stories said it would. He didn't experience a sensation of formless floating, wasn't gazing down at his own body lying on the operating table as the surgical team worked to save his life. One moment he was unconscious, the next he was wide awake, standing several feet away from the table, the doctors and nurses, and what presumably was his own body. He felt disoriented, disconnected, and he raised his hands to look at them, as if trying to assure himself of his own reality. His hands looked completely normal, but his forearms were bare – which only made sense because he was naked. It was at that moment he became aware of how cold it was in the operating room, and he began to shiver.

*A dream,* he thought desperately. *Please let this be a dream.*

He took a bit of excess belly flesh between thumb and forefinger and pinched hard, giving the flab a twist for good measure. He felt the pain, but the sensation didn't jolt him out of the dream. He breathed, could still smell the scents of the operating room: the tang of bleach combined with a harsh medicinal odor. He could feel his abdominal muscles tighten with anxiety, heard his stomach gurgle as it produced excess acid. This couldn't be real, but all his senses insisted that it was.

He remained standing, bare feet on cold blue tile, surgical team working with swift, economical motions. The atmosphere in the room was tense, and he could see beads of sweat forming on the head surgeon's brow. He waited for another member of the team to wipe away his sweat, but no one did. They were too focused on their patient—on him.

People who claimed to have near-death experiences reported feeling a calm sense of peace during the time their spirits were separated from their bodies. But he felt a mounting sense of panic that was swiftly becoming overpowering. Not because he appeared to be dying. He had no fear of death. He was afraid he would *survive* death…that his consciousness would continue to exist in some form after his body had long fallen away to dust. He could not imagine anything more terrifying.

He screamed, the sound coming from deep inside his being. The noise filled the room, but no one heard, no one turned to look at him, and he began to weep. Tears fell from his eyes, as solid and real as he was, and struck the floor with tiny, inaudible splashes. But they didn't land on blue tile. Instead, they hit white brick. He could feel the hard, uneven surface of stone beneath his feet now, and he knew he no longer stood on tile but on the—

*Road,* his mind supplied, and while the notion of a road inside an operating room was ridiculous, he knew that's exactly what it was: a white road. Although *road* did seem too big a word. *Path* might have been better. It was only four feet across, and it stretched from one wall to another, seeming to lead nowhere in either direction.

Phillip Price—fifty-six, overweight, poor eater and non-exerciser—had come to the hospital for a triple bypass. Technically, coronary artery bypass-graft surgery. His surgeon, who right now had his gloved hands inside Phillip's chest, had told him during their initial consult three weeks, two days, and four hours earlier that the procedure, while not without risks, was almost routine these days.

*Doesn't look so routine from where I'm standing,* Phillip thought.

He'd read an article on ScienceNewz.com one hundred and twenty-seven days ago that theorized the human brain retains consciousness for up to ten minutes after death. Maybe that was happening to him now. Maybe he was dead, or dying, and his mind was imagining he was outside his own body, maybe as part of some last-ditch but ultimately futile attempt at survival. He'd read—eighteen years, ten months, and six days ago—that men ejaculate at the moment of death, as if their bodies want to make one last longshot attempt to fertilize a woman's egg, life desperately trying to continue itself, regardless of how astronomical the odds were.

His mind was projecting his consciousness outside of itself, like forcing a passenger off a sinking ship onto a lifeboat and pushing them away so they wouldn't be pulled down with the vessel when it sank. If so, this projection—regardless of how real it seemed—would be no more successful than all those dying men shooting semen into nothing. All he had to do was endure this for another few minutes until his mind shut down for good, and then he would wink off as swiftly and easily as he'd winked on. He would be gone at last, and everything in his mind would go with him. It was what he wanted more than anything in the world. What he *didn't* want was something like what happened next.

Cracks appeared in the wall where one end of the "road" disappeared, jagged fissures that made harsh cracking sounds as they grew longer and wider. Chunks of plaster began to dislodge and fall to the floor—the pieces hit with loud *thunks*, but none of the doctors or nurses turned to see what was happening. Phillip watched the wall break apart, telling himself it was proof of his hypothesis, an indication that his mind was experiencing the first signs of its demise.

But then the wall burst inward and a large shape thrust its way through and into the operating room. It was twice Phillip's size and fashioned entirely from bone. Skulls, to be precise. Big ones, little ones, human, animal, and ones whose origins Phillip couldn't identify, all fused together to approximate a humanoid form—head, torso, trunk, arms, legs.

In the back of his mind, Phillip knew it was a ghost-beast. It was a dead thing from somewhere beyond reality. Was it coming to take his soul?

It paused for a moment, bone feet comprised of tiny bird and rodent skulls on white brick. Except the brick didn't remain white where the creature's feet touched it. Black stains spread outward from the two points of contact, as if the thing's feet were leaking thick black ink.

Its overlarge head was made of what Phillip believed were the skulls of infants, and that head oriented on him now. There were no eyes in the sockets—on any of the hundreds its skull body possessed—but Phillip nevertheless felt the weight of its regard settle on him. His thoughts hazy. Shouldn't he be too terrified to observe? He wondered how a ghost-thing could take the appearance of something solid.

It looked at him for several long seconds, its conglomerate body seemed to shake with rage, anticipation, or hunger—maybe all three—skulls *clack-clack-clacking* together like an orchestra composed entirely of castanet players. Phillip had never heard anything so horrible in his life.

But this *wasn't* his life anymore, was it? It was his death, and who knew what dark wonders lay in store for him as he faded from existence?

The lower jaws of the skull-beast's head dropped in unison, as if the creature bellowed a warning or a challenge, but no sound emerged. Instead, Phillip was struck by an utterly cold wind which tore at his naked flesh like knives of ice. The skull-beast started toward him then, hands raised, skull fingers curled into claws, feet rapping dryly on brick as it came.

Phillip did not question the skull-beast's reality, nor did he question its intentions. His body—whatever its current nature—acted entirely on instinct. He spun around and began running in the opposite direction, down the White Road and toward the unbroken surface of the other wall. Fat rolls bounced and his cock and balls jiggled as he went. He saw the wall rushing toward him, and he fully anticipated slamming into it. With any luck, he'd hit his head hard enough to render him unconscious before the skull-beast could catch hold of him and begin tearing him apart.

He didn't mind dying, but he didn't want to do it in searing agony if he could avoid it. But when he reached the wall, it gave before him, almost as if it were made of thin rubber no thicker than the surgical team's disposable gloves. For an instant he thought the wall would snap back into place, sending him flying backward into the skull-beast's less-than-tender embrace. But the rubber wall tore and Phillip stumbled forward, the wall closing up behind him like a giant soap bubble. He was through! He was safe!

And he was someplace else.

*****

Phillip first became aware that other people forgot things when he was a toddler. His mother was in the kitchen making lunch—tomato soup and grilled cheese—and she was frustrated. She'd bought a fresh package of cheese slices at the grocery three days, four hours, and twenty-two minutes ago. Phillip had been with her at the time, and he could've told her every item she'd bought in the order she'd pulled it from the shelves, as well as the order in which the woman working the cash register had rung them up, including the price of each item. He didn't even need to concentrate to summon all this information. His mind did it all by itself. Up to this point, he'd assumed everyone was like him, that they remembered every second of every day in perfect detail, and they could retrieve any of those memories with ease. But if that was true, why couldn't Mommy remember that she'd put the cheese slices on the refrigerator's middle shelf behind a carton of eggs, instead of in the meat compartment on the bottom of the refrigerator as she usually did?

He watched her standing in front of the open fridge, holding the door with one hand, the other resting on her hip while she glared at the fridge's contents, as if they'd somehow conspired to hide the cheese from her. Then he walked over to her, took hold of the egg carton, and slid it off the shelf, revealing the cheese slices. Mommy looked at him a moment, frowning, but then she smiled.

"Thanks, sweetie."

She grabbed the package of cheese, Phillip returned the eggs to their place, and Mommy closed the refrigerator door. She stepped to a counter and resumed making Phillip's lunch, and he watched her, wondering if there was something wrong with her, if she was sick. He would eventually learn that there was indeed something wrong with her, the same thing that was wrong with the whole damned human race. They forgot while Phillip remembered.

*****

After pushing through the wall, Phillip experienced an instant of darkness, which he hoped was the advent of death. He was sorely disappointed when his vision cleared and he found himself standing in the middle of a street festival. Booths and food trucks lined both sides of the street, and the crowd was so thick that people were forced to walk shoulder to shoulder at a snail's pace. The sun was high overhead, the day blisteringly hot. Everyone was sweating and most wore sunglasses to protect their eyes. Still, they seemed happy enough.

At first Phillip had no idea where he was, but then it hit him: The Freedom Festival, the July 4th celebration that his hometown put on every year. He'd come annually, up until he'd moved away when he was twenty-seven, and while he hadn't been back since, he'd heard the festival was still going strong. Given his inhumanly perfect memory, it only took him several seconds of looking around—at the booths, the people's hairstyles, their clothing—for him to know that this particular festival was the one he'd attended the summer before his senior year of high school. Which meant…

He looked to his right and saw Tricia Cole walking at his side. She was seventeen, also a soon-to-be senior, with curly brown hair and a round face that a lot of guys thought unattractive, but which he'd always found cute. She wore a yellow tank top, white shorts, and sandals. She didn't have sunglasses, and he could see her warm chocolate eyes. Even if he hadn't possessed a perfect memory, he could never forget those eyes.

He remembered that he was a middle-aged man—and worse, *naked*—but when he looked down at his body, he saw he was clothed in a *Star Wars* T-shirt, shorts, and sneakers. He wasn't skinny, but he was much thinner—he'd weighed 168 pounds that summer – and he realized, with more than a little astonishment that he was seventeen again. Someone else might've been thrilled to find themselves reliving a scene from their adolescence—*The best years of your life,* his father used to say—but these people didn't have his memory. He knew exactly what was going to happen next, and he dreaded it.

Tricia reached for his hand, her fingers hot and sticky from the heat, and when her flesh came in contact with his, he jerked away. She gave him a surprised, hurt look.

"Sorry," he said and made himself take her hand. His stomach gave a sick twist, but he did his best to ignore it.

Philip—the middle-aged version inside the teenager's body—did not choose to do or say these things. They happened automatically, repeating exactly what he'd done on that day. *I'm not living this,* he thought. *I'm reliving it.*

Tricia stiffened when he took her hand, but she forced a smile and relaxed a little. They'd dated for most of their junior year but had broken up a month before school let out. They'd only recently begun seeing one another again—six days, five hours, and twenty-seven minutes ago—but things were still not back to normal between them.

Tricia had starred in the high school theater production last year, *The Phantom of the Opera;* the play, not the musical. She'd played Christine, the object of the Phantom's obsessive desire. Daryll Burke had played her boyfriend, Raoul. In one of the scenes, Christine and Raoul kissed, and while Phillip knew Tricia and Daryll were only acting—and additionally there were rumors around the school that Daryll was gay—Phillip hadn't been able to keep from feeling furious jealousy whenever he saw them kiss on stage.

The problem was that, with his memory, he never *stopped* seeing them kiss. And his memories didn't merely extend to sight and sound.

He remembered his emotions just as vividly. When he recalled an emotion it hit him with the same force as when he first felt it. There was nothing between Tricia and Daryll—he sincerely believed that—but he could not stop remembering their kissing in the play. And the worst of it was when he and Tricia kissed. He saw her kissing *Daryll* then, experienced the same resentful jealousy. He would break off their kiss, they would argue, and before long she broke up with him, unable to stand his jealousy any longer. He'd tried to explain to her what it was like having a memory like his. But of course she couldn't understand, not fully. Who could?

*Maybe you have perfect recall,* she'd said. *But it's your choice whether or not you think about that memory, isn't it?*

So they'd split up. But partway through the summer, Tricia began having second thoughts, and she called and said she wanted to give "them" another try. Phillip feared the same thing—or something similar—would happen. It was why he didn't have friends, why his relationship with his parents was distant. Because he could not forget anger and sadness, could feel them anew at any time, and because of this he could not forgive. With a memory like his, everything was *now*, and how could you move on if everything you ever experienced was happening inside you all the time?

But when Tricia asked him if they could start dating again, he wanted so badly to make it work that he could learn to control his memory instead of letting it control him. If he worked at it, he worked *hard.* So far it didn't seem to be working, and Tricia seemed to be aware of it. Like him, she was going through the motions, but…

Out of the crowd, Daryll came walking toward them, a perfect smile on his perfect face. He wore a short-sleeved button shirt, top two buttons undone to show part of his chest, along with khaki pants and bowling shoes. Phillip had no idea why Daryll wore those shoes, but—with the exception of play performances—he had never seen Daryll without them.

Walking beside Daryll was Franklin Hoffstetter, equally handsome, equally well-dressed, but wearing regular shoes. Franklin was also in drama club, but he did behind-the-scenes stuff, such as makeup and set design. Maybe they were a couple, maybe they weren't. Phillip didn't know, and he was glad. With his memory, it was a relief not to know something.

When this incident occurred in real life, Daryll had greeted Tricia with a hug, they'd exchanged a few pleasantries, then Daryll had said hi to him, and he and Franklin had continued on their way. The whole time Daryll had spoken with Tricia, Phillip had been watching them kiss in his mind, over and over, jealousy boiling over inside him. He'd tried to ignore his feelings, but they refused to go away, and before long, Tricia and he ended up fighting again – for the last time.

But that's not what happened now. Before Daryll could speak, screams filled the air behind them, and Phillip—now able to command his body instead of just being along for the ride—turned to see people pushing toward him, expressions of absolute terror on their faces. Farther back, people flew through the air, hurled this way and that, faces, arms, and hands covered with ragged wounds.

*Bite marks,* Phillip thought. *Hundreds of them.*

People slammed into him, but Phillip managed to keep from being knocked down, and soon he saw the skull-beast. The thing had followed him from the operating room, and it appeared determined to reach him, regardless of who stood in the way. He turned back toward Tricia. There was no sign of Daryll or Franklin, and he assumed they'd fled with the rest of the people in the area. But Tricia was still there, watching with horrified fascination as the skull-beast tore its way through the crowd.

Phillip knew that Tricia wasn't *really* Tricia. Last he heard, she was a lawyer working in Milwaukee with a husband and two kids in college. But he still couldn't stand by and let this Tricia, the memory of a girl he'd once loved, be hurt. He was still holding onto her hand, and he pulled her toward the sidewalk, passing between a shaken lemonade stand and a booth where a woman was selling knitted hats and scarves. There was no way they could run in this frenzied crowd, but once they were on the sidewalk, they could—

Tricia's hand was yanked out of his, and he spun around in time to see the skull-beast wrap its arms made of skulls, all of which possessed teeth, and pull her into a deadly hug. Tricia screamed as dozens of skull mouths began tearing into her flesh. She thrashed in the creature's embrace, shrieking in agony, blood spilling from her wounds onto the ground. Phillip was overwhelmed by the awful sight, and his earlier resolve to save her melted away. He had a thought then. A terrible, selfish thought. Every detail of this awful moment would be recorded in his memory, and he would never be free from Tricia's blood and pain.

He tore his gaze away from Tricia, looked down, and saw he stood less than a foot away from the sidewalk—a sidewalk made from white bricks.

As he turned and ran toward the sidewalk, which in reality was the White Road, he felt like a complete shit-heel for leaving Tricia to be chewed to death by the skull-beast. He told himself that she wasn't real, was nothing more than an especially vivid memory, but it didn't help. He still felt like a coward for abandoning her, but he didn't turn back around. If anything, he ran faster, as if desperate to get away from her screams.

The White Road ran parallel to the street for a dozen feet or so before curving into the yard of a small building containing offices for a realtor and a massage therapist. The road terminated at the base of a large oak tree at the side of the building, but Phillip followed the road without question or hesitation. The road had taken him away from the operating room, and it would take him away from here. It *had* to.

Tricia's screams cut off, and he heard a loud *thud* that he assumed was the sound of the skull-beast slamming her body to the ground. This was followed by the *clack-clack-clack* of the creature's bony feet as it resumed its pursuit of him. Sweat poured off Phillip, and the hot air burned his lungs. What the hell *was* that thing? An emissary of Death, perhaps the Grim Reaper himself, albeit with a slightly altered appearance? Or was it a natural creature, a thing that appeared when someone died to devour their soul, kind of like an afterlife version of a vulture?

Or was the skull-beast simply a metaphor, an image his dying mind had conjured to process what was happening to him? If the latter was true, his brain was way more screwed up than he'd thought.

Then again, he *was* running straight for a tree, so how sane could he be?

The skull-beast caught up to him when he was three feet from the oak. The creature swiped one of its skull-fingered hands toward him, and he felt the tiny mouths of those fingers rake his shoulder, teeth tearing the cloth of his shirt and biting divots into his flesh. He cried out in pain and stumbled, but he didn't fall. He covered the last few feet to the tree and, unable to stop himself doing so, he closed his eyes in anticipation of hitting the trunk while running flat out. If he was lucky, the impact would knock him out, and he wouldn't feel the skull-beast savage his unconscious body.

But instead he felt the same rubbery resistance as he passed through the operating room wall, and then he was through.

*****

After Tricia and he broke up for good, he never dated again, and he didn't forge any friendships. Why bother? He knew his memory would eventually destroy any relationships he managed to develop.

With his gift (curse) he could've studied any field in college. Medicine, law, engineering, business…but money wasn't his primary concern in life. Living like a normal person, at least as normal as he could manage, was his goal. For him, that meant finding a job where he could work, a place where he would come into contact with as few people as possible. So he passed on college and took a job in data entry. He sat in front of a computer console in an office all day, inputting meaningless streams of random numbers. Later, when the technology was there, he did the same work, but now he did it at home, making the job even better. Without anyone around to interact with, his new memories weren't of hurt feelings—sadness, rage, betrayal, jealousy, envy—but rather calm, tranquil memories of typing at a computer all day. It was as close to bliss as a person like him could ever find.

When he thought about dying—which he did increasingly as the years passed—and considered the possibility of an afterlife, he hoped that, assuming there was one, it would be that of the ancient Greeks. Before the spirits of the dead could enter the paradise of the Elysian Fields, they first had to drink from the River Lethe, whose waters erased all memory of their mortal lives. Then, unburdened by the cares of their time on Earth, they could fully enjoy eternity. That sounded like Heaven to him.

A thousand hurts, all of them as fresh in his mind as the moment he experienced them, all of them *present* twenty-four seven. It was a kind of living hell, and while he didn't have the guts to commit suicide—he'd made a couple half-hearted attempts before admitting to himself that he could never go through with it—he looked forward to death, to the extinction, the *obliteration* of his consciousness. It was why he ate so badly, why he was so slothful. He didn't want to extend his life by as much as a single second. And when he died, all his memories would perish with him, and then, and *only* then, would he be free at last.

The worst thing he could imagine was surviving death with all of his memories intact, a million small ghosts that would haunt him for all time. It was his greatest fear and worst nightmare combined, and he was experiencing it now.

*****

The skull-beast pursued Phillip across an ever-changing landscape of memories. The funerals of his parents after they'd died in a collision with a semi when he was twenty-six. The burst appendix that nearly killed him when he was thirty-four. The heroin-addicted younger sister who'd continually hit him up for money, and who'd died from an overdose behind a Goodwill Store when he was forty-three. And more, so many more, all of them as alive and painful as when he'd first experienced them.

The further he ran, the wearier he became, until it was all he could do to keep putting one foot ahead of the other. He wanted to stop running, wanted to turn around and let the skull-beast have him, tear him apart, and in the process grant him the oblivion he so desperately craved. But he couldn't bring himself to do it…maybe because he feared the agony of hundreds of ancient dry teeth piercing his flesh. Or maybe because he feared that, as bad as this endless pursuit was, something infinitely worse than mere mutilation might be in store for him if he allowed himself to be caught.

Whichever the case, he forced himself to keep going. And then—after finding himself in a memory from last year in which he sat in his car after being rear-ended by a man in an SUV, a man who stood outside his window screaming at Phillip as if the accident had been his fault—the White Road veered away from his car toward a carpet store on the corner called We Got You Covered. He got out of his car, pushed past the red-faced screaming man, and followed the white brick over to the curb and to a section of the store's outer wall—less than ten feet from the entrance—where it didn't disappear but instead continued through a huge hole that looked as if it had been made by an exploding bomb.

When he saw what lay on the other side of the hole, he almost fell to his knees and began sobbing. It was the operating room where this mad chase through his memories began, and this hole was where the skull-beast had broken through the wall originally. The White Road, for all its twists and turns through his past, was a closed loop. He had gone nowhere, and he was exhausted.

Some last shred of survival instinct remained in him, though, and he jumped through the opening and into the operating room. The Road here was no longer white, but rather a black so cold that it burned his bare feet. He was naked again and back in his normal body.

He stepped off what he supposed was now the Black Road, bent over, put his hand on his knees, and gulped air. Was the Road—*his* road, he realized—entirely black now?

The skull-beast had pursued him across its entire length, spreading it corruption with every step, so yes, it was most likely entirely black now. He had no idea what that meant, but whatever it was, he doubted it was good. Still breathing hard, he turned to look back at the huge hole in the wall. The skull-beast had slowed as it approached the hole, and now it stood on the other side, watching him but making no move to join him in the operating room. His shoulder throbbed from where the skull-beast's claws had raked him, but the pain was the least of his worries now.

The surgical team had gone quiet and still. After a moment, the lead surgeon said, "I'm going to call it." He glanced at the digital wall clock. "Death occurred at 1:37 pm."

The atmosphere in the room became heavy and somber, and the surgical team began shutting down monitors and putting away instruments. The doctors were the first to depart, leaving the rest of the team to finish the clean-up. No one spoke as they worked, and no one was aware of his presence.

Phillip was too tired to feel anything other than mild melancholy at his own death. He'd wished for it so long, but now that it had happened, it was worse than an anticlimax: it was a non-event. His consciousness still persisted, and his perfect memory remained intact, only now his brain had added every instant of his flight from the skull-beast. People said your entire life flashed before you when you were about to die. *Looks like they were right,* he thought.

*Your kind always makes this process more difficult than it has to be.*

The voice—although that wasn't exactly what it was—sounded both amused and weary.

Phillip turned back toward the hole in the wall and watched as the skull-beast climbed through. It no longer seemed interested in attacking him and it moved slowly, almost casually toward him, arms at its sides. Phillip was still frightened of the creature, but that fear was a faint echo of what it had been, and his body didn't respond to it. He no longer felt an urge to run, no longer cared about preserving his existence on any level. Whatever was going to happen next, he just wanted to get it over with.

The skull-beast stopped directly in front of him, but it made no move to touch him.

*People always react so poorly to the life review. We thought you might be different since you retain such complete and vivid memories of your experiences. We thought re-examining them would cause you no discomfort. Ah, well.*

This was followed by a sound that was almost but not quite a sigh.

*Still, it is complete now, and that's what's important, yes?*

Phillip was so flabbergasted by the skull-beast's change in behavior that he had no idea how to respond. The ghost seemed to take his silence in stride and continued.

*You were right earlier when you recalled the article you read, the one about human brains only surviving a brief time after death. You have no souls to continue on after your bodies cease functioning, and once your brain finally shuts down, you are gone forever.*

Phillip felt the first stirrings of hope since waking in the operating room. The pursuit through his memories, while had seemingly gone on for so long, had in reality taken place in the ten minutes or so his mind needed to close up shop. Only a few moments more and he would finally be free!

*When my kind first became aware of yours—when we understood what happens to you when you die—we were filled with sorrow. You see, unlike you, we have no ending. We endure forever.*

As the skull-beast spoke, the edges of its body began to soften, and the white of its bone grew darker, until what stood before Phillip was a faceless human-shaped shadow. Still twice as large as him and still scary, but not as terrifying as before.

*When we first reveal ourselves to you, you see us through the lens of your fear, believe us to be demons come to steal your souls. Nothing could be further from the truth. We come to help.*

The shadow man put a cool hand on Phillip's shoulder, and the bite wounds healed instantly.

*Another willful misperception. I never tried to hurt you. As I said, we wish only to help. We appear when humans are near death, and we make a . . . I suppose you could call it a copy of their memories. We preserve them inside us, giving you an immortality that you cannot obtain in any other way.*

That was why the White Road turned black, Phillip realized. Once the skull-beast, shadow man, or whatever-the-hell-it-was had recorded his memories, the white disappeared, indicating the road had shut down.

Phillip didn't like where the shadow man was going with all this. He tried to take a step backward, but the shadow man still had a hand on his shoulder, and his grip tightened, keeping Phillip where he was.

*And then, once we contain your memories, we absorb your consciousness and allow it to dwell inside us. You can then experience whichever of your memories you wish whenever you like. In effect, you become your own Heaven.*

"No," Phillip whispered. Then he shouted, "No!"

He tried desperately to free himself from the creature's grasp, but he couldn't. It took hold of Phillip's other shoulder, as if to make doubly sure he'd stay put. Phillip continued repeating no, shaking his head back and forth so rapidly that the shadow man became a black blur in his vision.

*There's no need to fuss. This won't hurt a bit.*

An opening appeared in the thing's face where a mouth would've been on a human. It expanded, growing larger and wider.

The shadow man inclined his head toward Phillip and lowered his great maw over the man's head. And as the shadow man took him into his darkness, Phillip screamed—a scream which would echo throughout his perfectly preserved memories for all eternity.

# FILMORE

Shawn P. Madison

A loud crash sounded just outside the door to his bedroom and continued with several other loud thumps against the wall. Whitt jumped from the bed and made his way slowly toward the only door leading into his bedroom from the hall. Catching his breath, he knew he must make his way toward the bathroom to find his sleeping pills, although not even those, he knew, would calm his nerves tonight.

He knew the place was haunted. But he figured he could live with it… ghosts couldn't hurt the living. He had done a lot to acquire this home and he wasn't going to walk away from it now. Days were calm, but the nights were not. Some nights he depended upon those sleeping pills.

The building was old, once Filmore's Funeral Home, now Whitt's residence. Although the exterior was brick and stone, the entire structure still groaned and creaked as if made from old wood, graying with age and splintering. There were other sounds, too, most nights—sounds of metal clinking against metal, loud crashes upon the floor downstairs and, often times, what sounded almost like faint screams carried upon the wind.

Those last often seemed to be coming from the basement, from the dark depths of that cavernous space where many a soul's lifeblood had been drained away. Whitt had almost gotten used to the sounds of this place, the footsteps that always seemed to be climbing the stairs and the creaks of doors that he himself had secured before retiring to bed.

But lately the old building had seemed more lively than ever after dark. Perhaps it was because he lived alone, sharing his residence with the ghosts. Although his bedroom was tucked away in the far back corner of the second floor, no amount of distance ever seemed to suppress the night sounds.

Somehow, he'd known that this night would come. Knew that Filmore would have his revenge upon him—the signs had been growing. Even as he had been in life, shrewd and malicious, so Filmore was proving in death.

*****

The window leading to the woods out back let in little light and was filled with the shadows of many branches swaying in the storm. Rain pelted the glass and what light there was came from the efforts of the moon to shine its reflection through the thick dark clouds.

Once again he found sleep fleeting this night, coming in short stints and often ending with some dreadful nightmare that shocked him awake. He'd thoroughly soaked the sheets with sweat and every time lightning flashed across the room, followed by a crash of thunder, he sat up with a start, heart pounding in his chest.

He thought he smelled smoke, but when he sniffed again, the air seemed clear.

Across the room, his mirror fell from the wall, smashing to pieces against the hardwood floor. Glass skittered in every direction and his breathing grew quick, his chest tightening. The great piston-like battering of his heart would not slow. He knew he had some stronger pills to help with his nerves but decided he'd better investigate the house before he took them.

New anxieties manifested as he thought of the cold and darkened hallways and rooms of this old building. Searching for his slippers but not finding them led to dread as he thought of the icy cold that would seep through his feet and into the core of his being, especially on a wet night such as this.

He reached for the doorknob and felt an intense burn against his palm and fingers, sending a blazing shock of pain up his arm to the shoulder. Whitt gasped and, snatching his hand back, flexed his fingers to make sure they still functioned. With a shake of his head to clear the terror that was gripping him, he tried some of his deep breathing exercises and willed his body to calm down; for his heart to slow, for his breathing to normalize.

Slowly, so slowly, he managed to achieve a state where he felt he could reach for the doorknob again and, this time, its temperature was as it should be—cold to the touch due to the early winter storm battering away at the old brick and stone structure. It cost a fortune to heat the old place, especially at night, so he piled on the blankets and suffered through the cold.

The door creaked open—slowly—on rusted hinges and he lumbered his way into the dark hall. The walls were a deep earthy brown, the rugs a moody burgundy along with some other shades of brown and dark blue, lending more depth to the cloying dark. Not his particular decorating style, to be sure, but it had been this way for decades upon decades.

Filmore Funeral Home and Crematorium had been built over a half century ago on top of a low hill overlooking the main streets of town—built with massive columns supporting the front entryway. It looked more like a medieval castle—all dark and brooding grays—than a place where the dead were either prepared for their funeral or burned to ashes.

Only the tall chimney, reaching toward the heavens and dwarfing the line of trees that dotted the hillside behind the great structure, gave the building away for what it truly was. A long winding drive led up from the entrance on Mission Hill Road and ended in a small parking area toward the right of the building. Otherwise, the woods surrounding the property had long been given to scaring the local children when they dared each other to come here at night. The small Filmore family crypt, tucked away several yards into the woods, also provided many frights to the local youth. Long feared haunted in local legends, the building had been passed down from Filmore to Filmore until only Richard Filmore had been left.

But Whitt's recent fears came not from the outside, but from the inside of this old lonely place. Every shadowed corner, every crevice, held the ghosts of his newly dead partner and the other dead Filmores who once walked these very halls. Every step he took seemed to echo with the steps of those Filmores who had dwelled here before. That family had built this place with their bare hands and broad backs, brick by brick and stone by stone.

Just a few steps down the hall, Whitt found himself staring into the main foyer. Nothing was there but the fluid movement of shadows cast about the floor and walls as more lightning raged outside.

A shadow, more solid than those being cast by the swaying

branches outside, slithered across his field of vision in the dark, stopping Whitt dead in his tracks. It had been there but a fleeting moment and thoughts of dead Filmores filled his head.

The phone sitting on a small stand—just a yard away—chose that moment to ring, shattering Witt's trance at the top of the stairs, and he nearly jumped from his skin. Looking at the large clock, fashioned with roman numerals, hanging also at the top of the stairs, he wondered who could be calling him this late.

With trembling fingers he snatched up the phone. "Hello?"

Static met him on the line along with a sound reminiscent of a fire crackling.

"Who is this?" Whitt whispered and only more static met his question.

He was about to hang it up when, through the earpiece, in a raspy voice as if scratched out of a rotting throat, came one word…*Flames*…

Whitt slammed the phone down and raced to the bottom of the stairs, determined not to be caught on the second floor if there really were to be a fire. At this point, he would actually welcome the destruction of this old place—the reduction to ashes and a pile of gray bricks of the entire establishment. He was insured.

The first-floor phone rang—from its position on a small desk just inside the main doors—adding it's shrill to the storm still pounding at the walls outside. Whitt picked it up and immediately screamed, "Leave me alone! You are dead! Dead, you hear me?"

"Whitt?" the voice belonged to Deputy Helmsley sitting at the Dispatch Desk of the Mission Hill Sheriff's Department. "Are you okay? What are you doing in there?"

"Everything's fine," Whitt managed. "Why such a late call?"

"Are your ovens lit tonight of all nights, with this horrible storm?"

"No, of course not…"

"Then why is the Sheriff on the radio reporting a great cloud of smoke coming from that chimney of yours?" Helmsley asked. "It may be the mother of all storms out there tonight but he tells me he could see that thick cloud of smoke half a mile down Mission Hill Road…"

Whitt dropped the phone and ran to the front windows. Through the pelting rain he could make out a County Sheriff's car parked at the bottom of the driveway. A flash of lightning blinded him for a moment and when his vision cleared, reflected there in the glass he saw the specter of Filmore—hunched over, face bloodied and head bashed in. The apparition's left hand was outstretched and reaching toward him with trembling fingers.

Whirling to face this monstrosity, Whitt found nothing there but dancing shadows. He scrambled frantically to the end of the hall, descended another flight of stairs to the basement, threw open the door to the large room where the bodies of the deceased were prepared and stood frozen at the sight before him. No lights were on within the large room but the ovens were burning at full heat and, with their doors wide open, the space was filled with an eerie orange glow.

He screamed and shut his eyes. This was impossible, he knew. The ovens had been off for months. No remains had been left inside them. There was a process to get the ovens lit and going and none of it had been performed tonight.

He heard a voice whisper, *Flames!*

Whitt found himself scrabbling to get out of there, but the great oaken door slammed shut and he hit his cheek hard against the solid wood. Blood dribbled down his face and his heart raced faster than ever in his chest.

From all over the large room, the tools of his trade rattled, tables rocked side to side and the smell of burnt flesh overpowered his senses. A skull skittered close to the edge of the oven and Whitt could see where part of the bone had been cleaved in by a blunt object. The cause of death—in obvious detail before him. But there was no way that skull or those other bones could be in that oven. He had removed the ashes of those bones from that same oven just two months earlier.

Richard Filmore had been a doddering old fool, afraid to retire from his business and meet what was waiting for him outside these stone walls. Whitt had toiled for him down in these ovens for years, waiting to take his place at the helm of the operation but Filmore just wouldn't call it a career. He kept coming in, day after day, as his brain continued to pickle itself and his mind faltered to the point where Whitt had to do twice the work just to fix the senile old bastard's mistakes.

There were no more Filmores to will the place to. There was no one else who could take over but Whittington Montgomery. And yet the ancient old relic just wouldn't let go.

So Whitt let go for him. Upstairs in the apartment. The fireplace poker was just the tool. He came up on the older man from behind after they'd argued about when Filmore would finally retire. The obstinate old fool just didn't realize that his time was up.

One swing—that was all it took. One swing and the last of the

Filmore clan was no more. And Whitt had stepped up and taken possession of this stately, lovely home. Cause of death: an old man took a horrible fall. A quick cremation and it was over…until it was not. It would never be over.

Whitt felt a bony finger trace itself down his back, a ghastly, rotten fingernail caught its ragged edges on the material of his night shirt, and he leapt back from the door to the staircase. He clambered around desperate to put space between himself and whatever was playing out in front of him.

"No, no, no, no…" he stammered as he stumbled about the cavernous space. "You were going to die anyway! At any moment! I didn't change things. Your time was up with or without me, right?"

*Flames*…came the raspy reply from nowhere and everywhere at once.

Whitt scooped up a long, metal tool and held it out in front of him, determined to do some damage to his attacker, whoever or whatever it may be. He swung the implement weakly from side to side as he banged into tables and slammed into equipment.

*Flames*…the word came again, louder this time and from what seemed to be several voices and from all directions. *Flames…this home needs to die.*

Fire erupted out of the two remaining open ovens then, leaping across the room to brush against Whitt, searing his eyebrows. A scream escaped him at that point, his terror never at a higher point than now. He knew he had to get out of this basement and quickly if he were to survive this insane experience.

Something flew across the room at ground level, banging against his shin and ankle, nearly taking him down. He looked down and shrieked. It was a skull! A skull had flown out of the oven.

Another skull flew into his back with a heavy impact, causing a shock of pain down his spine. Another slam, this time delivering the hit to his head. More blood coursed down Whitt's face as he cursed and moaned and tried to find another way out of the lowest level. The heat was intense. Sweat poured off of Whitt in steady streams. He felt as if his head were going to explode and he could barely catch his breath.

Yet another skull in the oven merged with several other bones now, all glowing red with flame. The impossible jumble gathered itself at the edge of the oven and fell to the ground in a languid, liquid motion. More bones flew around the room. They impacted against Whitt's chest, his arms, and his torso, battering him without mercy. Whitt could hear himself crying, first in fear, then in pain. His forearms and midsection were bruised, and his face swelling.

All the while he could not tear his eyes from the pile of bones as they pulled themselves upright and began to drag themselves closer to where he knelt against a wall made of white tiles. "Leave me alone!" he screamed. "You're dead! I know you're dead because I made you dead!"

*Flames…*Whitt cried more heavy; great heaving sobs that wracked his entire body. All of the memories of the night he murdered Filmore came crashing back and he knew he deserved this death, deserved to meet his end just as had his victim. Because the one memory that he had been suppressing about that horrific night came flooding back to him now—overwhelming him with dread and grief for what he had done.

As the bones dragged themselves closer to where he knelt crying, battered and bruised, Whitt looked up into those empty sockets feeling the heat coming off of those bones in waves and understood the wrath of this spirit, understood the reason why it could not rest until it had its revenge.

Whitt had not killed Filmore with that one single blow to the head. No, the old man had regained what passed for semi-consciousness, despite the huge gash that had been struck through his cranium, and started to struggle feebly against his killer.

Although the first hit hadn't killed him, it was the way Whitt put the old man into his bedroom, lying on the floor, that led to a slow and painful death. Filmore died a horrible death all alone on his bedroom floor. Whitt let him suffer, knowing it would lead the authorities to believe that Filmore had taken a fall.

One last heavy object slammed into the side of Whitt's head and he blacked out for an instant, it couldn't have been more than just a few seconds, but when he came to he could feel bony hands as they effortlessly pulled him closer to the red raging blaze that had burned many dead bodies during its use.

With the fists of the Sheriff pounding against the front doors, Whitt's screams were lost into the wind of the storm outside, and the flames leaped out of the ovens and grew higher until they engulfed the entire structure.

## GREEN SHADOWS

Neal Privett

When Carter turned the corner, the house appeared suddenly, rising above the trees and brush. The structure was ancient and antebellum, a mute monument to lost times and almost forgotten ways that stretched back to the previous century. It loomed above Carter, three stories plus an attic, and had an atmosphere of mystery and decay. The house was a corpse from some invisible enemy.

And that is exactly why Carter had returned to this place of horror: to do battle with an enemy. Perhaps even with himself…a half-insane idea to conquer the very fear that had eaten him alive for two decades. It was a fear that grew like a cancer deep inside his gut and spread.

The fear of this house.

Soft, cold drops of rain began to fall as the dark evening clouds rolled in and the wind picked up. He crouched beneath an old pine and peered through the limbs at the house. The yard was overgrown with brush and littered with debris. The house had lost random pieces over the decades. Bits of shingle…some rotted wood…broken glass.

He traveled through the overgrown weeds and found his way to the front porch. There he stood for a long while, peering through the smudged glass into the darkness within as if he were staring down the throat of an awful beast.

Every atom and every cell of Carter's body—as well as his mind—screamed at him about what a bad idea this was. He recalled the recklessness of when he was a boy and the dark night so very long ago when he ventured into the house to prove to his friends that he was brave enough to find what the old place hid behind its stone and timbers.

He fought off the fear as he took another step closer to the house. He understood that sleepless nights and psychiatrists' office visits would never end unless he now confronted what was inside this house.

Back then, when he had been so young and naïve, he had entered the house.

When they found him the next morning, he was lying semi-conscious in the cellar, almost dead. His mind was a muddled maze. His clothes were ripped, as if by talons.

He lived in terror of the house every second since. And now he returned, armed with a flashlight, ready to finally exorcise the ghosts out of his life.

The sound of a branch snapping caused Carter to jump. He couldn't believe his eyes. He turned around on the porch and watched as a boy raced frantically across the overgrown front yard. Carter tried to call out to the boy to warn him away, but he couldn't find his voice.

The boy stopped beneath a low hanging pine. Carter's heart froze in his chest. *That kid needs to stay out of this house,* he thought. *I remember what happened to me when I was his age.*

He decided the boy was out of his control, so he continued his mission. He glanced around nervously and threw his shoulder against the massive oak door. The giant hinges were rusted and creaked like a coffin in an old horror film, but the door finally opened.

The tension boiled inside him as he teetered between the urge to run in terror and a deep-seated sense of purpose. He took a deep breath and ventured into to the dark world that had haunted his life for decades.

He turned on his flashlight and stepped into the front parlor. He glanced nervously around, not wanting to alert the things that walked the silent halls. He could feel a familiar chill in his bones as he moved through the front parlor.

From out of nowhere, an unnatural wind blew through the house, making the cobwebs dance and the dust rise into the air, then fall gently back to the floor. He heard something move in the rooms above.

They knew he was here.

To his right, the decaying stairs rose steadily to the floor above, winding like a venomous snake into the darkness. He tried to remember what had happened up there twenty years before, but strangely enough, his mind was a blank. He only knew that whatever he saw that night was terrible and that his amnesia was a small blessing. Something had found him in the upstairs rooms and somehow, he had ended up in the dark cellar, more dead than alive.

He aimed the flashlight beam into the main gathering room on the other side of the grand staircase. The light cut through the darkness like a scalpel, feeling its way into the corners and crevices of the room where the southern aristocracy of a different age once displayed and exercised their social graces.

He moved silently beneath a giant chandelier that was caked with a century of dust and spider webs. The light from his flashlight made the crystal glitter and sparkle, betraying the old glamor that once graced this place.

The chandelier began to sway.

Carter moved through the gloom into the far hallway. The dusty curtains shifted a little as he walked by. His spine tingled. He could not be sure if it was the draft of his movements or something else that made the curtains move as if touched by invisible fingers.

He whispered a small prayer of thanks for the flashlight with the addendum that the batteries hold up. He moved stealthily through a couple of side rooms and into the old dining hall.

He briefly thought about the boy he had seen in the yard. He hoped that whoever the child was, he had enough sense not to enter this house.

Carter navigated his way toward a covering of gossamer spider webs draped across one of the doorways. The webs emanated with a ghostly glow in the light. He hesitated, then pushed his way through and almost panicked when the webbing hugged his face.

He rubbed his face frantically, trying to stay quiet. He calmed down and kept moving.

The floor creaked under his weight and he silently prayed that it would not collapse and send him reeling down to the cellar below. His breath caught savagely in his throat as a memory wracked him…*the cellar*. That night in the cellar…there were *rats*. It was a roomful of yellow-eyed rodents scratching and clawing. But the memory stopped there. What happened beyond that was a mystery to him.

A sudden sound made him stop in his tracks. He listened intently, pointing the light around in frantic circles in the hope that nothing surprised him there, all alone as he decided to climb the stairway to the second floor. The sound came again…something fell to the floor and crashed in a room upstairs.

Something moved suddenly to his right and he jumped.

A possum appeared in the flashlight beam and scurried away, its rest disturbed. Another movement made Carter spin around. An owl launched itself from its nest built in a convenient hole in the wall. Its great wings stirred the musty air, and in an instant, the creature of the night was gone. The room was quiet again.

He sighed with something akin to relief and turned to the long hallway on the second floor.

He took a few more steps and stopped again. Another sound. There came a soft voice from below.

Had the boy entered the house? Of course, that was it.

Carter bit his lip so hard that the taste of blood rose up into his mouth. He backed against the crumbling wall and closed his eyes, focusing on keeping his sanity intact. The voice faded when a strange burst of air almost froze him.

He continued to lean against the wall, trying to summon the nerve to continue. He wrestled with his fear, reminding himself that this was something he had to finish, no matter what…or else he would never find peace in his life.

Letting go of the wall, Carter moved to the next room. The light revealed nothing. The room was empty, save for a crumbling fireplace against the far wall. He pictured a lot of cold winter nights with one of the old family huddled around the warmth of the fire before they retired to a bed piled high with quilts.

He studied the room with his flashlight. All the furniture was long gone, probably taken by the locals. That furniture would be worth a fortune now, most likely. He glanced at the walls; crumbling wallpaper and great brown water stains where the roof had leaked. The floor was cherry wood…durable, but even the advent of time could not keep it from buckling. He took one last look and moved back into the hall.

A rush of fear hit him square in the face and he froze in his tracks.

A small shadowy figure appeared suddenly at the far end of the hallway.

Carter thought it was the boy. With a sinking heart, he realized that the kid had entered the house after all. A savage chill washed over him yet again as he called out and received no answer. The figure stayed stone-statue still, staring at him.

Carter called out once more. “Hello? I saw you out in the yard.” His voice echoed throughout the still of the night and shattered his nerves. He began to tremble uncontrollably, but he could not take his eyes from the figure at the end of the hall.

When the shape came into the light, Carter gasped. It was a child's charcoal effigy…a living shadow, solid as a mortal entity but as soulless as damnation.

Cold sweat broke out on his face and rolled down his neck, saturating his collar. He did not budge but watched the thing as it watched him. He did not know what to do, so he waited for it to make its move…and it did.

The mysterious small effigy turned suddenly and raced away from him. To his utter horror, Carter then took a step forward…much against his will…as if something was forcing him to follow the boy. Before he knew what he was doing, he was racing full speed down the hallway. He realized very quickly that the deafening sound ringing out all over the house was his own screams.

He descended the great stairs, still screaming. The beam of his flashlight danced on the walls and floor sporadically as he raced like a burning meteor falling to earth in the deep black of night. The darkness closed in on him and all he could see at the end of the tunnel of light was that boy…that shadowy, inhuman *thing* running ahead of him, pausing for a second here and there, almost gleefully, as if to make sure Carter was still in pursuit.

It *wanted* him to follow…it *beckoned* him…led him down to the first floor and into the kitchen. Carter's mind howled in defiance…on the far side of the kitchen was the doorway to the cellar! The boy was leading him to the cellar!

All of the revulsion bubbled to the surface as he tried to stop himself…to put the brakes on…but it was no use. He was pulled along in the wake of the boy and could not free himself.

As his foot hit the first step leading to the cellar, the voices from beyond came howling throughout the house—hundreds of voices—forming one long wail of corruption. The sound of the McAllisters: murderers, extortionists and thieves.

*His ancestors.*

He remembered now. *This* was his ancestral home. He had visited it for the first time on a dare that night twenty years ago. And the guilt of his family name had almost drowned him alive in the pit of the cellar.

Translucent shades of glowing green appeared in the walls as he raced past, en route to the kitchen. Wanton and tortured visages leered at him from the ancient wallpaper…from the holes, crammed with rat nests and spider webs. The ghosts of his family jeered at him…as if welcoming him back to the hell that was his by birthright.

The child's dark effigy stopped on the bottom step and turned once more to see if he was coming.

The child's shape vanished into the cellar. Carter followed down the stairs, and his legs gave out suddenly. He felt himself falling through space…down into the black pit of the cellar.

He panicked as the flashlight flew from his hand. It went dark as it hit and rolled on the ground.

Carter landed with a thud amidst a cloud of dust that clogged his nostrils and choked him. Pain shot through his aching body. He felt the rusty taste of blood and vomit in his mouth as his stomach finally gave way. He vomited violently, then collapsed onto his back, groaning and staring up into an inky sea of nothingness.

And that's when Carter felt the scraping horror of sharp fingers in his eyes and on his throat. He writhed on the cellar floor in agony as great gashes of stinging pain ripped his face.

The ghosts of his ancestors glowed…their spirits raked his flesh, desiring his blood and his soul.

He tried to shield himself, but they kept coming and emanating their essence in the cellar.

He tried to shut out their luminescent faces as they bore down on him…the demonic masks of those who had damned his family name and condemned him to hell. They snarled and ripped at him with their ghostly hands.

There came a pause, then the cessation of the ghostly attack, followed by an unexpected hot crimson rush of rats. The cellar filled with them. Hundreds of squeaking, stinking, blood-hungry burning-eyed rodents …and suddenly Carter knew that the rats were the children of this house.

The burning red pain of the ghosts was nothing compared to the gnashing of yellowed teeth and the acid of rat saliva coating his wounds. He screamed to save his soul and pushed upwards with all his strength, sending the river of rats sliding and scurrying all around him. Then he picked himself up from the cellar floor and tried for the stairs, feeling his way through the darkness.

He could smell the dirty yellow stench of the rats and feel the claws of the undead on his back as he stumbled desperately up the stairs to the kitchen. When he reached the top, a bright light hit him in the eyes and he heard a human voice. Carter fell to his knees and tried to shield his eyes.

A young voice startled him. "You're okay! I'll help you!"

It was the boy from outside.

Then what boy was in the cellar? Was the charcoal effigy that lead him down here one of his ghostly ancestors?

Carter took a chance. He reached out to the only other human being in the house, the boy from outside.

They exited through the back door, which collapsed from its rusted hinges and tumbled to the ground. Carter stumbled out behind the boy, trying to regain his balance and stay conscious. The night had cooled a little and the breeze made his lacerations sting. But he was free.

They paused in the overgrown back yard. The boy stood before Carter, eyeing him curiously.

"What are you looking at?"

"You, Mister…"

Carter snapped at his young benefactor. "Why did you come here?"

The boy hesitated, then spoke. "I came here to see you."

"*Me*? How did you know I would be here? You don't even know me!"

"You're Carter McAllister."

"So what?"

"I came here to find you. They say you haunt this place every night. People hear your screams from the cellar and your footsteps up and down the dirt road here. I had to see for myself."

"I came back here to find out what nearly killed me twenty years ago!"

"You *died* twenty years ago…I've seen your grave!"

"No!" Carter cried. "I'm an adult."

"I see someone my age when I look at you."

The boy's words took the rest of the air out of Carter. And just as quickly, he knew and understood.

He glanced up at the night sky. The storm had passed, and the clouds parted, revealing a cool velvet section of stars. The moon appeared, bathing Carter in its soothing light. He felt numb suddenly, as if he were made of air. He felt his face. The stinging had stopped and the flesh melted away. He felt the ivory Death's Head on his shoulders.

The boy stepped aside and watched him vanish.

## BECKON U

Dean H. Wild

The opportunity was too good for Jan Slager to pass up. At the moment there was no younger daughter to shield from the potential unpleasantness of a stranger's preferences (Vivian was conked out on the couch, her fourth grade homework spread across her chest in an untidy drift) and no older daughter to hover with varying expressions of disapproval and judgment (Corrinne had mumbled something about stopping after the movie to do whatever fourteen year olds did before weekday curfews took hold). And of course there was her own curiosity, dull but constant since she'd found the laptop. It churned into a flurry as she slipped past the apartment's tiny bathroom, around a row of yet-unpacked boxes, and up to her bedroom door.

Pessimistic logic descended as she stepped inside. A hacker's toolbox was all that waited to be found on the orphaned computer's hard drive. Or a disappointing yet extensive collection of porn. What else was to be expected from something deposited in a hastily gouged hole in the wall? A hole covered up, no less, by a broken dresser abandoned by the previous tenant. She'd relocated her find to a spot under her bed, and it was there she slid her hand with a hopeless chuckle. This was her excitement for tonight. This was how one's life degraded once you were left to raise two daughters alone—

An electric shock strong enough to emit a bluish flash stung her fingertips. She drew back and aimed an accusatory glare at the under-bed darkness and the hard shell laptop case couched there. Damn thing still possessed a little juice. A silly notion, since the apartment had sat empty for six months. The landlord said so himself. Too long for a battery to hold a charge, wasn't it? She reached in again, dragged the computer out and plunked it on her bed with one smooth motion. No shock this time. Of course not. Static electricity did not a sign of life make.

"Let's see what we've got," she said to the dull silver housing.

The laptop was an older model, heavier by far than the cut-rate units she bought for the girls to use at school, and the hinged screen-to-keyboard separation worked with deliberate slowness. She snatched the power cord for her own laptop from the dresser and connected it, then tapped the boot key. The screen winked to life followed by a metallic chime.

With a slight but undeniable tremble, she closed her bedroom door, switched out her lights and settled in, cross-legged on her bed with the glowing screen perched in front of her like a naughty child up to after-hours mischief. Ah, the simple desperate joys of a degraded life.

Three icons populated the plain blue-gray desktop screen; none of them common or familiar. She slid a finger across the navigation pad at the bottom of the keyboard and skated the cursor arrow past the upper left icon, a plain rectangle labeled DRIVE. She likewise bypassed a more eye catching sigil marked APPS WORKING. Not hacker's files, but those of a designer or programmer, perhaps.

"Pretty boring desktop for a creative type."

She said it as she navigated to the olive drab rectangle in the lower right of the screen. The one labeled BECKON U.

"Maybe the University of Come Hither," she said.

More likely a hook-up site, something of little interest to her, no doubt requiring a password or other unattainable credentials. Yet, she allowed the cursor arrow to hover atop the icon, her taut smile meant to ward off the tingling of her scalp and the rise of tiny hairs across her body. This was, after all, a night of opportunity. She clicked. An off-white chat box blinked onto the bottom of the screen. Simple. Waiting. Just like that. "You're in," she breathed, her heart's cadence nearly keeping time with the expectant blink of the box's cursor.

The quick keystrokes she made felt natural and yet reckless. H-E-L-L-O.

She tapped the "send" button with an almost blithe giddiness.

A second box appeared below the first, a narrow gray field with its own cursor. For replies, she assumed, as if there were any respondents out there, as if Beckon U was something other than a work in progress connected to nothing more than an APPS WORKING folder. Upshot shadows thrown by the screen's glow leaned close to her, she was suddenly sure of it, to warn her enough was enough, it was time to bring up the lights and put away this suddenly reckless-seeming thing—

The gray box took on creeping dark strands like the flow of congealing watercolor, forming shapes. Letters.

HELLO BACK.

An icepick chill pierced her bones. Dankness filled the room like a massive passing breath, there and then gone. Gray perfume, a waft of moldy concrete perhaps, touched the air. The raspy sound of someone coughing or gasping swelled and then faded behind her—or was it above her?—with the frailty of a lost radio signal. Some sort of sensory misfire, she guessed. A product of silly excitement blended with a dark and uncharacteristically quiet apartment. Not a misfire, however, was the third word bleeding into the chat box behind the others.

HELP.

She was grateful for the grounded, rational part of her awakened by the word. Almost immediately, she typed. *TROUBLE?*

The response formed with the delicacy of rolling fog. SEE KIMBER.

*WHERE?* She replied with barely a thought.

The next compliment of letters stopped her breath.

COMING TO YOU. NOW.

She glanced at the bedroom window awash in night, glowered at her door, closed but unlocked. Thoughts of Vivian asleep and vulnerable down the hall rushed up amid a vision of Corrinne, home unnoticed and raiding the refrigerator, the front door ajar and unguarded behind her.

She suddenly needed to check on everything so foolishly put at risk, yet her legs were locked up and useless. Only her hands seemed capable of motion.

*NO. STAY AWAY* she typed.

She drew a long, creaking breath as the gray box refreshed. New letters took shape like the stretching of a sinister smile.

ALREADY HERE.

A cold hand gripped the back of her neck. Squeezed.

She leapt to her feet to break the grip. The computer crashed down and threw gray light and angular shadows around her. She spun around to evaluate the room. Empty. She was alone. No intruder. Certainly no hand. And yet a residual chill remained at her nape.

"Mom?" Corrinne called from the apartment foyer amid a rustle of coat sleeves and a jingle of keys. "I've got homework so I'm going to stay up a while. Don't have a shit fit, okay?"

She gathered a series of composed breaths and at last opened her door. "Okay, you get a pass this time. And don't say shit, it's unladylike." Speaking seemed to steal the air from her lungs. "Did you lock up?"

Desultory. "Yeah."

Jan closed her door again, rubbing the cold place on her neck. In the returning, familiar quietness, she wanted to be amused, wanted to shake off the last few minutes like the memory of a funhouse ride. Only when she switched on her bedside lamp and took another assessing gaze around the room did the tension in her muscles lessen. The Beckon U laptop was splayed open on the floor, cracked, leaking components, ready for tomorrow's trash. Good. Good.

"Kimber," she said once she was undressed and under the covers, her door cracked to let in a streak of hallway light, her eyes straining to evaluate every corner again and again. "I didn't mean to beckon you. I don't want to see you. Stay away."

*****

"Question for my whiz kid," Jan said as she cleared the breakfast table.

Corrine put down her phone and stared across the bright kitchen, impatient enough to seem nearly formidable. "What?"

"Ever hear of Beckon U?" She was barely aware of how her hand rubbed the back of her neck. "It's a computer thing."

Corrinne gave it real thought. No cursory dismissal for a change. "Becky New? Is she on YouTube?"

"No. Beckon. You. Like waving you over from across the room."

"Peck on you," Viv piped up from the table, silken pigtails flopping, her toothless smile radiant. "Sounds like a chicken."

"Bring your cereal bowl over here, little miss. You're going to be late." Jan told her. Then to her older daughter. "Just something I came across last night."

Corrinne slouched. "Oh God, is it some sort of old people's dating site? Gross."

"I don't think so," she said and took Viv's offered bowl. "Now get down to the bus stop. And hold hands."

The girls traipsed out loaded down with their school gear, Viv performing some sort of impromptu hopscotch dance while announcing "Peck on, neck on, wreck on you," while Corrinne made it obvious this was a chore beyond all reason. Jan stared at the door after they closed it behind them.

"YouTube," she said under her breath, took up her phone and dialed her work number. She was going to be late today.

*****

"It's your own laptop. You've had it for years for Christ's sake, so relax." She said it while the sleek Asus booted up on her kitchen counter.

What she might find during her Beckon U search hung before her unknown and troubling. More worrisome was the possibility a computer savvy deviant might already have her street address thanks to last night's antics. Hacker's skills scored just this side of black magic, it seemed. Inscrutable, arcane. And why not add a replay of cold fingers on her neck, whatever that was about? Join the party, jump on in. The paranoia's fine.

*Just launch the damn search engine.*

Her hand froze in mid motion when a new icon winked to life at the bottom of her screen. Olive drab. Beckon U.

"How—?"

Her hands hovered in an attitude of typing as her on-screen cursor drifted on its own toward the icon and then selected it. Twin chat boxes appeared. The lower incoming message box already contained two words.

HELLO AGAIN.

Her fingers descended to the keyboard with a type of desperation and fluttered like frightened birds.

*STOP. DON'T WANT YOU.*

The reply rose, fog-like.

NO CHOICE NOW.

Her logical side took over, fueled by a surging sick fear. She shot a confirming glance at her phone on the counter while she typed.

*HARRASSMENT. WILL CALL POLICE.*

The reply materialized. COPS BAD.THEY BROKE IN HERE.

ANGRY…

Here? Her heart thudded harder as she again glanced her surroundings, so much like their other drab apartments—three in the last two years—but this one tainted and unsafe.

She dragged her gaze back to the rest of the reply.

…THEY HID ME AFTER THEY BEAT ME TO DEATH.

*Done*. The word was a loud demand from somewhere in the back of her head, an accompaniment to the clack of her finger stabbing the boot key to shut everything down. Chilled air whorled around her. Across the way, the living room floor muttered, low, sustained. An announcement of presence.

*Don't touch my neck again. Just don't. Please.*

The door to Corrinne's room, visible from where she sat, juddered in its frame as if tested by curious hands. From the living room, the yellow indicator on the virtual home assistant came alight like a hectic eye, ready to search the internet or recite the weather forecast or compile a shopping list, although she had called for none of those things. "KIM-ber," its inflectionless voice declared . "See…KIM-ber… find KIM-ber…"

The dangling light fixture above her head described a circular pattern in the air as if stirring the cold, or tracing a barrier around her.

"Who are you?" Jan said, all logic consumed by sensory stitches of movement around her like unseen straw caught in a whirlwind.

"Find KIM-ber…or KIM-ber will take…" the home attendant continued, joined by the flutter of papers and a rattle of tumbling boxes in Vivian's room.

The sleeve of her blouse twitched, tugged by petulant invisible fingers. An exploratory arm circled her waist and then slid free. The need to move burned bright in her, but one step in any direction might mean collision with an icy, unseen form waiting to embrace her and drag her away.

Her voice was nearly a shriek. "Take what? What will you take?"

Silence dropped around her, full of dark promise. She glared at the Beckon U incoming message box, at the single word there.

BOTH.

A new logic, nourished by ideas as gossamer as fairytales, took over. Restless spirits (that's what you've got here, Jan. A bona fide, beaten-to-death ghost. Don't doubt it. Denial would be an arrogant lie in the face of what's happening) always wanted something. Redemption, forgiveness. But bargaining—practically extorting—

seemed like a new entry for the books and movies and television shows on the subject.

Her fingers tapped the keyboard as coldness returned to the air, accompanied by a suffocating, squeezing sensation.

*BOTH OF WHAT?*

Corrinne's door unlatched and swept open with a slow creak, affirming the words which materialized in the reply box.

YOUR DAUGHTERS.

She slammed the laptop lid as if the screen might open up and bite her. The overhead light bulb shattered as if in response and pelted her with glinting bits. Her hands clamped over her mouth, her gaze straining to every corner, every visible shadow in the now-quiet space.

"You can't have them," she said at last and reached for her phone.

No work today. There were new priorities.

*****

"Kimber," Mrs. Diller in 4B sat back in her chintz chair, an aroused and clearly knowledgeable smile working across her seamed face.

Jan was glad her suspicion about the little widow who occasionally brought cookies for the girls and seemed to have her wizened finger on the pulse of the whole building turned out to be correct. This was better than a computer search, the thought of which left her cold. This was safe. "You know the name?"

Mrs. Diller nodded. The late morning sun blazed in the patio door and set her coiffed white hair aglow. "What puzzles me is how you came to know it, dear. You're not a local."

"I've heard it twice now in the last twelve hours or so." She took a polite sip of instant coffee and tried not to tremble. "Did he live in my apartment at one time?"

"For a short while, yes. And then, gone." The woman shrugged and brushed her fingers in the air as if to say *that's that*, her eyes bright and unblinking. "They stopped searching for him only a few weeks after they found the bodies, which we always thought was odd."

A dark bloom unfurled deep inside her. "Bodies?"

"Girls." Mrs. Diller delivered it with the conviction of a long-awaited punchline. "*School age* girls. Beaten, strangled. You people with ground floor units have basements. He used his to keep his victims piled like cordwood. I've got some newspaper clippings in my scrapbook if you want to see them."

She managed to set her rattling cup on the end table. "Yes, I would. Thank you," she said.

*****

One way to measure the depth of this thing; ask her girls if they'd noticed anything strange without igniting any unwarranted terror or any underlying questionability of true sanity. She weighed her options as she swept up the kitchen and changed the broken light, driven by the facts laid out for her in three brief and yellowed newspaper articles. Gerald Kimber, 28, single, employed as a computer programmer, last seen the night before the gruesome discovery in the basement storage area of his apartment building. The bodies of nine girls between the ages of thirteen and fifteen were found tucked under a plastic tarp. Each one was positioned in a proper hands-folded repose, each one crudely embalmed with hastily injected chemicals. At least three of them were reportedly enticed from their homes by an unnamed friend they met online.

"Beckon U," Jan said, her throat hot and tight, her hands atremble as she assessed the silent rooms around her and the door just off the kitchen which now loomed like a grim totem in her thoughts. The door to the basement.

"Find KIM-ber," the virtual assistant announced.

"Shut up." She whirled toward it.

The living room lamp blinked on, then faded to dark like a seductive wink. What was next? Hands cupping her elbows from behind, grave cold, and the flutter of lips at her ear. "*I just want to be found, Jan. Don't we all?*"

She stifled a cry when the front door flew open. No threatening shadows, only Corrinne with Viv in tow. Three o'clock already. Her words spilled out. "We need to talk about something right away."

Her older daughter offered a condescending scowl. "Really, Mom?"

"I'm serious. I think something is wrong with this apartment."

Corrinne produced her phone with an eye roll. "I'm talking about this." The olive drab square declaring Beckon U amid the cluster of phone screen icons seemed to still Jan's heart. Corrinne then plucked the electronic tablet from her sister's hands and flashed it forward. Beckon U loomed next to a colorful title called Krazy Kitties like an infection ready to spread. "This is not funny."

"No, it's not." Jan snatched the devices from her daughter's hands before she was truly aware she was moving. "Did you click it? Did either of you open Beckon U?"

Corrinne's provoked "No," was followed by a sincere yet troubled head shake from Vivian.

"Good." She managed to find some welcome authority in her voice. "It spreads, whatever it is. It's getting into everything. Even the lights. Have you noticed anything strange here? Last night? This morning?"

Corrine stepped toward her, hands out as if to reclaim her precious phone. "Like a virus?"

"Strange like this, Mommy?" Viv waggled an index finger at the white cloud of breath vapor that drifted near her pink lips. "Is this strange?"

"Jesus," Corrinne's hands drew in and clamped over her own forearms. "Cold."

"Listen to me." Jan cursed the way the authority ran out of her. A door down the hall banged closed, opened, closed again like a show of force, a display of presence. "Let's go out to the car and we'll—"

Hands gripped her from behind, one on her neck, the other tangled in the back of her blouse. Icy strangler's hands made powerful by their desperation. They yanked her backward. The basement door rattled open, the startled screams of her daughters enraged her. Her shoulders barked the frame of the basement door as she was pulled through. Next would come the brutal, repeated assault of the stair risers as she tumbled down.

*Is this how you took them all, Kimber? Threw them downstairs so they landed broken and stunned on the cement floor?*

But she felt no stairs, just a rapid downward rush and a rough pushing sensation that deposited her in a sitting position at the foot of the stairs. It was punctuated by the slam of the door above. She jumped to her feet and searched the near-gloom. Viv's tablet had tumbled down with her and lent a hazy illumination to the room. Corrinne's phone rested on the floor nearby, blazing at the ceiling like a startled eye. It bore the Beckon U chat screen. She drew a shuddering breath as her gaze brushed across it, picking out the words UNCOVER KIMBER NOW in the top text bar.

The screams of her daughters as they tugged and pounded on the unyielding door, seemed to fade as her eyes lifted farther. Figures—she was sure there were none only a moment before—stood a few feet away, forward facing, hunched and still as if holding a vigil in the gloom. Girls.

She knew there were nine without counting (the Beckon U girls, part of her chirped, wild, like a hysterical laugh). Their vague pubescent curves and lithe limbs knew no real substance, bore no weight. Their heads remained downcast, their longish hair shielding faces she was sure held dreadful knowledge.

"I know what he did to you," she said wincing as a new, bitter chill rolled toward her in waves. "Does that help? Does that bring you any peace?"

A graceful arm stretched out from the most forefront of the shapes and indicated the back wall of the basement. Near the floor, a singular square of plywood was bolted to the painted cinderblock like a miniature door. The means, she suspected, to finish this.

The phone chimed and flashed as if in acknowledgement.

UNCOVER KIMBER NOW NOWNOWNOW

She turned a wary eye toward the upstairs. Grating wood joined her daughters' calls. One of them, Corrinne no doubt, was prying at the door with a knife or perhaps a claw hammer.

"I'll go over there," she announced to the air, "but I want to know Kimber is down here with me. Nowhere near my girls. Got it?"

A beat of contemplative silence. Then cold fingers clamped back of her neck. Forceful. Not *hello* but *get moving*.

She stepped toward the Beckon U girls, anticipating a rare melancholy cold as she passed between them. They swirled apart like fog before she reached them, however. Less substantial than Kimber, an essence trapped in the vacuum of a corporeal world.

Vagabonds in an endless loop of self-memory.

She snatched up Corrinne's phone to light her way and kicked small boxes out of her path. Kimber's grip steered her toward the left side of the plywood, where a small gap between wood and wall stood out in the gloom. An anxious yet gleeful trembling emanated from the presence behind her.

"I'm not doing this for you," she said as she slipped her fingers in, pulled at the edge of the wood.

It did not so much break as disintegrate into brittle scraps of cheap wood, revealing a narrow plumbing access niche. The rancid stench from inside was like a singular expelled breath. She thrust the phone forward with the conviction of a warding talisman and the light revealed a tangle of pipes in the upper portion. On the floor, an adult sized huddle of human bone and desiccated meat.

"There you are," she said to the dark remains. "Exposed. Found, just like you wanted, you twisted piece of filth. Now get out. Go to Hell."

The fingers against her neck lost firmness, the presence at her back became a breeze that soughed through the fabric of her being. It trailed thoughts and joys and sorrows shot with dreadful embers of compulsion as it departed from her. A vile intimacy. No sensory misfire but real revulsion over the contact of foul hands on her skin, of vile ideas skittering through her mind. Broken remnants that at last dissipated.

The door at the top of the stairs popped open and Corrinne turned on the lights. The place seemed too large, over-bright and somehow hollow.

"Stay up there." Jan rushed to the stairs and climbed up on shaky legs.

"What happened?" Corrinne embraced her at the top step with a type of desperation. "It was so weird. The cold. The door. The TV came on and the washer tried to start up by itself."

"I took care of it, I think. And when I figure it out, I'll explain it." She put Corrinne at arm's length to evaluate her expression. "Okay?"

Corrinne nodded and allowed herself to be led back into the apartment. The warm apartment. The *calm* apartment.

"Get us some overnight stuff," Jan said with a final sweeping glance at their surroundings. "Make it quick."

From the living room, Viv evaluated her, pale and stricken in a pool of shadow. Jan scooped her up, surprised when she pushed back with a swimming but direct look. Her words were slow and grave.

"Wreck-on You isn't done?"

Jan followed the twitch of her daughter's eyes.

The living room television displayed a glowing menu screen, normal and orderly except for the new icon in the lower right. Olive drab. Beckon U. Under it, two stacked chat boxes. Blank. Waiting.

"Maybe never," Jan said and put Viv back on her feet while Corrinne rushed toward them clutching a bulging duffle bag. "Wait for me in the car. Both of you."

She watched them go but did not immediately follow. Her gaze locked on the basement door, her thoughts consumed by what might be standing in wait on the other side. What new grim shadow dances played out at the bottom of the stairs? All she needed to do was turn the knob.

*Done*, a bright and deep logic awoke and put her in motion. Her phone was in her hand and with a groan—or was it a humorless chuckle?—she set it aside without checking the screen and hurried to the car.

Behind her, the television winked off and its cooling insides ticked with slow, lingering patience.

## THE HOUSE ON HENLEY WAY

Jeani Rector

"You should tell them," Nick said.

Mandy sighed. "I'm so close to a sale. I can feel it in my bones. The wife loves the house."

"At least be glad your buyers aren't looking at the Dorothea Puente house over there on F Street," Nick said. "Those weren't exactly flowers that old Dorothea planted in the ground."

She ignored his sardonic grin. "Well, it's just that I need a sale."

"Don't we all?" Nick said. He grinned again as she went out.

She drove to Henley Way, where she was going to meet the young couple interested in the house. She pulled up in front of the house, turned off her engine, put her hands on the steering wheel, and stared.

It looked like any other house.

It was tan with white trim; a typical tract house. It was a ranch-style one-story, just like every other house on the block. Who would figure that this house was any different? Nothing about its appearance made it stand out from the rest.

She had a decision to make. And so she made it. The wife loved the house, and she needed the sale.

*****

Amber opened one of the many boxes that littered the kitchen floor of her new house.

It was taking her all day to unpack. Her husband wasn't any help since he was working. It seemed that just as soon as they closed escrow and moved in, Kevin had to attend to his business…always his business.

In fact, that was one of the reasons they bought a home. Kevin felt that Amber needed something to take her mind off the fact that she was alone a lot of the time. He told her that if they bought a house, she could decorate it any way she wanted.

Amber had been thrilled. There was only one thing she wanted more than a house, and that was a baby. Kevin had told her they weren't ready for that kind of responsibility, but Amber figured that since they had bought a new house, it would make sense to fill it with a baby. She felt that with time, she could talk Kevin into it.

Certainly they had the space now, and she loved this house; for some reason, when she had looked at it with the realtor, it had spoken to her…whispering promises.

The new house wasn't exactly new, having been built in 1980. Still, it was a three bedroom, two bath, ranch-style tract home that had over 1,500 square feet. That was a lot of space for only two people. A baby could fill the space.

And so Amber unpacked by herself in her new home. She hadn't had time to look for a job in this new town, and reveled in the idea that at least for a while, she could live a life of luxury by not having to go to work. Of course, once they started paying the mortgage, she would need to find a part-time job.

But on this day, she wasn't going to worry about it. She was going to unpack a few things and begin nesting; preparing for the baby that she knew would arrive.

She glanced at a window, and couldn't believe it when she saw it was raining. How could it be raining? The weather had been so beautiful just the day before. It rarely rained during May in Sacramento, but it was sure coming down now. The dark sky seemed to dampen Amber's mood, and her high spirits changed to anxiety.

Because of the rain, night came faster, throwing its ebony blanket over the city to change it from a place of friendly openness into a place of menacing shadows. Amber found herself wishing that Kevin were home. Earlier, she had been enjoying her new house, but now that it was night, she found herself nervous to be there alone.

She had nothing to do. She didn't have cable hooked up yet, and there was no antenna, so she couldn't watch television. She tried to read a book, but it was a murder mystery and that made her more nervous. She didn't want to unpack anymore, because she had been doing that most of the day and she was sick of it.

Amber found herself walking around; wandering from room to room. She held her cell phone in her hand, trying to resist the urge to call Kevin. Outside, the storm was at full force now, raging in its fury. Lightning flashed and thunder soon followed; the sound rumbled and growled throughout the house.

It made her feel better to turn on every single light. The kitchen, bathrooms, and dining room all had ceiling lights, but the living room and the bedrooms did not. Amber was glad she had thought to unpack lamps earlier in the day; now she plugged them in and turned them all on.

In one of the empty guest bedrooms, the lamp was shining its light at an angle upon the wall. Something about the wall didn't seem quite right.

She put her cell phone down on the floor to free her hands for the lamp. She picked up the lamp and moved it a bit, trying different angles to shine upon the wall. It looked like some sort of bulge was pushing out about halfway up the wall.

She wondered why she had not seen it when the realtor showed her the house. Maybe the room had looked different in the daylight.

*Great*, Amber thought, *do we have structural problems already*?

She put down the lamp and walked over to the wall, running her hands over it. There was definitely a bulge in the wall. It was all bumpy and uneven. And now that she was close to it, she could see that it looked as though someone had done a makeshift repair job; probably there had been a hole in the wall and someone had haphazardly patched it and painted over it.

It was a very bad patch job.

Amber heard of people stuffing newspapers into holes in the wall so that they could have something to spread the spackle upon. That sort of idea made her very nervous. She didn't want paper inside her wall; it could be a fire hazard.

Would it hurt if she took a look? After all, wouldn't Kevin want to do the same thing, since the patch job had been done so poorly? Either way, the hole in the wall would have to be done over and patched correctly, so there would be no harm in opening it up now. Hadn't Kevin given her free rein with the house? Besides, she had nothing else to do.

She went into the kitchen and grabbed a knife. Returning to the guest bedroom, she punched the wall with the knife. She was not surprised when the knife went through the patch job very easily and that she could hear rustling on the other side.

So she had been right: newspaper.

She fumbled at the wall but managed to begin tearing away at the plaster. She used the knife to create openings and then pulled the makeshift spackle patch job out. The spackle crumbled, falling into little pieces upon the floor.

The hole opened up. Amber reached inside and started pulling rumpled newspapers out. Finally when she had them all removed from the wall, she decided to sit down and take a look at them. The date on the newspapers would tell her how long ago the wall had been patched.

She picked up one of the newspapers and un-wadded it. It was yellowed, so she figured it must have been in the wall for a while. She placed it on the floor and tried to smooth out the wrinkles with her hands.

When it was free of most of its wrinkles, she picked it up again and looked to the top of the page for the date. It said: *The Sacramento Bee, Sunday May 8, 1988.*

How ironic that that paper was dated the same month in which she found it, May. She skimmed the page and saw advertisements that proclaimed it was not too late to buy a Mother's Day gift.

So May eighth must have been Mother's Day in 1988, she thought. *Maybe it's an omen.*

She started reading the paper, glad that it wasn't the Sunday funny pages. Her eyes stopped on an article. She read:

> *A 23-year-old woman was arrested last night on murder charges in connection with the death of her son, according to a police report.*
>
> *Sacramento paramedics responded about 10:15 PM to a 911 call to a home on the 1900 block of*

*Damn!* Amber thought. The page was torn, so the rest of the article was missing.

Then she remembered how she had believed that finding a

newspaper dated on Mother's Day had been an omen. She shuddered, and instinctively reached for her belly, even though there was no child inside.

She connected the article to her own address, which was 1924 Henley Way. Too bad the article had been torn before the name of the street could be given.

*There are lots of streets in Sacramento that have 1900 blocks*, she thought. It could be any house on any street between the addresses of 1900 and 1999.

Still, it made it even creepier to be reading about a murder at night while she was in an unfamiliar house with a thunderstorm raging outside. The effect of the bad weather was apocalyptic to her mood, and she had feelings of melancholy and paranoia. She decided to start a fire in the fireplace, using the old newspaper pages as fuel. It would add more light in the house. Plus, she was feeling cold.

Grabbing the newspapers, she wadded them all up in her hand again. She took them into the living room, placed them into the fireplace, and grabbed the book of matches that she had placed on the mantle earlier.

Amber crouched to touch the flaming match to the newspapers, when suddenly the front door blew inwards, blowing out the match. She screamed in frightened surprise.

The rain gushed into the room, and the wind howled with a furious aggression. Running towards the door, Amber pushed to try to slam it shut, and was astonished at the resistance of it. Was the wind really that strong? She shoved even more forcefully, using all of her strength, and finally she managed to close the door.

After locking it tightly, she stared at it, trembling and fearful. Hadn't she locked it earlier? Of course she hadn't, or else it would not have blown in.

Then came the thought: *If I didn't lock the front door, then maybe I didn't lock the back door or any of the windows, either.*

She would have to make the rounds all through the house to double check all of the locks.

She took a step forward to start making sure everything was safe when suddenly the front doorbell rang. She glanced at her watch. It was 10:15 PM. Who in the world would be ringing the doorbell at this late hour? And who would venture out on such a stormy night?

Should she answer the door? She was so glad that she had locked it before there was a visitor.

The doorbell rang again. It seemed so loud in the quiet, empty house. She felt frozen. She waited a few minutes, then took a deep breath.

Slowly she walked to the front door, listening to her own footsteps thudding dully upon the hardwood floor of the entranceway. She peered through the peephole, but she couldn't make out anything on the front porch because of the dark night.

Amber next turned to the window by the door. Slowly and carefully she pulled a corner of the curtain aside, and looked out. Rain was running in rivulets down the windowpane, blurring the glass, and making visibility close to impossible.

She didn't know what to do. She was all alone. Anything could happen to a woman who was all alone in a strange house. She certainly couldn't open the door to who knew what.

She backed away from the door. It was quiet now. Maybe whoever it was had left. After all, no one knew yet that she and Kevin were moving in, so perhaps whoever had rang the doorbell had been looking for the previous owners. If so, they kept odd hours.

"Calm down," Amber told herself, not even realizing she was speaking aloud.

She held her hands up to gauge the amount they trembled. Then she wiped her forehead, surprised at the sweat, considering how cold it was in the house. She turned away from the door.

She heard something, and stood stock still, her mouth slightly open so that her ears would work better. It sounded like the groaning of a door opening down the hallway. One of the bedroom doors. *It must be the house settling*, she told herself. *I'm not familiar with the sounds of this house yet.*

Despite the logic, she was afraid. Damn that Kevin, leaving her all alone in a foreign place! She didn't know any neighbors, and had no family to call in Sacramento. If she called the cops, what could she tell them? That she was afraid of the thunderstorm? Or of a boogeyman who went around the neighborhood ringing doorbells at night? Or of the foundation settling down the hallway?

The only thing she could do was to go back to checking all of the doors and windows to make sure everything was locked.

She double-checked the front door almost obsessively, even though she had already locked it. She reached for the handle and jiggled it. She touched the dead bolt and assured herself that it was also locked solidly.

On to the windows. She checked the living room windows. She went to them one by one, feeling the cold panes, fumbling with her fingers for the latches. There were no curtains, making her feel even more vulnerable. Anyone outside could see in, but when she looked at the glass, all she could see was her own reflection because of all the lights turned on inside the house.

She stopped for a minute at one of the windows and studied her face. She was startled at the fear that showed on her features. She saw that her eyes were wide with the whites visible, giving her a wild, crazy look. Her face in the glass was too blurred to see the sweat that she felt slowly dripping down her temples.

Next, the back door. Amber hesitated, then walked through the living room to the kitchen. The only window there was too small to worry about, but the door…it looked like it wasn't even closed all the way! It stuck out a bit, half-latched. She could see it moving as the wind pushed against it but the half-latch held. She felt her heart thud against her chest as though it was trying to escape her body. Her mouth dried up and she almost choked.

She made an almost demented sound as she raced to the back door. Shoving her body against it, she slammed it shut, the latch catching completely. She grabbed the handle and locked it. She was shaking so badly that she barely was able to position the guard chain.

*You left the door half-latched when you were moving boxes inside,* she told herself. It had to be true. She would have heard someone enter the house if anyone did. There was no one in the house but her.

*But what about whoever rang the front doorbell?* a voice in her head nagged. No, that person went away.

She realized she was frightened out of her wits.

And then she heard that groaning sound again down the hallway. It really did sound like a door slowly swinging open. Pausing, she could feel her heart thudding in her chest once again. She had to call Kevin. He needed to come home.

Oh no, where was her cell phone? Damn it; hadn't she left it in the empty guest bedroom when she had picked up the lamp and found the newspaper earlier in the night?

That meant she had to go back down the hall. Could she summon the courage to go back through the house to get her phone?

*This is my house,* she told herself. *This is a good house. This is where Kevin and I will get our new start. I am a grown woman. I need my phone. The sooner I get it, the sooner I can talk to my husband.*

Silently she crept to the start of the hallway. All of the lights in the house were still brightly lit. She could hear the thunder booming outside, and rain pounded on the roof. The sound of a tree branch creaked against the house somewhere; and she thought, *That's what the noise was, a tree branch, right? Not a door opening*?

Slowly she entered the hallway. She could smell floor wax that was somewhat masking the underlying, musky scent of a house in which no one had lived for a while. Hardwood ran all the way down the hall, and she was glad she had taken her shoes off and was wearing only socks on her feet. She had the irrational idea that she wanted to sneak up on the bedroom.

She saw that the door was indeed half open.

She hesitated just outside the bedroom door and listened. Nothing. It must be okay for her to go into the room and get the cell phone.

But as she entered the room, before she could take it all in, she knew, *she just knew*, that she was no longer alone in the house. She could hear the rhythm of blood pounding in her ears, pushed by her rapidly beating heart. Once inside, she gasped, and clutched her chest.

A strangled cry escaped her throat when she saw what waited for her in the room.

Sitting cross-legged on the floor was a child. He was barefoot, wearing jeans and a blue-and-white striped shirt. He looked up at her with soulless eyes, and Amber could see the gash in his skull.

He made an attempt to get up. His hand reached out towards her as if imploring her to come to him; to touch the flesh that looked cold and bloodless. He moved in a series of jerks and spasms, and then his body listed to the left as though he had no sense of balance, and he fell back down.

"Where's my mother?" the child spoke through cracked and swollen lips. One of his front teeth was missing. "I keep looking, but I can't find her. I've been looking a long time."

He straightened his body and leaned forward. He crouched close to the floor and began to crawl. He dragged his body across the wooden surface and came at her with a slow, scrabbling motion, pulling himself along, coming right at her. She could hear shuffling as his knees brushed across the floor, and his hands slapped the wood with a wet sound as he alternated between using them to crawl and to reach for her.

He was coming closer. He would be able to grasp her legs in a moment.

Screaming in fright, Amber whirled around and ran from the bedroom. She fled down the hall, slipping on the hardwood. Catching herself before she fell, her arms flailing, she regained her balance and continued to run. Reaching the front door, she fumbled with the locks. She didn't dare to look behind her to see if she was being chased. She needed to unlock the door to escape out into the night.

She flung the front door open, and bolted. She ran from the walkway into the front yard, sliding when she hit the slick mud on the ground. She was instantly drenched by the raging storm, freezing and soaked in her wet clothes, her hair in dripping ribbons around her face. She ran as fast as she could, splashing in the mud, running for her life.

Then suddenly rough hands grabbed her shoulders.

"Amber!" came a man's voice, as his hands closed tighter on her shoulders, preventing her escape.

It was Kevin. Kevin was there!

Amber collapsed in his arms. She sobbed into his shoulder.

"What are you doing outside in the storm?" he asked her, sounding upset and baffled. "Come on, let me get you back inside so I can warm you up."

"No!" she shrieked. "Don't make me go back into that house!"

He stood there in the downpour, holding his wife, the water running in rivulets down his rain slicker. "All right," he soothed her. "Get in my car."

Leading her to his car, he held open the passenger side door. Then after he made sure she was belted in, he went around the car to the driver side. Starting the engine, he turned the heater up to high.

"You don't even have shoes on," he said. "Listen, I was worried about you. I tried to call you all night but your cell phone was turned off. I asked Roland to check on you. You remember Roland, don't you? You know, my business associate? I asked him to drop by to see if you were okay. When he called me to say you didn't answer the door, I decided to come home."

"Someone rang the doorbell," Amber said. "I didn't see anyone on the porch."

Kevin sighed. "Why were you in the yard?"

"I saw a ghost in that house," she told him. "A dead child. A five-year-old boy; oh Kevin, he was dead!"

"Amber…"

She grabbed his arm. "You do believe me, don't you? Tell me you believe me!"

He glanced sideways at her as he drove. "Sure, honey, you know I always believe you."

"Always? What do you mean, always? This has never happened to me before."

"Don't you remember?" he asked gently.

She looked out the window, as though suddenly realizing she was in a car. "Where are we going?"

He sighed again. "Amber, I'm taking you to a hospital. Then tomorrow we can go on a trip to see Doctor Robinson. Remember Doctor Robinson?"

"No," she said.

"Remember how much help he was to you after our son was hit by that car two years ago?"

She was flabbergasted. "What son? Damn it Kevin, you know I've never even been pregnant. What are you talking about?"

"That's okay, Amber," Kevin told her. "Doctor Robinson will explain it all to you. He'll tell you all about how you keep seeing our son."

She buried her face into her hands and sobbed. "Yes, our son. Did I see a ghost in that house? Maybe I was just seeing our son again. Now I feel so confused that I'm not sure."

He told her softly, "There's no such thing as ghosts."

*****

It was a magnificent July morning when Mandy walked into the office that she shared with Nick.

"Hey," he greeted her. "You'll never guess what house is already back on the market."

Mandy froze, her heart slowing. "It can't be. Not again. Not this fast, anyway."

"Yep, 1924 Henley. The one with the murder in 1988. Just how many times have you sold that house, anyway?"

She continued to stand still for a moment. Then she walked to the coffee pot and poured herself a cup. She felt she needed it.

## Other HellBound Books Titles
## Available at: www.hellboundbookspublishing.com

### Ghosts Spirits and Specters: Volume 1

Compiled and edited by the Dark Poet Princess herself - Xtina Marie - Ghosts, Spirits, & Specters boasts eighteen terrifying tales of ethereal and ghostly goings-on from the gloriously fevered minds of:

Michael J. Moore, T. Fox Dunham, Richard Raven, Sarah Cannavo, DJ Tyrer, Kev Harrison, David F. Gray, Jon O'Bergh, Dustin Chisam, Bill Davidson, Nathan Helton, Brian James Lewis, Trevor Newton, R.C. Mulhare, Nikki D. Freeman, Laszlo Tamasfi, Dawson Goodell, and Eric Nash

## The Toilet Zone

*"Restroom reading at its most terrifying!"*

Compiled and edited by the grand master of 80's schlock horror, Bret McCormick, each one of this collection of 32 terrifying tales is just the perfect length for a visit to the smallest room....

At the very boundaries of human imagination dwells one single, solitary place of solitude, of peace and quiet, a place in which your regular human being spends, on average, 10 to 15 minutes - at least once every single day of their lives.
Now, consider a typical, everyday reading speed of 200 to 250 words per minute - that means your average visitor has the time to read between 2,500 to 4,000 words, which makes each and every one of these 32 tales of terror - from some of the best contemporary independent authors - within this anthology of horror the perfect, meticulously calculated length.
Dare you take a walk to the small room from where inky shadows creep out to smother the light and solitude's siren call beckons you?
Dare you take a quiet, lonely walk into… The Toilet Zone

## The Horror Writer

***"The most definitive guide into the trials and tribulations of being a horror writer since Stephen King's 'On Writing.'"***

We have assembled some of the very best in the business from whom you can learn so much about the craft of horror writing: Bram Stoker Award© winners, bestselling authors, a President of the Horror Writers' Association, and myriad contemporary horror authors of distinction.

The Horror Writer covers how to connect with your market and carve out a sustainable niche in the independent horror genre, how to tackle the writer's ever-lurking nemesis of productivity, writing good horror stories with powerful, effective scenes, realistic, flowing dialogue and relatable characters without resorting to clichéd jump scares and well-worn gimmicks. Also covered is the delicate subject of handling rejection with good grace, and how to use those inevitable "not quite the right fit for us at this time" letters as an opportunity to hone your craft.

Plus... perceptive interviews to provide an intimate peek into the psyche of the horror author and the challenges they work through to bring their nefarious ideas to the page.

And, as if that – and so much more – was not enough, we have for your delectation Ramsey Campbell's beautifully insightful analysis of the tales of HP Lovecraft.

Featuring:
Ramsey Campbell, John Palisano, Chad Lutzke, Lisa Morton, Kenneth W. Cain, Kevin J. Kennedy, Monique Snyman, Scott Nicholson, Lucy A. Snyder, Richard Thomas, Gene O'Neill, Jess Landry, Luke Walker, Stephanie M. Wytovich, Marie O'Regan, Armand Rosamilia, Kevin Lucia, Ben Eads, Kelli Owen, Jasper Bark, and Bret McCormick.

And interviews with:
Steve Rasnic Tem, Stephen Graham Jones, David Owain Hughes, Tim Waggoner, and Mort Castle.

**A HellBound Books LLC**
**Publication**

www.hellboundbookspublishing.com

**Printed in the United States of America**

Printed in Great Britain
by Amazon